# A LADY OF

# INTEGRITY

A steampunk adventure novel
Magnificent Devices Book Seven

Shelley Adina

Moonshell
Books

Moonshell Books, Inc.
www.moonshellbooks.com

This is a work of fiction. Names, characters, places, and incidents are a product of the author's imagination. Locales and public names are sometimes used for atmospheric purposes. Any resemblance to actual people, living or dead, or to businesses, companies, events, institutions, or locales is completely coincidental.

Book Layout ©2013 BookDesignTemplates.com.
Art by Claudia McKinney at phatpuppyart.com, with images from Shutterstock.com, used under license.
Design by Kalen O'Donnell.
Author font by Anthony Piraino at OneButtonMouse.com.
All rights reserved.

A Lady of Integrity / Shelley Adina—1st ed.
ISBN 978-1-939087-21-8

*For Linda McGinnis and Nancy Warren
the placemat plotters*

1

*London, October 1894*

"I absolutely, positively forbid it," Lady Claire Trevelyan said with the firmness that comes of complete conviction. "There will be no pink of any kind at my wedding—and that includes flowers and your dress, Maggie."

"But Lady—"

"Of *any* kind."

Maggie Polgarth gazed longingly at the illustration of the latest creation by Madame du Barry, its roseate glory taking up the entire center spread of *London Home and Hearth* magazine, that popular glossy publication that came in the Sunday edition of the *Evening Standard*. Having remembered her travails at the hands of that same modiste, Claire was seriously reconsidering the renewal of her subscription.

"Don't you think you are being somewhat harsh, dearest?" Andrew Malvern inquired from his chair by the fire, where he was engaged in a lively hand of cowboy poker with Snouts McTavish, Lewis Protheroe, and Lizzie Seacombe, none of whom were showing any respect whatsoever for his age and consequence.

"Pink is far more harsh to me than I am to it," Claire informed him, her heart warming at the contented if keenly competitive picture they made. "On this point I will not be moved. The Mopsies will precede me down the aisle in cream *peau de soie* with emerald-green and sapphire-blue velvet sashes, and Snouts will escort me wearing a green waistcoat with as much embroidery upon it as he pleases."

"Peacocks won't have anything on me," Snouts said absently. "I'll see your toothpick and raise you a thimble, Mr. Andrew—though it will do me no good. Lizzie is going to trounce us all and you'll be wishing you'd folded five minutes ago."

And so it proved to be. With a cry of aggravation, Andrew threw down his unsuccessful hand, congratulated Lizzie on her victory, and came to join Claire on the sofa, where she was curled up with her engineering notebook and several sharp pencils she'd barely managed to keep the boys from tossing into the pot as bets.

"Is it time to order more toothpicks?" Claire asked, raising her face and receiving a kiss that was not quite proper considering they were in front of the children.

"We can get another night out of this lot." Andrew folded himself next to her and had a look at her drawing. "It's a lucky thing no one actually uses them for picking teeth. What are you working on? A wedding gown?"

She poked him in the ribs with the eraser end of the pencil. "This is an airship, sir, and if you are implying I ate one too many Yorkshire puddings at dinner, then you had best watch out for the business end of this pencil."

"I would never imply any such thing. You are perfection, and would be even if I were Jack Spratt and you his legendary wife."

Claire narrowed her eyes at him and hastily, he returned his attention to the drawing. "Ah, the automaton intelligence system."

"Indirectly," she said, her pencil once again busy on the paper. "Of course Count von Zeppelin has already adapted Alice's and my design for the long-distance ships that fly to the Antipodes, though they are so much larger than *Athena*. But efficient flight is more than simply increasing the number of automatons built into the hull. It is also a matter of engines. There simply must be a better way to power these great Daimler engines. Half the holds are filled with coal, and water condensers are heavy. I will find it, Andrew. Before I arrive next week, I want to have a design firmly in my mind, so as to waste no time once I actually take up my work in the laboratory."

"And you have settled this with Count von Zeppelin?"

"No," Claire said with some reluctance. "We have not actually discussed my duties in detail yet. But I am quite sure he will allow me to work on this project. It can only benefit the Zeppelin Airship Works in the long run."

She spoke as though it were a foregone conclusion, when in fact she did not know exactly what the count had in mind for her when she took up her position at the greatest manufactory of airships in the world. Their correspondence had not gone into detail, and their many conversations during her university career had been directed more toward philosophy and mechanics than specifics such as where her laboratory would be or whom she would hire to assist her.

"I wish Alice would write again," she said, following that thought. "She and I would make a marvelous team, and I have heard nothing since I answered that peculiar letter."

"At least she says she and Jake are all right," Maggie put in, now engaged in doing the crossword puzzle in the back of the newspaper with Lizzie while Lewis diagrammed the hand they had just invented. He sent the spreads in once a month for the paper's back page. No one had yet discovered that the mysterious poker player who provided the most maddeningly clever variations on the popular game was actually the owner of the Gaius Club, membership to which was so sought after among the young and wealthy that there was a waiting list a year long.

"I am dying to hear the story," Claire admitted, "but I confess I am a little worried about what could have made her flee the Duchy of Venice in such a fashion, and why she asked for my help when she is safely in Bavaria. It does not add up."

"I hope Claude is all right." Lizzie looked up from the crossword. "He's still in Venice, you know, so I wrote after we heard from Alice. All I got back was a postcard from that big exhibition they're all attending.

He sounded his usual self ... though there's no room to say much more than 'Having a grand rumble' on those little bits of cardboard. The picture was lovely, though."

"I'm glad he is out of France for the time being, at any rate, and unlikely to be used any longer as a means of blackmail," Andrew said. "It has been a number of weeks, and yet I am still wondering if it is safe to assume that Gerald Meriwether-Astor perished in the Channel when Maggie scuttled his great undersea dirigible."

Maggie abandoned the crossword altogether and stood in front of the fire, as though she had suddenly become chilled. "I hope so," she said fiercely. "I hope he got exactly what he deserved for trying to mount an invasion and make himself a king—killing all those poor bathynauts in the process."

"Maggie," Claire said softly. "Do not make yourself distressed. You have just managed to sleep through the night without nightmares, and neither Polgarth nor I wish you to lose the ground you have gained."

At the mention of her grandfather's name, some of the tension eased out of Maggie's lovely young face. "Must I go back to Bavaria?" she pleaded, flinging herself on the rug at Claire's feet. "Can't I go down to Gwynn Place and stay with him and Michael and my aunts while you and Lizzie are gone?"

"And not finish your education?" Lewis looked up from his spreads in astonishment. "If I had half your advantages, Mags, you can bet I wouldn't be throwing them away."

"You've done pretty well for yourself under your own steam, I'd say," Snouts told him, "but it's different for girls. Don't you think about quitting, Mags," he told her, a hint of their old gang leader's authority flashing through the façade of the fashionable young business-man. "We see a job through, and always have, innit?"

Claire fought the temptation to marshal her argu-ments, and instead let the boys do the job she hadn't exactly been prepared for. Was this how Maggie really felt? That she didn't want to finish her studies and graduate? The prospect horrified Claire—but at the same time, Maggie had always been of a gentler persua-sion than her cousin Lizzie, more inclined to value home and hearth than either Lizzie or Claire herself.

Not that Claire didn't value her homes. She did, deeply—both here at Carrick House in London, and the little cottage in Vauxhall Gardens where they had cre-ated their first refuge. But her deep-seated need to se-cure her own engineering degree had driven her actions since the age of fifteen—and led her into such adven-tures that she had been changed forever.

She passed an affectionate hand over Maggie's hair—put up now that she was a young lady, and her hems lowered in equal measure. "I will not say whether you must go or not," she told her. "But I would be sad-dened indeed if all your work were left unfinished and you did not get the credit for it."

"You can't stay here," Lizzie said firmly. "What would I do with myself all alone at school?"

"Become better friends with the other girls?" Maggie suggested.

"I'm as friendly with them as I intend to be."

"Wait about for Tigg to get leave?"

"Oh, yes," Lizzie nodded. "I shall run to meet the post every single day and weep all night when there's no letter." Her mouth pursed up in disdain at such missish behavior. "Tigg would wash his hands of me if I did such things. No, Mags. You're coming back with me and that's that. Nothing is going to hurt either of us, if that's what you're worried about."

"I never said so." Maggie traced the rose design in the carpet by her knee with one finger.

"But I know you. You like things peaceful-like. The thing is, trouble found you as easily in Cornwall as it did me in the Cotswolds and the Lady in the Canadas. We can't hide from adventures—they find us whether we want them to or not."

"They don't seem to find me," Lewis pointed out, clearly somewhat disappointed.

"Give them time," Andrew advised him.

Since in her mind the matter was closed, Lizzie returned to the crossword. "What's a nine-letter word for 'young lady of marriageable age'?"

"*Elizabeth,*" teased Snouts.

Lizzie swiped the box of toothpicks and threw it at him. Since she very rarely missed, Snouts exclaimed in chagrin and returned it to the mantel where it belonged, rubbing his shoulder.

"Lizzie, really, where are your manners?" Claire wondered aloud.

"*Debutante*, you gumpy," Maggie told her cousin. "Even Willie might have got that one."

Happily, Lizzie filled in the last space and closed the paper. "Speaking of Willie, has the invitation come for his birthday party? It's bound to be a—"

Someone pounded on the street door, sounding as though they meant the lion's-head knocker to break right through the panel.

"I'll get it." Snouts went out of the family parlour and into the hall, moving on the balls of his feet in a way that told the observant eye he believed trouble lurked even behind the laurel hedges and glossy iron railings of Belgravia.

Claire put her notebook aside and stood, Andrew beside her.

"Snouts," they heard a familiar voice say, "is Claire here?"

"Captain! She is, but—"

"Thank heaven. And Mr. Malvern?"

"Aye, but—"

Claire started forward, but before she could even reach the door, a blond, disheveled wreck of a young woman fell through it, the tracks of tears cutting lines through the dirt on her face.

"Claire—Andrew—thank God," Alice Chalmers said breathlessly, pulling the flight goggles off her unruly hair. "You've got to come with me to Venice and get Jake out of that underwater prison before he dies in there."

## A LADY OF INTEGRITY

2

"When was the last time you had something to eat?"
Claire handed Alice a steaming cup of tea and a healthy
piece of fruitcake.

Alice snuggled more deeply into the comfortable sofa
and reflected that it was lucky the two of them were
much of a size. Claire's blouse and knitted cardigan
were comfortable enough, particularly now that she'd
had a bath, but the black raiding skirt was a bit short.
Not that she was in the habit of wearing skirts.

"And do you have anything else to wear?"

"I don't remember ... and no."

"We'll take care of you, our Alice," Maggie said,
curling up against her side as though to give her both
comfort and warmth. Alice was grateful for the thought,
though comfort of the mental kind was a stretch at the

moment. "One of the girls tried to launder your pants and they fell apart in her hands. The Lady won't mind you borrowing a few things until we can get you your own."

Those pants were about the last things she *could* call her own, save her goggles. How could she have gone from self-supporting captain of her own ship and crew to such poverty and dependence in such a short time?

"I didn't have myself smuggled here in a rifle case to get a repeat of our shopping trip in Edmonton," Alice said, too exhausted by despair for politeness.

"In a what?" Claire nearly dropped the teapot. If it had not been for Andrew's quick steadying movement, she might have. "Alice, you must tell us what is going on now that you are clean and able to think clearly."

Alice was not so incapacitated that she didn't notice the very modest ring containing three pearls set in gold upon the fourth finger of Claire's left hand as she returned the teapot to the low table. Since to her knowledge, the only jewelry her friend owned was her grandmother's emerald ring and the St. Ives pearl necklace, this could only have come from Mr. Malvern. How long had they been engaged? And when was Claire planning to tell her?

Oh, she'd never had any hope of Mr. Malvern's regard, except for a few brief hours during their adventures in the Canadas five years ago. Claire's letters since then had not revealed much—but so much air had passed under her own hull in the intervening years that she was practically a different woman.

Or maybe hardship and experience had convinced her there were more important things for a woman to think about than a gentleman's affection.

# A LADY OF INTEGRITY

The cake fortified her enough to speak coherently, and promising smells coming from downstairs in the kitchen gave her hope that a proper meal would make an appearance soon.

"It was Count von Zeppelin's idea." She began at the end instead of the beginning, because the beginning was too painful to talk about just yet. "When it began to look like my troubles had followed me to Munich, it was either get rid of me or arm himself and the baroness as they went out in their landau. So he acted. He got me out to the airfield disguised as a member of his party, and when he asked for a tour of one of his new M7 cargo ships, two of his men popped me into an empty crate filled with straw. They made sure there was just enough space between the slats that I could lift the latches with my knife when we got to England. At Hampstead Heath, I simply climbed out and disembarked with the other members of the crew." She leaned over and took another piece of cake, and Claire pushed the plate closer. "From there it was a matter of hitching a ride into town and finding your address."

"You could have sent a note from the mooring station," Andrew said. "We would have come to fetch you immediately."

"But then someone might have seen you," Alice said. "I came on the sly in hopes that no one would twig to me being on this side of the Channel. Not before we're rigged and ready."

"Ready for what?" Lizzie asked, her eyes wide, maybe at the thought of being shut up in a rifle case for all that time. Alice couldn't blame her. It wasn't an experience she wanted to repeat. "Who is chasing you?"

"That's just the thing. In Venice I had my suspicions, but no proof. And by the time I realized the danger, it was already too late. They'd impounded the *Stalwart Lass* and taken Jake as insurance for my cooperation. But as I found out, they had no intention of setting him free."

"Alice, you're getting ahead of yourself." Claire's tone was calm, but the pads of her fingers on her teacup were turning white around the edges from tension. "Of whom are you speaking?"

"The Famiglia Rosa," Alice whispered, her voice dropping to nothing. This was Wilton Crescent. Claire's home. She'd only been here twice in five years, but those visits had been enough to tell her that this house was one of the safest places in all of London.

If London could be said to be safe—and Alice wasn't one hundred percent sure of that.

Blank, expectant faces told her she'd better get on with it. "The Famiglia Rosa—that means Red Family in the Venetian tongue—owns the shipping trade from the Levant to the north coast of Africa, and all the Adriatic. Everyone thinks it's the Doge—that's the Duke who sits on the throne—but he's just one of three brothers who pretty much run the tables in that part of the world. One brother rules Rome, one controls Naples, and the third is the Doge."

"And how did you and Jake run afoul of them?" Andrew asked.

Alice sighed. She'd give a lot to know that herself. How kind Andrew's eyes were, yet how intelligent and alert. Oh, if only …

*Never mind.*

"It was just an ordinary job, or so I thought. A month or so ago I got orders from the Dunsmuirs to take a cargo of furs from Charlottetown to Byzantium, and do a deal with a contingent from the Tsar of Russia."

"In Byzantium?" Claire sounded puzzled. "That's a long way from the Tsar. Why not go directly to St. Petersburg?"

"It might be autumn here, but it's already too cold there. Airships can't fly directly to the Russias after October, just like at the Firstwater Mine, remember? The gas contracts in the fuselages if the weight of the ice doesn't collapse them first. So the solution is to go to Byzantium, where it's still temperate, and put things on a train. Of course, Byzantium is just close enough to the Famiglia Rosa territory to give them itchy fingers. If they can coerce an airship to go through Venice instead, they can extort what they call a 'transfer tax' ... which can be as much as half the value of your cargo. And where is a rope monkey like me going to get cash like that?"

"From the outfit you contracted with?" Snouts said. A reasonable suggestion. Too bad it hadn't worked out so reasonably. "How much were you carrying?"

"About six hundred pounds' worth—so the tax would have been three hundred."

Good heavens. Claire's spine wilted into the back of her chair. She could almost buy *Athena* over again for that price. If she had in fact bought *Athena*. Which she had not.

"But if you were going to Byzantium, how did you come to be in the Duchy of Venice?" Now Claire put her teacup down altogether, and it rattled in the saucer before she let go of it.

"Stupid me—I put down for water and repairs. It's

halfway, you know, and getting over the Alps is a tricky business at this time of year. The poor old girl still has your power cell in her, which runs like a clock, but the rest of her is beginning to show her age. I no sooner reported to the port authority when this gang showed up to confiscate my cargo. Illegal import without authorizing papers, they said. Oh, they'd give it all back once I had the paperwork, but what they didn't tell me is that you have to get authorization before you leave your home port, as part of filing your flight plan."

"But that's ridiculous!" Claire exclaimed. "No one does that. Shipping would slow to a crawl."

"It's just an excuse," Andrew said, "to seize and extort whatever tariffs they wish."

"Seize is right." Alice nodded. "Before I knew what was what, they had the *Lass* locked down and Jake in quarantine so I'd do what they said. But when I didn't—because I couldn't—I went into hiding. Next thing I find out is that they've run poor Jake through a sham trial and clapped him in gaol. And he wasn't alone. There were ships—and presumably prisoners—there from England and Prussia and France. And from the Americas, too." She lifted her gaze to Claire's. "Meriwether-Astor ships."

"That's impossible," Lizzie piped up, evidently recovered from the thought of the rifle case. "One, he's dead, and two, his ships aren't allowed to leave the Fifteen Colonies."

Andrew was about to reply, but a boy Alice had never seen before appeared in the doorway to the dining room. "Beggin' your pardon, Lady, but Granny Protheroe says to tell you dinner's on the table."

"Thank you, Charlie. We will be in directly."

## A LADY OF INTEGRITY

Claire rose and shook out her skirts. "We'll stand on no ceremony. I want to get food into you, Alice, before we ask any more questions. I do not like your color at all."

Alice had eaten unidentifiable dishes in Na'nuk villages and exotic ones in the Dunsmuirs' castle in Scotland, but she'd never tasted anything better than the golden pheasant pie at Wilton Crescent that night. Rich with gravy and vegetables, and accompanied by potatoes and roasted onions, it could have rivaled anything set before the Queen.

Claire allowed her enough time to wolf down her first helping before she said, "Alice, is there any evidence to indicate Gerald Meriwether-Astor is alive?"

Her mouth full, Alice shook her head. When she swallowed, she said, "He don't need to be alive for his ships to fly into the Levant. The company would go to his girl, wouldn't it? What was her name?"

"Gloria," Maggie said, exchanging a glance with her sister that Alice couldn't read. All she could see was the mischievous smile that played around her lips, as though she'd put one over on the absent Gloria and still enjoyed the joke.

"Surely not," Andrew said. "She didn't seem the sort to break the law—although she certainly did you and Claire a service in the Canadas."

"Lot of rope pulled up since then." Alice addressed herself to her second wonderfully runny slice of pie. "Anyhow, that edict only applies to the Prussian Empire and England. If Meriwether-Astor Shipping wanted to run cotton over to Byzantium or Venice, I suppose they could. It's not like the Famiglia Rosa are going to pay attention to anybody's edicts—and the Turks certainly won't."

"Enough politics," Snouts said around his potatoes. "Can we get to the part where we spring my brother from gaol?"

"One must know the lie of the land before one goes barging in to break someone out of gaol, Snouts," Claire told him, her tone soft with understanding. "Even we reconnoitered Bedlam before we freed Doctor Craig."

"Claire, you are not seriously thinking of going to Venice?"

Both Alice and Claire stared at Andrew in shock before Claire found her voice. "Andrew! If not we, then who?"

"He is there under contract for the Dunsmuirs," Andrew pointed out. "Between her ladyship and Her Majesty, it should be a simple enough matter to send an envoy and free an innocent English subject from what is clearly a gang of criminals. At gunpoint, if necessary. There is no need for *you* to go."

# A LADY OF INTEGRITY

3

Claire was not certain what shocked her more—that Andrew believed she needn't assist in Jake's rescue, or that, engagement notwithstanding, he believed he was able to prevent her.

"Do you think I haven't already thought of that?" Alice said impatiently. "The first thing I did when I got to Bavaria was send a pigeon to Scotland, only to be told by return that the Dunsmuirs are back in the Canadas, seeing the last convoy out of the Firstwater Mine."

Claire recovered enough to speak. "Even if they left tonight, they would not reach England for a week or more, and by then—"

"Did you say 'underwater'?" Snouts asked.

"I did." Alice's color, which had begun to return,

faded once again. "It ain't pretty. Maybe we should wait until everyone has finished dessert and had a thimble or two of port before I go any further."

"With all due respect, Miss Alice, I want to know my brother's situation."

"As do we all, Snouts," Maggie said gently. "But it may be hard for Alice to tell us. Give her a moment to collect herself."

Alice took a fortifying sip of wine. Then she addressed herself to Claire, as though she felt safer saying these things to her rather than directly to Jake's half brother.

"The thing you have to know about Venice is that it ain't like other cities."

"Clearly not, if ruffians and criminals are in charge of its economy," Andrew said.

"Hush." Claire touched his arm. "Let Alice speak."

"I mean physically not like other cities. Most places sit on the land, but Venice … she sits on the water."

"On islands, I understand," Claire said.

Alice shook her head. "Maybe back in Roman days, but not now. See, hundreds of years ago, Leonardo da Vinci was the most famous engineer in the world. The Doge who was in power back then hired him to make Venice the most difficult city to conquer in all of the Levant. So da Vinci turned the city into a giant moving clockwork. That way, an enemy could never pin down the Doge's exact location, nor that of the shipyards, nor the armory. It would be different every day."

"What?" Snouts shook his head, as though a fly were buzzing around his ears. "I don't understand."

"It takes some getting used to," Alice said. "Even now you can't post a letter to an actual address, because the postmen could never find it. Everyone goes to a central post office on the mainland for their mail."

"But what of Jake, then?" Snouts asked, looking more and more confused and angry. "How are we to find him? And how does it work, exactly?"

"I suppose if you hovered over the city in your ship for a good long time, you'd see all the neighborhoods moving on their individual pieces of the mechanism," Alice explained, "but when you're on the ground on foot, all you know is that every so often, all the church bells ring, all the bridges go up, and you feel a little seasick while the gears underwater grind into action, moving the neighborhoods into their next position. How they dodge around one another is a mystery, but they do—and have been for five hundred years."

"How does it not fail?" Andrew asked, clearly interested in spite of himself. "The corrosion of the parts from seawater alone—barnacles—algae—heavens, even an errant fish if it were large enough—could damage the workings and bring the city to a grinding halt."

Alice swallowed, and Claire put down her fork. Here it was. Here was the part that she had been unwilling to share with them until now.

The worst part.

"That's a very good question. And the answer is—convicts."

Now Snouts put down his own fork with a clatter. "Convicts?"

"That's who they use to clean and repair the gears and workings. That's why going to prison in Venice is so dadburned awful." Tears began to swim in Alice's horizon-blue eyes. "The ground crew on the mainland told me. Ships don't moor in the city proper because there's no free space to put down—it's all taken up with palaces and houses and court buildings for the Doge. They ... they send the convict crews out along the great arms of the gearworks in diving bells, where they spend their days cleaning off barnacles and algae and everything you said, Andrew. The convicts are the ones who keep the city oiled and operating—because no sane person would volunteer to do it. Venice has the lowest crime rate among ordinary folks in the whole Levant—if you don't count the crimes the Famiglia Rosa gets away with. And since no one wants to make a misstep and spend the rest of their days under the sea, the powers that be have taken to preying on foreigners like us. One false step on that moving ground and you're snatched up and put under with only the barest excuse for a trial, like they did with Jake." A single tear tracked down her cheek as she finally raised her chin and met Snouts's horrified gaze. "Hardly anyone is found innocent. And so they stay down there until they die—or go mad."

The last words seemed to echo in the silence of the dining room, and when Charlie came in with the treacle tart, everyone jumped.

"Claire, please, for the love of God—" Andrew began.

"How are we going to get him out from under—" Snouts cut him off.

"What about Claude?" Lizzie's voice rose in shrill concern. "He could drop a handkerchief and be arrested!"

Claire put her hands to her ears, both to shut out the cacophony and to squeeze out the awful vision of Jake, that independent, brave, conflicted young man, forced under the waves for the rest of his life. A large body of water had been instrumental in saving that life earlier in their acquaintance, when the sky pirate Ned Mose had pushed him out of an airship in a rage. She would not allow it to be the end of him now.

"Girls. Gentlemen." She was not in the habit of raising her voice, only because her occasional use of her mother's tone of authority usually produced the desired result. But she did have to speak twice, which only went to show how upset and agitated were the people around the glossy table—the people she cared about most in the world. "I agree that what we face here is nearly insurmountable." Snouts drew in a sharp breath, and she moved on quickly to spare his feelings further laceration. "But it is not impossible. Around this table are some of the bravest hearts and finest minds in all of England—quite possibly in all of the world. When we apply all our resources to the problem set before us, I have every confidence that we will find a solution."

It did her heart good to see both Alice and Snouts relax visibly. It would have done it far more good had Andrew done the same, but her brave words only seemed to inflame him further.

"Claire, may we speak privately?" he said with an evenness of tone that she knew must have cost him dearly.

"Of course, Andrew. But for the moment, surely we can agree on one point—Jake must not be left in that place an instant longer than necessary."

"Of course I agree. I am not a monster," Andrew said, still with that calm control. "But it is in the means of carrying this out where I believe we differ."

"Then let us agree on our first steps." The treacle

tart was set down before her, along with a knife and a stack of small plates. "Thank you, Charlie. You must have some of this with us, so that you may receive your payment in praise." She smiled at the ten-year-old urchin, who had been discovered in the garden by Lewis several weeks previously, sleeping stretched across the threshold of the hens' coop, as though guarding them. Or, more likely, their eggs. "I know you had a hand in making it."

The boy smiled shyly, wriggling onto a chair next to Maggie. "I did, Lady. Granny Protheroe says I have the touch—she let me make the pastry."

The boy was never happier than in a kitchen, where he could not only learn a trade, but also keep an eye on all the foodstuffs and prevent their escape. Having known debilitating hunger herself, Claire fully understood his reluctance to leave apples and cabbage and beef alone and undefended, even in Belgravia.

When everyone was settled with their tart and cream, Claire seized the metaphorical bull by the horns. "We had planned to leave London for Bavaria on Sunday, so I believe we must follow that plan." Snouts began to speak, but she forestalled him. "I know you believe we ought to lift at once, as do I, but hear me out. It is quite clear that Alice is being pursued by unknown parties who mean her harm."

"That's putting it mildly," Alice said. "It's got to be the Famiglia Rosa. I just had no idea their reach was so long."

"Precisely. But by all accounts they do not know you are in London, so we will keep it that way. We will act as though no news or visitors have come, and leave in two days, as we do every autumn, for Munich. Once the girls are comfortable in our rooms at Schloss Schwanenburg, they will begin classes as pl—"

"Classes?" Lizzie interrupted her with a complete lack of propriety. "There's no point in beginning classes if we're only to leave to go to Venice."

"My darlings, you will not go to Venice. It is far too dangerous, and you have responsibilities of your own at the *lycée*."

"So do you, at Uncle Ferdinand's manufactory," Maggie riposted with needle-like skill.

"I agree with Maggie," Andrew said promptly. "The Count expects you to take up your new position on Wednesday."

"He will understand when I tell him I must postpone." Really, must she explain herself on this point? "I'm sure you see this, too, Andrew. It is clear we cannot rely on the Dunsmuirs now. Jake has only us to count on, and we cannot let him down."

"Of course not. Once you add your pigeon to Alice's and notify Lady Dunsmuir that she must solicit Her Majesty's help, and that is secured, Jake will be a free man within days."

"You can depend on Her Majesty's help, just like that?" Alice asked, clearly impressed.

"We have not had to ask for it before this," Andrew admitted, "but she holds Claire in high regard. And even if she did not, Lady Dunsmuir is one of Her Majesty's closest confidantes. Any request from that quarter is fulfilled instantly, though governments go a-begging."

In the Canadas, Claire had swung from a mooring rope high above the earth, and Andrew had been instrumental in drawing her to safety. But the sense of vertigo and weightlessness she suffered from now was the emotional kind, brought on by his inexplicable reluctance to handle this matter themselves. Since when had they ever called upon governmental resources to solve their problems?

At the same time, the possibility did have its merits.

"Very well," she conceded at last. "I will send a pigeon tonight giving further details of the situation, and adding my plea to Alice's, with the addition that Davina communicate with Her Majesty on our behalf. We will remain in Bavaria until we have heard from Windsor Castle."

"And what about me?" Alice said, cleaning up the last of the pastry crumbs on her plate with her forefinger. "Where am I to remain while I'm standing around being invisible?"

"I wish you *were* invisible—it would make the logistics much easier." Claire made her best attempt at a smile. "You will come with us, disguised as—oh, I don't know. Which would you prefer? A man or a woman?"

"If a woman's disguise involves corsets and petticoats, I'll go as a man, thanks," Alice said with most unladylike decisiveness. "I could use new pants and a decent coat anyway."

"I can give the order to my haberdasher and you will not even need to leave Carrick House," Andrew said. "But you will not be able to leave the ship in Munich, either, unless it is under cover of darkness. For all your pursuers know, you are still in that city, where no doubt they have been turning over every stone in search of you."

"Dunno about that," Snouts put in. "Can't see them sticking to the job very long if they don't have any success. They'll be wanting to go home to Venice to lie in wait for the next poor blighter."

"I agree with Andrew," Claire told them, hoping this sop to his gentlemanly pride would go a little way to softening the discussion she knew they must have. "Alice must stay aboard *Athena* and avoid the viewing ports."

She rose, and the girls rose with her. After a moment and a pointed glance from Lizzie, Alice did too. But Claire did not go to the drawing room, as was usual after dinner. Instead, she went upstairs to her private study, where the Mopsies, clearly not finished with her yet, advanced.

"Lady, you cannot leave us behind," Lizzie said, sinking onto the sofa beside her and clutching her hand. "You're going to need scouts, and you said yourself we have brave hearts."

"I did, and I meant it." Claire's grip tightened. "Falling afoul of danger while one is going about one's life and minding one's own business is one thing. But sailing straight into it on purpose is quite another. You must see, my dears, that I cannot take such a risk with your lives. It is not right."

"But you will risk your own? What will Mr. Malvern have to say about that?" Oh, Lizzie had not lost any of her logic because of her recent adventures, it was clear. Or her powers of observation.

"I am hoping he will not need to say anything at all, if the Queen agrees to send assistance." Lizzie gazed at her, and Claire felt her face heat. "Do not look at me in that way."

Alice's lips twitched. Maggie studied a watercolor of Gwynn Place upon the wall.

With a sigh, Claire gave it up. "Andrew and I are going to have words, and it will distress me, but I must not give in," she said as Maggie cuddled up on her other side and Alice leaned protectively over the back of the sofa. "I cannot. When I think of poor Jake—"

"So you will let us come and help?" Lizzie said slyly.

Claire shook her head. "I am sorry, darlings. For once, you must think of yourselves before others. Of your futures. Of your own safety. And if you will not, then it is my responsibility to do so. There will be three capable individuals in this rescue party, which by any reckoning is more than enough. For I will have to convince Snouts that his place is not with us, as well."

Pulled in three different directions, horrified, saddened—was she about to weep? For here was her lower lip, actually trembling with distress. Maggie gave her one keen look and got to her feet. "Lizzie, you have made the Lady cry. Apologize at once."

To Claire's astonishment, Lizzie looked as though she was about to burst into tears herself. "Lady, I am sorry. Never mind. We'll go to Bavaria, as you said, and do as we ought."

She pulled Maggie and Alice from the room. Claire would have been grateful for a moment's privacy to collect herself if at that moment she had not heard a heavier step upon the stairs. It would have taken a great deal of distress to force Andrew up into the family regions of the house—indeed, both of them would likely blush at the impropriety of it tomorrow.

If they were still speaking tomorrow.

Claire took a deep breath and braced herself to disagree with the one person for whose good opinion she cared most deeply in all the world.

# A LADY OF INTEGRITY

4

But it was not Andrew who stepped into the room and closed the door behind him. It was Snouts.

Claire had known this conversation was coming, but she had not expected it so soon, with Andrew still downstairs. But whether soon or late, it must happen, so she patted the sofa next to her and he sat, remembering in spite of his agitation to tug on the legs of his trousers as a gentleman did.

"In all your plans, Lady, it was not clear what my part was to be," he said without preamble.

"What should you like it to be?" she asked softly.

"You know what I do," he said with his customary bluntness. "These years running the Morton Glass Works haven't changed the part of our lives that we keep under wraps. I would be your second, as I always am. Whether we waylay a man or eavesdrop or use our fists to get the information we need, I'm the one who takes care of it for you."

"Not for years now, Snouts."

"I haven't lost the hang of it."

"And what of our operations here? What of Lewis, and the glassworks, and the others here in the house who look to you for leadership?"

"With Tigg in the Corps, Lewis is my second. He can fill in for me." He gazed at her, his eyes full of the determination of a man much older than twenty-one.

"Lewis cannot protect Granny Protheroe and a house full of children under fifteen," she pointed out with gentle logic. "I depend on you to provide that protection. Imagine if it got out to the south side that my entire inner circle and I had left Carrick House defenseless. What then?"

He was silent, the truth of the matter doing full battle with his need to help his brother.

She pressed on. "Jake has myself, Alice, and Andrew to help him, and if Her Majesty responds to our plea, the resources of the government will be brought to bear as well. But what will the inhabitants of Carrick House have if you come with us?"

Claire saw color flood into his face as he realized the truth of the situation. "But he's my brother," he said at last. "It's my place."

"Your friends may stand in your place for you," she said. "But no one can replace you here. You have been my second for four years while the girls and I were at school. Would Jake wish you to abandon your post to come to his aid if it meant endangering the defenseless in your own home?"

## A LADY OF INTEGRITY

Slowly, Snouts shook his head, and Claire took heart. "I give you my word, Stephen, that I will not come home without him, though it means I die in the attempt."

"Don't say that, Lady." His lips barely moved, he was struggling so hard not to reveal his emotion to her.

"I mean every word. You protect and keep the ones I love, and I will do the same for your brother. Are we agreed? Is it a fair exchange?"

After a moment, he nodded, and then did something so out of character she was left speechless with surprise. He reached out and hugged her. For a moment she felt his cheek against her own, burning hot with his emotion, before he pulled away and fled the room.

Outside, she heard a murmur and realized that he had met Andrew at the top of the stairs.

She braced herself. For she knew perfectly well that all the carefully reasoned arguments she had just given Snouts were about to be used on her.

*

Andrew rapped lightly on the door and when he heard Claire's voice, stepped into her inner sanctum. From this room she ran what Andrew jokingly referred to as her empire—the airfield in Vauxhall Gardens, her investments in steam transportation, her patent registrations—and from which she maintained a lively correspondence with Lady Dunsmuir, Dr. Rosemary Craig, Dr. Frieda Schmetterling of the University of Bavaria, and a number of other women of singular intelligence and vision.

The room, he understood, had once been her parents' bedchamber, but now it was tastefully furnished with a mahogany desk and a smaller desk of teak, where Snouts and Lewis might work on matters concerning the Morton Glass Works and the Gaius Club and consult with Claire as often as needed. A few good landscapes by Cornish artists hung on walls painted a soothing pale yellow, with white wainscoting, and the windows overlooked the garden where Lewis's hens pecked and hunted.

Two of those happy individuals, Holly and Ivy, were usually to be found somewhere in Claire's vicinity, but he supposed that with the lateness of the hour, they had gone to the walking coop that stood under the beech trees below.

Andrew took his seat next to Claire on the sofa and searched her downcast face. "Having second thoughts, dearest?" he asked gently.

"Second ... and third ... and probably fourth by morning." She raised her gaze to meet his own. "But they all circle back to the most dreadful one. I cannot bear to think of Jake in prison. He is not the sort who will survive in such circumstances. His own temper at being unjustly accused will precipitate him into even greater peril—perhaps even mortal peril. I am afraid, Andrew, that if we do not act soon, we will have no reason to act at all."

He took her hand in both of his. "Her Majesty will not allow an English subject to be treated in such a fashion. Even the most humble of her subjects deserves the process of law to prove his innocence."

"But this was not a legal matter. It was a shanghai, and I cannot see Her Majesty bringing the force of our government to bear on criminals such as these. They will simply deny that any such person exists in the Duchy, and if forced to prove otherwise, they will simply dispose of him before her representatives arrive."

"We can only hope she disagrees with you."

"And if she does not? What then, Andrew? Will you disagree with me, too, once all hope of help is lost to us?"

Trust Claire to come to the sticking point immediately.

"Is it so wrong of me to fear for your safety?" Clearly unwilling to reply, she turned her gaze to the silk draperies. He went on, "Or to ask you to think before you plunge headlong into a situation for which you are not prepared?"

"How can one prepare for this?"

The truth was that one could not. But his fiancée was very good at thinking on her feet—and this was what frightened Andrew the most. That, and the thought of a failed rescue resulting in the woman he loved being imprisoned under the water herself.

Or worse.

"Let us consider the situation," she said. "Should Her Majesty not be willing to assist us, what then? Will you allow Jake to die there before you will allow me to go?"

"I do not recall any situation in which I have been called upon to *allow* you to do anything," he pointed out. He must say something while he tried to marshal his panicked thoughts.

He had experienced terrifying danger at Claire's side—including the imminent threat of death and imprisonment. Why, then, should the thought of this voyage loom so darkly in his mind? Was it that it contrasted so completely with the bright picture of happiness he had been entertaining of late? Was it that, having secured her affection, he now valued it even more than the life of a young man?

Andrew shuddered away from such an estimation of himself.

"I know you are afraid for me," Claire said, her face softening at the distress he could not hide. "Since you will be with me, I shall be just as afraid for you. But do you not see that if we do this together, we have twice the chance of success?"

"Do what, exactly?" he replied, keeping his voice steady with difficulty. She responded best to a calm discussion of facts, so he must school himself to calm. "We cannot land, guns blazing, and expect to succeed at all. This Famiglia Rosa will see us coming from fifty miles off."

"Of course not," she said, evidently heartened by his willingness to talk the matter over instead of locking her in her room, as his former business partner and her erstwhile fiancé had once so foolishly done. "We must approach this as a woman does—pleasantly, innocently, twirling our parasols and remarking upon the scenery. We shall attend the exhibition in full view, securing Claude's safety while we are at it, and spirit Jake away by ... by ..."

"By what means?"

Crestfallen, she admitted, "I have not yet worked out that part, but I am sure I shall once we arrive." She brightened. "It is Friday. Can you not contrive a strategy for rescuing someone from underwater by Sunday?"

This was too much. "I suppose now is not the time to remind you that you were to have ordered your wedding gown by tomorrow?"

"Wedding gown?" She looked so completely at sea over the change in subject that he had to laugh.

"Yes, dearest. If we are to be married at Christmas, I am told one must do these things in advance. See? It is marked on your calendar." He nodded at the wall calendar, scribbled over and crossed out to the point where it was difficult to see. But on October third it clearly said *wedding dress*, twice underlined.

"Oh, dear," Claire said. "That's not the order, it is merely an appointment. I must remember to cancel it. I'm afraid I haven't given much thought to the arrangements—dress, church, flowers." She brightened. "But one isn't required to carry flowers, is one? Many brides carry a Bible or a prayer book or some such."

"I think you have the wedding ceremony confused with an execution, dear."

"Do I? No, surely not. Oh, bother. It is three months off, and now is not the time to think of such things. A boy's life is in danger."

Andrew held back a sigh. She was utterly right—and therein lay the only cloud upon their nuptial horizon. Not for the first time, he wished that her loyalty and love for those around her would not precipitate her into rash action. She was forever charging off to save people, which someone had to do, of course. But it came at the expense of her own domestic felicity, to say nothing of his peace of mind.

But if it was to be his fate to love a woman of resources and integrity, then the least he could do would be to live up to her. She believed him to be the partner best suited to a common happiness, and he would do everything in his power to support and protect that belief.

Which is why he finally said, "We shall have a simpler wedding that requires less advance planning. If I am to build a prototype of some kind in two days, I shall have to visit the metal yard tomorrow." The walk would give him time to think and possibly even come up with a design. "It is at times like this that I wish Tigg had not chosen the Corps as his career. I could use his skill."

"Oh, Andrew." She flung herself into his arms, and he took a selfish moment to enjoy the warmth of her embrace and the scent of her auburn hair under his cheek. "Thank you."

"I shall seriously consider an elopement if this is to be my reward," he murmured.

"Not for that, you gumpus, though I am grateful you favor simplicity. I meant for throwing your lot in with mine, foolish and hopeless though it often seems to be."

"If we are to be married, we shall be throwing our lots in with each other," he said with a slight return of his usual good humor. "It is wise to practice as much as possible beforehand."

This earned him a kiss, but as he held her, perhaps his arms were a little tighter about her slender form than usual. And he tried not to think of what would happen to his heart should she be torn away.

\*

Alice may have been forbidden to leave *Athena*, but Claire was simply unable to.

Her personal vessel, while not quite as shabby as it had been when she'd originally acquired it, still looked as out of place as ever in the grand park that doubled

as an airfield at Schloss Schwanenburg, the Munich estate of Count Ferdinand von Zeppelin. Moored around
her were examples of the finest air fleet in the world,
with the possible exception of that of Her Majesty's
Aeronautic Corps, shining silver and blue in the late
autumn sun. *Athena*, in contrast, was the brown of a
sparrow, of canvas left too long in adverse conditions,
and possessed a gondola not of brass, but of a material
that might have begun as teak but was now built up
and built on in a manner understood only by her present captain.

"I cannot bear it." Claire paced the narrow corridor
between the engine compartment and the navigation
gondola, from whence she would be able to hear the
arrival of the pigeon from England. "It has been three
days since Lady Dunsmuir's message went to the
Queen. How long does it take to decide whether or not
one is going to save a boy's life?"

"Claire, you need to get your mind off it. Let me do
the pacing," Alice suggested, not for the first time.
"You should be dressing for dinner with the count and
his wife. They'll be here in half an hour. Do you want
them to find you in your shirtwaist?"

"I don't care if they find me in a pair of your pants
and one of Mr. Stetson's hats." Claire reversed direction
past Alice, who was holding up the wall near the cabin
she tended to call her own when she was aboard. "I'm
going mad."

"We all are, dearling."

Claire ran her hands over her face, as though that
might help rub the worry wrinkles from between her
brows. "I know you are right. Very well. You must
come and change, too. You have a new middy now—

assign Mr. Stringfellow to pigeon watch."

Alice pushed herself off the wainscoting. "I have to say this is a new one on me. Having a middy, I mean. That poor kid—are you sure he wouldn't be happier back at Carrick House?"

"He would not." Claire looped her arm through Alice's and together they made their way to the crew's quarters. "The children may arrive in Wilton Crescent as street sparrows, but they stay with the understanding that they will make something of themselves. Mr. Stringfellow has proven himself able at mathematics and reading, and has shown an aptitude for heights—meaning he retains his meals during lift. When we find the *Stalwart Lass* and Jake, the latter may be incapacitated. You will be glad of another hand then, I daresay."

"He doesn't leave *Athena*. I don't want another boy's fate on my conscience—especially one barely out of short pants."

"Of course not. His duties are aboard ship." Briskly, she knocked on the closet-sized cabin that had thrilled the boy's heart. Had he been a prince given a country of his own, he could not have been happier. "Mr. Stringfellow, are you within?"

The door opened at once to reveal the black-haired, red-cheeked urchin. "Yes, Lady. What is it, Lady?"

"Captain Chalmers and I must dress and receive dinner guests—since she cannot go out, they are coming to us. I would like you to stand watch in the communications cage. The instant that pigeon arrives from England, I want the contents brought to me, no matter where I am or what I am doing."

"Yes, Lady."

Before she could take another breath, he dashed off down the corridor to carry out his orders.

"Can't fault his obedience, anyway," Alice said as he disappeared from view. "Come on. Let's get you dressed."

"What about you?" Claire poked her in the ribs. "Whatever happened to that aquamarine dress Lady Dunsmuir had made for you in Edmonton?"

Alice huffed a laugh. "That thing? I haven't seen hide nor hair of it since then. I think it got spoiled somehow during our escape. I must have thrown it out—or used it to patch a gas bag, maybe. There was enough fabric in it to make a touring balloon."

"Such a shame. You looked well in it."

"If you're hinting that I ought to dress up for dinner, you're bound for disappointment. I'll put on one of your navy skirts and a shirt, and that will have to do."

"Believe me, I wish I could do the same. But the von Zeppelins know perfectly well the contents of my wardrobe, after four years here, so I'll be expected to put on evening clothes. It shows them respect, you know, since they will certainly dress to greet us."

Alice looked a little anxious. "They won't think I'm not showing respect, will they? Because all I have to stand up in outside of what I can borrow from you are the things Mr. Malvern got from his haberdasher."

"Certainly not. A man who secretes you in a rifle case knows precisely the extent of your resources and will not hold them against you."

Claire had not seen the count and the baroness since she had taken her leave of them following her graduation from the University of Bavaria the previous June. So their arrival here yesterday had been a happy one, with tonight's invitation being contrived so that the count, ever alert for the engineering talent he enjoyed nurturing in others, might converse with Alice without danger of her being seen.

Claire had kept the menu simple out of consideration for the von Zeppelins' cook, who had prepared the meal in the palace and was simply adding the finishing touches in *Athena's* spartan galley. A cold shrimp cocktail, soup, and a game course with roasted vegetables were all easily transported across several hundred feet of lawn.

They had barely begun the haunch, which may as well have been porridge for all the attention Alice and the count were paying to it, so deep in conversation were they, when running footsteps could be heard in the corridor.

*The pigeon. Thank God. Oh, let it be good news.*

Claire intercepted Mr. Stringfellow at the door and he handed her a thick, creamy envelope bearing the royal seal in a dollop of red wax. Her stomach dipped and righted itself, as though *Athena* had hit a wind shear.

"Alice, Count, Baroness—it is the Queen, at last."

*To our right loyal subject Lady Claire Trevelyan, greetings.*

*We are in receipt of a message from our dear friend and counselor, Lady Dunsmuir, on the subject of one Jake Fletcher McTavish, navigator of the Charlottetown-registered vessel Stalwart Lass, recently under contract to Lord John Dunsmuir as a cargo ship. We understand that he and said vessel*

## A LADY OF INTEGRITY

*have been seized and imprisoned as collateral against*
*payment of transit taxes.*

*At least, so we are informed by the Venetian am-*
*bassador, who is presently in London to invite us to*
*next year's art exhibition. He assures us that once*
*the transit taxes are paid by the captain of the ves-*
*sel, navigator, cargo, and ship will be released and*
*sent upon their way. We view this as the reasonable*
*cost of commerce and fail to see the necessity of our*
*intervention. Indeed, the Dunsmuirs will send what*
*is needed immediately.*

*Lady Claire, please accept our felicitations and*
*those of our dearly beloved Husband upon the recent*
*news of your engagement to Mr. Andrew Malvern.*
*The Prince Consort wishes me to convey his particu-*
*lar delight at the news. He looks forward to securing*
*a dance with the bride, with fond memories of a past*
*occasion.*

*By our own hand and seal,*
*Victoria Regina*

5

"Oh dear," Claire said in tones of despair, her spirits falling into her shoes. "There go all our hopes of a simple wedding ... to say nothing of our hopes of assistance for Jake. How can she possibly call kidnapping the 'reasonable cost of commerce'? It's absurd. She has been completely misinformed about the case."

Now Alice was on her feet, the Queen's letter in both hands as if a reading by a different pair of eyes would produce a different message. "I don't understand," she said blankly. "I already asked the Dunsmuirs for the money for the transit tax, and it wasn't forthcoming."

"At a guess, might it be because they refuse to be the victims of extortion?" Andrew mused aloud. Alice passed the letter to him, and when he'd read it, he gave it to the count and his wife, who perused it together.

"Then why 'send what is needed' now?" Claire said. "The Dunsmuirs are not so small that they would withhold money in a circumstance like this—not if it means Jake's freedom—his very life. It does not seem like them at all."

"Maybe they mean to cut me loose." Alice had gone pale. "Maybe I did something wrong—made the wrong person angry—and they're disavowing me and breaking the contract."

"Not at all." Claire gave her a squeeze that somehow made her feel a little better, herself. "They are sending what is needed. No matter what political maneuverings are going on in London at the moment, we must hold to that."

Voices sounded below in the landing bay, and for the second time in ten minutes, footsteps pounded down the corridor. "Lady!" Mr. Stringfellow shouted, heedless of the impropriety of raising his voice in front of their august company. "Lady, it's—"

"Don't spoil it, Benny—we told you, it's a surprise," came a laughing voice from the deck below.

Lizzie gasped and pushed back her chair with such suddenness it fell over behind her. "That's—"

Claire, standing nearest to the door, bolted out, Lizzie hot on her heels. And there, emerging at the top of the stairs between decks, was a familiar, beloved coffee-brown face and lively dark eyes.

"Tigg!" she exclaimed.

"Tigg!" Lizzie shrieked, and threw herself with most unladylike abandon into his arms. He hugged her so hard it was a wonder she could breathe—and then kissed her with a calm possessiveness that told Claire that there had been much more to his letters than the snippets Lizzie had been reading to them over breakfast.

He set Lizzie down and turned to Claire, who hugged him in her turn. Goodness, he was strong, his body filling out and coming into its own with vigorous, satisfying work. He was a man now, and she smiled into his eyes with all the pride that welled in her heart.

"All right, Lady?" he asked.

"More than all right now," she said. "What have we done to merit this gift, so unexpectedly?"

Now a new voice, equally familiar and unexpected, sounded behind him. "Did you not receive Her Majesty's letter?" Ian Hollys, captain of the Dunsmuirs' flagship vessel, *Lady Lucy*, climbed the last of the stairs and emerged into the receiving salon beside his lieutenant.

Her mind spinning in joy and confusion, Claire gave him her hand. "But … I don't understand. What are the two of you doing here when we understood you were at the Firstwater Mine, on the other side of the world?"

"Then you have not received her letter."

"We have indeed, not ten minutes past. But it does not explain your presence—welcome as it is." She collected herself and remembered her manners somewhat belatedly. "Do come into the dining salon. We were just at dinner with Count von Zeppelin and the Baroness. Will you join us?"

"I wouldn't turn down good grub." Tigg took Lizzie's hand and led the way back along the corridor. "Nor the chance to shake the count's hand again."

Which left Claire alone with Ian Hollys, a situation in which she had not found herself since she had declined his proposal in June, practically on this very spot. "Will you come and have something to eat?" she said, a little diffidently. How did one treat the worthy and noble gentleman one had refused? The etiquette books her mother was so fond of did not cover such a situation, she was quite sure—and even if they did, Claire had not read them. "You can tell all of us the story at once. Each person here is exceedingly anxious to know if you have any more information than Her Majesty gave us."

"Claire, a moment." His gaze had not left her face, and if not for the ring upon her finger, she would have felt quite uncomfortable.

"Of course."

He lifted her hand as if to kiss it, and saw the ring. After the briefest of hesitations, he patted the back of it and released it. "Please accept my heartfelt felicitations upon your engagement to Mr. Malvern. I heard of it only recently, when Tigg came to Hollys Park."

"Hollys Park?" she said blankly. What had he been doing there? And when had he come home? Goodness, he must tell them what was going on at once. "Thank you, Ian. We are very happy, and planning to say our vows at Christmas."

"I am glad." They walked down the corridor, toward where she could see Alice and Andrew crowding the door, astonishment written on their faces. "Your happiness means a great deal to me, and the fact that I can respect and admire your choice makes me happy, as well."

It was gallant of him to say so, but there was no time for more. Ian and Tigg were borne away to the table, where the von Zeppelin staff lost no time in setting two more places and offering food. Lizzie, glued to Tigg's side, peeled shrimp and would have fed them to him one by one, too, if she had not caught Claire's eye and straightened in her chair enough to pay attention to her own plate.

Claire handed Ian the letter from the Queen. "We have all read it. I do hope you can shed some light on it, for it makes no sense at all even to the fine minds gathered here."

Ian scanned the lines, then handed it across to Tigg, who put down his fork and did the same. "She has succeeded in her intent, then," Ian said. "She is emulating her predecessor, Queen Elizabeth the First, in that her writing says what it must, while she herself does what she can. She is, of course, quite powerless to act openly, with the Venetian ambassador camped upon the doorstep."

"So we assumed," Count von Zeppelin said, "but it does not explain the help she refers to. Will the Dunsmuirs pay the transit tax, or not?"

"Certainly not," Ian said crisply. "It is extortion, pure and simple, and they will not be a party to it."

"Then how will we get Jake out of prison?" Alice asked, her eyes filling with tears. "Surely you didn't come all this way just to give us bad news."

"Of course not," Tigg said. "What do you take the captain for?"

"I hardly know." Alice's fear made her tone sharper than it might have been, given her present company. "It appears I have to take him or leave him, when a bag full of money would have done the job faster. No offense."

"None taken," Ian said. Then he smiled—a dangerous smile that Claire suspected put fear into the hearts of air pirates and extortioners alike. "The Dunsmuirs could not send money, and the Queen could not send an envoy that might hint in any way at interference in the Duchy's affairs. But they could do the next best thing."

"They sent us," Tigg said with satisfaction. "Pulled us both off leave and popped us on the first transport out, quiet-like, so that we could come and help. And the topper to it all?"

"I can't imagine," Claire said.

Ian took up where Tigg left off. "We have *carte blanche* from Her Majesty to do whatever is necessary to retrieve 'her most loyal subject, Jake Fletcher McTavish' from the hands of these miscreants, up to and including deadly force."

Claire's breath went out of her in a long sigh of admiration at the Queen's cleverness. Across the table, Alice covered her face with her napkin and burst into tears, as though a terrible burden had just been lifted.

*

"But of course you need not go." Count von Zeppelin's grip tightened upon his glass of port, and Claire saw Lizzie and Maggie exchange a glance of trepidation.

The dining salon and the family salon in which Claire and her guests now gathered after dinner had once been a cargo bay. A little elbow grease and the removal of several years' worth of packing material, bullet casings, and insects; the laying of a new hardwood floor; and the addition of comfortable furniture, carpets, and books had gone a long way toward making *Athena* into what she was today: an airborne home.

Viewing ports had even been added, but the drapes had been drawn and lamps lit, which now illuminated the count's lowered brows and tense hands.

"If Captain Hollys, Lieutenant Terwilliger, and Mr. Malvern make up the rescue party, there is certainly no need for young ladies to go. Young ladies, I might add, who are expected to take up their duties here in Munich tomorrow morning."

The Mopsies wisely remained silent, leaving Claire to have the conversation in public that she had most hoped to have in private.

"Count, perhaps I might walk with you, the Baroness, and the girls to the palace?" she suggested. On Lizzie's other side, Tigg sat, his fingers entwined with hers. "And Tigg," she added. He would not stay aboard *Athena* in any case, if it meant Lizzie crossing the park without his protection to the suite she shared in the palace with Claire and Maggie. Not after what had happened only a few short weeks ago, when Lizzie had nearly been blown up by a pocket watch.

Well, that meant only half the party would be witness to the lecture she was about to receive.

The count and his wife made their farewells and in a few minutes, they were crossing the familiar lawn, with its double avenue of linden trees and the fountain playing softly in the middle of the lake. At this time of the evening, though, the swans for which the palace was named were nowhere to be seen.

Lucky creatures.

The three younger members of the party melted discreetly away when they reached the French doors of the pretty suite that had been their home thanks to the count's hospitality for the last four years. Was she really prepared to show herself so ungrateful for everything he had done for her by abandoning her position before she had even taken it up?

She thought of Jake, and did her best to firm her resolution.

She sank onto a delicate Rococo chair when he and the baroness seated themselves on the sofa. "You must understand my feelings," she began. "Jake is practically a member of my family. He is Alice's navigator. We cannot go about our normal lives when one of our friends is in danger. You would not expect it of us."

"I would expect you to take the sensible view," the count said gently. "What can you add to the expedition that an experienced military man, a scientist, and a capable aeronaut do not already possess?"

*Brains, bombs, and a modest amount of beauty if necessary* would probably not be the most prudent reply.

"I have a plan," she said. "I believe we stand the greatest chance of success if we pose as visitors to the art exhibition. As English tourists, we may explore the nooks and crannies of the city unmolested, and as a woman, I would not be suspected of any behavior more threatening than a fainting spell."

"And then?"

How fortunate she and Andrew had talked this over. "And then Mr. Malvern plans to devise a—a mechanism by which we may effect a rescue. But it will all depend on what we discover there, after we reconnoiter."

"This is all very well, but there remains one other question."

Here it came—the point where she must bring shame upon herself. "I know I was to begin work in the laboratory tomorrow, and Count, you cannot know how much it distresses me to disappoint you."

"Then do not," the baroness urged her. She spoke so rarely that Claire blinked in surprise. "Ferdinand has been waiting eagerly for this day. To launch you upon a career that will put many others in the shade."

"And I am equally anxious to begin my career," she said quickly. "But can you not see that it would only be delayed by a week at most? Surely, for the sake of a young man's life, that is not too much to ask?"

Von Zeppelin's gaze did not soften into sympathy or agreement. "It reflects poorly upon us two," he said at last. "You, for unnecessarily putting yourself in the way of danger, and I, for allowing my expectations and those of my senior staff to be toyed with. It is not necessary for you to go, and I find it difficult to have my offer and my hospitality of the last four years repaid in this manner."

Claire tried not to wilt, to meet this charge with the straight spine of a woman and a lady, not a child, but it was difficult. "It is only for a week," she said faintly.

"And what if it is not? What if some disaster strikes and we lose you? Will the life of young Jake balance the loss of yours, Mr. Malvern's, and Lieutenant Terwilliger's, to say nothing of those others who go with you?"

Well, this was simply not fair. "One cannot declare the worth of one by the measure of another. And besides, it does no good to borrow trouble, only to prepare for it."

"And will you be prepared? Will you go, despite my wishes?"

She was silent.

"Because I cannot guarantee that upon your return,

the position will be waiting for you, if you will treat it so cavalierly."

"Ferdinand." Even the baroness's eyes widened as she put a hand upon his arm.

Claire felt as though she might be sick. "Please," she whispered. "You cannot expect me to send others in where I am not willing to go."

"Your Queen is perfectly satisfied to let capable men handle the task. Are you so much better than she?"

He had never spoken to her in such a tone before, nor used such words. How dreadfully she must be disappointing him—and how afraid for her he must be! She could feel his distress from where she sat—and it did not make this any easier.

"Do not make me choose between my family and my career," she said brokenly, her throat closing up. "I cannot bear to disappoint you … and yet I cannot bear to stay behind while others risk their lives."

"I am the last man to say that a woman cannot prove herself in laboratory and manufactory," he said heavily. "Mrs. Bertha Benz—to say nothing of my own dear wife—would never let me hear the end of it if I did. But this is not the first time you will have to make this choice, Claire. Tonight it is young Jake. Tomorrow it may be Elizabeth, or Marguerite. Five years from now it may be a youngster with your eyes and Mr. Malvern's smile. How will you choose then?"

"How did you?" she had the temerity to ask. "How did the Baroness?"

"I raised our family while the count was in the army and the government," that lady said quietly. "My place was in the home—and in my office here in the palace."

"Times have changed since then," Claire said. "A

woman may employ her talents outside the home."

"And is that fair to her family? You see, Claire, these are difficult questions. But you must ask them of yourself—and when you know the truth, you must act upon it." The count paused, his eyes at last softening to more resemble those of the man she had come to know since she and their friends had saved his life in the Canadas. He seemed to remember that, too, for he said, "I owe you my life and am the first one to say so. I will repay my debt … but you must be willing to take up the responsibility I give you."

He rose, and offered the baroness his hand. "We will wish you a good night, and will see you in the morning."

Claire kissed them both, and the door closed behind them.

She sank onto the sofa, her lips trembling, her back straight now that she was alone.

The Mopsies came in, murmuring quietly between themselves, and hesitated on the threshold. Then they crept away to the bedroom they shared.

When the suite was silent and a very terrible hour alone with her conscience had passed, she crossed the room to the writing table and got out paper and ink. She wrote one letter to the girls, and took it into their room. Lizzie was a sound sleeper, and Maggie only murmured as she kissed them both. The second letter she addressed to the count, and left it propped against the vase of flowers on the mantel in the sitting room.

Then she went out and crossed the vast darkness of the park, the glowing lamp on *Athena*'s mooring mast guiding her back to the one place on earth she needed to be.

# A LADY OF INTEGRITY

6

Dawn lay upon the horizon, a line that might have been drawn in watery gray ink if one had been on the ground, but up here, it was a sky-wide glow in the viewing ports that promised a clear day and good flying.

"Nine, continue on this course, and I will take the helm when we approach the Alps," she instructed the automaton intelligence system that she and Alice between them had invented. She had never flown over mountains so high, but they could not be higher than the Rocky Mountains of the Canadas. Claire had rebuilt *Athena*'s engine from cell to screws over the last several years, with Andrew's assistance, and had complete confidence in her ship's ability to manage, no matter what was demanded of her.

"What in God's name have you done?"

Claire turned in some surprise at having her communion with the skies interrupted in such a manner. "I have lifted," she told Alice calmly as the latter came into the gondola, tying her hair up with a ribbon that had seen better days. "I acted as my own ground crew—no easy feat in the dark, I assure you. I'm glad you're up. I shall likely need your help with wind currents and altitude as we cross the Alps."

Alice checked the viewing port, as if she needed the proof of her own eyes that yes, there were the Alps rising blue and serrated in the distance. "But the count—last night—he seemed adamant. Did he relent and allow you to go?"

Claire busied herself with charts and general tidying up of the navigation table. "I don't know if *allow* is the right word," she said slowly. "He was very honest with me about the consequences of the two courses of action before me, and taking those into account, I chose one."

"You lifted before dawn—without consulting Captain Hollys or Mr. Malvern or even me," Alice said flatly, seeing right through this prevarication. "Claire, what were you thinking? What if I had gone to a beer garden? What if the men have? Do you even know who is aboard?"

"I know who is *not* aboard." Fine. Yes, she had been rather peremptory about whisking people into the air who might not even have loaded their bags yet. But there was a greater good to be accomplished here. "Lizzie and Maggie," she added when Alice remained silent and aghast. "Can you imagine the fuss if I had taken a conventional leave and forbidden them one last time to go? This way, the thing is done, the girls are safe where they belong, and while Captain Hollys may not have a spare shirt if his flight gear was not brought aboard last night, at least he and Tigg will have two fewer worries on this voyage."

"Provided either Captain Hollys or Tigg are even with us. Since they're the official members of this mission, shouldn't someone take the time to check?"

"Check what? Claire, why are the engines—" Andrew Malvern stopped in the doorway, the view through the windows clearly not the trees and lawns he had been expecting. "Dear heaven. Where are we? What have you done?"

Alice filled him in with rather more pointed brevity than Claire thought necessary, and he spun on his heel and ran back to the cabins from whence he had come.

Claire braced herself.

Sure enough, five minutes later Captain Hollys and Tigg spilled into the navigation gondola, tucking in their shirts, Tigg hopping on one foot as he dragged on his second boot.

"Lady Claire, explain yourself at once!"

Alice levered herself off the table and put her hands on her hips. "Now, now," she said to the captain, "there's no need to take that tone."

"There certainly is," he contradicted her bluntly. "We have been shanghaied and I demand to know why!"

"I should think it quite obvious, Ian." Claire forced herself to speak calmly instead of matching his indignation with her own. "If we had not left with some stealth, there would have been no way to prevent the Mopsies from coming along. I am sure you agree that the absence of two young ladies of strong wills and irrepressible spirits will simplify our expedition at least a little."

"I still have two of the same on my hands." He glared from her to Alice. "I am of half a mind to turn this ship about and take you back to Munich before we fly another league."

Alice's eyebrows rose.

Claire had to agree. Had he really had the temerity to say such a thing to her? If in the very beginning she might have had the smallest of regrets at declining his offer of marriage, now she was conscious of a feeling of relief at having her instincts confirmed by his own actions. "You forget, Captain, that *Athena* is my ship. If anyone is to be put off, it will not be me."

He managed to haul back on the headlong gallop of his temper with difficulty. "You are right. Forgive me. However, there still remains one young lady whose presence aboard you ought to have considered. For heaven's sake, Claire, you are returning Alice straight into the danger from which she risked her life to escape."

"She is not returning me," Alice corrected him with some spirit. "I am going back voluntarily."

"I hardly think so, if she lifted with you asleep in your bed and not even a *may I, please.*"

"Do you seriously think I would have stayed in Munich or gone back to London while other people go to pull my navigator out of trouble?" Alice demanded. "You have a poor idea of the capabilities of women, sir."

"I do not," he retorted with heat. "You forget that I fly for one of the most important and capable women in England."

"And what would she say of this lecture you're giving us?" Alice flung at him. "I'd lay a bet you wouldn't say such things to her."

"Lady Dunsmuir is not in the habit of lifting without the permission—or at least the knowledge—of all aboard."

"Permission?" Claire repeated. "Captain, Alice, do calm down. I admit my actions were peremptory—and I do hope you and Tigg were able to get your bags aboard last night—but do you not see that we all share a common purpose? Come. I beg that you forgive me for my haste in leaving and realize that it was for a greater good—the safety of Lizzie and Maggie."

A bubbling cluck sounded behind Ian's trouser leg, and Holly and Ivy popped through the door, heading at a brisk trot for Claire and the treats that usually resided in the pockets of her raiding rig.

If Alice had been surprised by the view outside the windows, Claire was now equally astonished by the view within. For the birds were certainly not supposed to be aboard.

"Where did you come from?" she asked the small golden hens, picking up Ivy and allowing her onto her left shoulder. "Surely the girls did not leave you aboard when they took their trunks off. Why are you not safe in your coop in the count's garden?"

Ivy cooed happily next to her ear, but it was not a reply. It was a greeting.

"There you are, you fluffy rascals," Maggie said, squeezing out from behind Tigg and picking up Holly. "Is there a chance of breakfast yet, Lady? Why is everyone up so early?"

*

Claire's stomach dipped with horror as she stared into Maggie's innocent face—entirely too innocent—while her own cheeks flooded with color and then began inexorably to blotch. "Maggie," she said quietly, "is Lizzie aboard as well?"

"Yes."

"And when did the two of you manage this?"

In the dreadful pause that followed, Maggie seemed to realize the depth of the trouble she was in. "Last night."

"After I checked on you in your room in the palace? After I returned to the ship myself?"

"Yes, Lady. We came in through the communications cage, where the pigeons dock. It—it's a flaw in *Athena*'s design, and a squeeze now that we're older, but—"

Claire's razor-quiet voice cut her off. "Is there a reason for this deceitful behavior?"

A rustle near the door produced Lizzie, just in time to hear this question, take in the silence in the room, and observe the state of Claire's complexion. Claire saw the moment when Lizzie came to the conclusion that innocence was futile and they would have to employ a different strategy.

"We knew you would need us, Lady," Lizzie said, her tone cautious, as one might use when approaching a lion. "It wouldn't be proper for an unmarried lady to attend the exhibition in a company of gentlemen, so we came along to make the numbers more believable."

Another silence. Any other response would dignify this nonsense far too much. And she needed a moment to take a firm grip on her temper—and her fear.

## A LADY OF INTEGRITY

"First," Claire said, "I am engaged to one of the gentlemen, so your concerns are groundless. Second, Alice, too, was a lady the last time I looked. Third, do you realize you have put your final year at the *lycée* in jeopardy? Do you really have so little respect for yourselves that you would risk losing all for which you have worked so hard? And *fourth*, the count and the baroness will be frantic with worry, thinking you have been kidnapped. Have you no regard for them, after all they have done for you?"

Maggie shrank under the lash of her tone. Lizzie did her best to bear up, but by the fourth point, she, too, could only gaze at the floor, blinking, her lips trembling and her fingers pleating the skirt of her raiding rig.

"You will send a pigeon at once," Claire said, "informing them of your whereabouts and asking them to send a landau to the commercial airfield to meet the packet from Geneva. We will re-route our course and have you on it this afternoon."

"But Lady—"

"I will hear no arguments. You have disobeyed and deceived those who love you most with no regard for our feelings, and I can barely look at you for disappointment. Go aft now, please. You may leave Holly here."

Meekly, Maggie put the hen on the teak floor, and the two of them trailed out the door, faces red with shame, tears standing on their lashes.

Alice gazed after their retreating backs, then turned to Claire as though she didn't know who to offer comfort to first. "Claire," she began, "surely they—"

But Claire turned away, blinking back the tears she would not shed in front of the girls.

Tigg had already gone out after Lizzie, but the two men still stood there, gawking and unwelcome during this moment of feminine emotion. As though realizing that such a moment demanded privacy and consideration for finer feelings, Alice took the elbows of Captain Hollys and Andrew, and steered them toward the door.

"What—"

"Give us a moment, gentlemen," she said.

"I hardly see why—"

Alice glared, and Captain Hollys abruptly closed his mouth, turned, and departed, Andrew on his heels.

Gently, Alice removed Ivy's feathery self from Claire's shoulder and passed a comforting arm about her. Claire leaned her forehead on her friend's shoulder and let the tears come. "There, there. It will be all right," Alice said softly as she patted her back, as though Claire had been one of her little half-sisters back in the Canadas.

"I'm just—so afraid for them—and for you," Claire finally managed between sobs.

"Don't be afraid for me," Alice said in some surprise. "I made sure I stocked up on bullets for the Remington before I left."

"But the girls—if anything should happen—"

"I would put those two up against just about anybody," Alice said. "Don't forget that one foiled a plot to kill the Prince of Wales, and the other stopped a French invasion. These are no ordinary young ladies."

"Believe me, I have not forgotten." Neither had she forgotten the knifelike terror during the final moments of each of those occasions, when she had thought them dead. "But in striving to give them as normal an upbringing as possible, I fear they may never forgive me."

# A LADY OF INTEGRITY

Claire sniffled and wiped the tears off one cheek with the flat of her hand, then pulled a handkerchief from her sleeve and used it with vehemence. "But if I let them come, I may regret it for ever."

"Forgive me for saying so, but our sudden lift tells me that you defied the count this morning in a way not so different from the girls' behavior last night. You just got away with it and they didn't."

Trust Alice to bring her face to face with the truth she had been trying to avoid. "Thank you for the reminder of my own poor example," Claire moaned. "Honestly, I am the worst guardian anyone ever had—and if they are killed or taken prisoner and forced underwater, I do not know what I shall do."

"The same thing we're going to do for Jake," Alice told her firmly. "This is no time for you to lose your nerve, Claire. We have work to do, and I can't do it alone. We need every hand on deck. If I have to walk back into that boiling kettle of a Duchy, I tell you what, I'd be glad of Lizzie or Maggie watching my back."

"I would too—but their educations, Alice." Shouldn't a guardian look at the longer view, not merely the current emergency? How was one to know the right thing, when what was right at one moment might be wrong for the next?

"Send a pigeon to their headmistress and say that a family emergency has come up. All we need is a week. They won't be booted out of school for missing that, will they?"

"No," Claire said slowly. "I do not suppose so." She couldn't keep the plea out of her gaze. "Do you really believe we ought to take them?"

Alice's mobile mouth took on a rueful cast. "I believe that if we don't, they'll bribe an aeronaut in Geneva to get them over the Alps themselves, and that poses its own problems."

The corners of Claire's own lips twitched, and the tension in Alice's shoulders eased a little.

"Thank you, Alice," she said. "I am glad I can count on you to tell me what I need to hear, not merely what I *want* to hear. And now I must hurry back before they release that pigeon. On the way I shall decide how best to recant my position. Will you take the helm?"

"I'd be happy to." Alice turned to relieve Nine of his duty, blowing a long breath up through her curly fringe, as if she'd had a narrow escape.

# A LADY OF INTEGRITY

7

Alice gripped the wheel with a sense of relief, the familiar course scrolling beneath *Athena*'s hull like a map being unrolled on a giant's table. Flying she could handle. It was straightforward. You calculated your course, prepared as much as you could for the unexpected, and kept a weather eye out.

She supposed that motherhood—or being a guardian standing in a mother's or an older sister's place—was somewhat similar, if you got right down to it. But she wasn't sure she'd be able to manage the Mopsies if she were walking in Claire's shoes.

Still, her relief at having those two irrepressible girls along felt like a child's balloon under her breastbone. She hadn't been telling Claire a story—she'd meant it when she'd said she'd rather have one of them at her back than just about anybody. And what did that say about her own maternal instincts, such as they were?

"Captain Chalmers?" Ian Hollys stepped into the gondola, looking about him as if he were expecting to be snapped at. "Permission to enter?"

"Granted," she said, and he strolled over to the viewing port, taking in the landscape and no doubt pinpointing exactly where they were. Well, one look and anybody could see that. The Bodensee spread below them, a silver sheet in the morning sun, like a flat doorstep before the wall of the Alps.

"I take it the contretemps with the girls has been resolved satisfactorily?"

"Yes."

"So why then are we bearing due south rather than west, toward Geneva? This route will take much longer."

She suppressed a tingle of irritation at having her course questioned, even by an aeronaut of his standing and experience. It was a fair question, but if their positions had been reversed, she would have kept her mouth shut and assumed the other person knew what they were doing.

"Because our plans have changed," she said. "We're not going to Geneva. We're heading straight for the Duchy and the girls are coming along."

"After that lecture, Claire is backing down?" His eyebrows rose. "Is that wise, to give such strong-willed young ladies as these the upper hand?"

"She isn't backing down, and if you think they have the upper hand with her, you haven't been around them much." She adjusted course a slight degree. "I simply convinced her that we can use their help, and she's gone to send a pigeon to the school to say they'll be delayed a week with a family emergency. And another, I expect, to the von Zeppelins letting them know the girls lifted with us."

"She was quite right, you know. Their behavior was deceitful. But she is not without culpability, either, lifting like an owl in the night."

"Did you manage to get your bags aboard?" Alice asked.

"As it happens, we did. But that is completely beside the point."

"Oh, do give over, Captain Hollys. What's done is done, and grumbling about it isn't going to change anything. She did what she believed she had to do—and so did the girls. Their motives were for the best and sometimes you have to look past the means to the end."

"Is that your philosophy?" He clasped his hands behind his back and gazed out the bow, as if checking that the course she'd set was the correct one. No, that wasn't fair. She was probably reading too much into it. It was a bad habit. "That the end justifies the means?"

"Why don't you ask me that when we have Jake and my ship safely back in hand?"

"Perhaps I shall. Would you like me to take the helm as we pass over the Matterhorn?"

"Why?" she blurted. The nerve of the man! "Claire gave it to me, and I'll hang onto it until she relieves me, if it's all the same to you."

His skin reddened, as if he wasn't accustomed to being spoken to in such a way. Well, maybe he wasn't, in his own gondola. But she could speak any way she wanted to in her own—or at least, as long as she had the helm.

"I simply did not know if you had planted the flag."

Hmph. So of course he had assumed she hadn't. "Yes, we did, in the *Stalwart Lass* on the flight down."

It was a crazy custom—almost a rite of passage among the rope monkeys. You'd fly so close to the famous peak that you could plant a small flagpole bearing the pennant of the country you flew for and the call numbers of your vessel. It signified both skill and the extent to which you'd traveled. Jake had hung on a harness below the *Lass*'s engine compartment, hooting like a cowboy riding a bull, as he'd planted the flag in the frozen snow while she steered overhead, and then been reeled up before the tricky winds and the cold punished them for their impudence.

"Congratulations," Captain Hollys said, somewhat stiffly.

"Have you done it?" If they were to work together on this mission, then she supposed she should be polite. Really, he'd given her nothing but courtesy in the past, so she should be a little nicer.

Besides being a baronet, and Lord Dunsmuir's cousin, he was good-looking—if you liked the tall, dark, and masterful type—and captain of one of the most recognizable ships in the world. If what Claire said was true, he was making quite a splash among this season's debutantes, with Miss This on his arm one evening and Lady That dancing with him the next, to say nothing of enjoying the opera with the Honourable So-and-So the night after that, while he looked for a wife to suit him.

The man had everything going for him and probably didn't even need to earn his living. Could she really be blamed for giving in to the temptation to cut him down to size once in a while?

## A LADY OF INTEGRITY

"Yes, on our first voyage to Byzantium," he replied, shaking her out of what was fast becoming a mood. "It only counts if you do it your first time across, you know, so one of my lieutenants came prepared. I had the helm while he dangled from an access hatch on a safety line. I must confess I was glad when the job was done. One moment of wind shear and we'd have been picking ice out of our teeth while we waited in line at the pearly gates."

She'd had a moment of fear herself, wondering what she was doing as she risked life and ship to participate in such a crazy custom.

"I am surprised at your temerity, with only your navigator as your crew," he added.

"One to fly, and one to plant the flag. That's all you need."

"But the loss of one would mean disaster for the other. I hope you come to your other decisions as captain with greater thought and less daring."

Well, if that didn't beat all!

"We survived, didn't we? And besides, I have one of Claire's and my automaton intelligence systems in the *Lass* now. If there are only the two of us, it's because I don't need more." She paused. "Until Mr. Stringfellow joins us. Then we'll be three."

"This ship has the same, does it not?" He gazed above her head, where the cables ran like nerves between the brains of her original automatons, still running like clocks, bless them.

"It does. So you'll excuse me when I disagree with you."

Again, his skin reddened. With the world's briefest bow, he said, "Forgive me for intruding." And he turned on one boot heel, as though he were on parade, and marched out the door.

Hot blood cascaded into Alice's cheeks with chagrin and remorse. The man was risking life and liberty to come to her assistance and this was how she treated him? What was the matter with her?

Now she would have to go and apologize. And he would take it as his due, which would mean she would lose his respect.

Fiddlesticks.

Why did she care?

Because earning someone's respect meant something. It cost dearly, and few people in her experience had that kind of coin. With a few prickly words, she had thrown it away, and now, too late, she would give anything to get it back.

\*

Because of the general trickiness of flying over mountains, with their updrafts and sudden wind shears, Claire could not simply leave the flight to the automaton intelligence system and go to bed that evening. Luckily, she had two other experienced captains and two engineers aboard, which neatly solved the problem.

"I shall take the graveyard watch," Captain Hollys said when she laid her plans before them.

"You shall not," Claire objected. "When we land in the Duchy of Venice, we will need you sharp and observant, which you will not be if you have been flying in the night. Alice and I will divide the task in four-hour watches. Andrew, if you act as Alice's engineer and navigator, I shall be as happy as it is possible to be with Tigg once again at my side." She smiled at the young lieutenant, who leaned back in his chair in the dining saloon and passed an arm about Lizzie's shoulders.

"Nothing would make me happier, Lady—with your permission, sir?" he asked Ian.

But Ian clearly was not of a mind to give in just yet. "It is not right, Claire, for a man to leave his duty to women."

In the silence, there was a tiny clink as Claire's thimble of port touched the table, and a gulp as Alice tossed back hers.

"I believe your duty as conceived by Her Majesty has not yet commenced, Ian."

"That may be so, but I am still quite able to assist you in this manner. I have stood many a double watch with no reduction in my faculties, I assure you."

"I have no doubt of that at all," she said with a softening of her tone. "But it is only four hours, and will pass quickly."

"All the more reason for me to assist. With three, we may reduce it to three hours apiece."

"But we don't have a third engineer," Alice put in. "Please, Captain. Claire is right. We need you fresh for our landing." He gazed at her for a moment, until her cheeks flushed under his regard. "Perhaps I might offer my apologies for my hasty words earlier," she went on with difficulty. "We are not trying to keep you away from the helm. Truly, we're not. We are simply trying to do what's best for our mission, and if that means dividing up the watch, then that's what we have to do."

To Claire's astonishment, Ian cleared his throat and nodded briefly. "Very well. Lieutenant," he said to

Tigg, "I would say I needed you just as rested, but the young have amazing powers of restoration. You have my permission to act as engineer with Lady Claire."

"You speak as though you were as old as Count von Zeppelin, sir." Maggie, clearly sensing that a storm of some kind had been narrowly avoided, had the temerity to tease him a little.

"Some days I feel that way," he murmured, and reached for the bottle of tawny port.

Her earlier color faded from Alice's skin, leaving her looking sad and chewing on her lower lip.

Now what was this? Claire was tempted to ask, but for all she knew, Alice's mind had gone back to Jake and it would be best to let sleeping dogs lie. No good ever came of prodding and prying.

So it was that at ten of the clock, when the three-quarter moon rode high in the sky, she and Tigg took possession of *Athena*'s helm and charts for the first watch.

"I miss the old boat," he said affectionately, patting the frame of the starboard viewing port. "Even with all the ships in the Dunsmuirs' fleet, there isn't one quite like her."

"That is because she was made in the Americas— and built for speed," Claire said. "Do you remember the night she came into my possession?"

"Do I," Tigg said. "I remember the Mopsies loading me up with ordnance and sending me back to the *Lady Lucy*, frightened out of my wits but determined to free our crew or die trying."

"And that is precisely the meaning of courage," she told him fondly. "To be frightened, yet to stand up and do what is right. And your courage saved a ship, a family, and a crew, and led to your first promotion, if I recall."

"It did. Perhaps our mission here will lead to another, and I can afford to—" He stopped, looking closely at the cables overhead as though checking that they were operating properly.

"Afford to what, Tigg?"

"Nothing, Lady. Is this what your work is going to be with the count—adapting the automaton intelligence system for the passenger liners?"

"You know perfectly well that it is not," she said, undecided whether or not to allow this conversational dodge. "He has had the systems in place for several years now. My share of the income from the patent is what is paying for Lizzie's and Maggie's educations."

There, now. She had given him an opening. It would be up to him to take it. An updraft pressed the deck against the soles of her boots, so she bent her knees and steadied the helm as they passed over the lights of a town far below. The chart told her it was St. Moritz.

"Has it been expensive, their education?" Tigg asked.

"It has not been inexpensive," she allowed, "but it has been greatly offset by the count's hospitality. He has acted like the best, most generous sort of uncle to the girls. It is partly what angered me so when I discovered them aboard. I do not wish anything to upset him and the baroness, though," she amended, "I suppose I am as culpable as they."

"I'm glad Lizzie and Maggie are with us," he said. "It will be almost like old times."

"But you are not children anymore, Tigg," she reminded him gently, "and it seems we play on a broader stage than the old neighborhood in Vauxhall Gardens. We are no longer merely defending our cottage against marauders."

"I think we are, still," he said. "They're still marauders, only they've got a better hideout and sneakier tactics. But we'll outfox 'em, you'll see."

He sounded so much like the Tigg of old, ready to take on any challenge even if he only had a rock for a weapon.

"I shall depend upon you to see to the girls' protection," she said, her smile fading. "I mean it, Tigg. They are as precious to me as one, at least, is to you."

His dark eyes met hers, and in them she saw the determination of a man to protect his own. "If anyone so much as touches a hair on Lizzie's head—or Maggie's— he'll answer to me, all right, and he won't like it."

"Your feelings for Lizzie have not changed, then?"

"No, and they're not likely to. It's been Lizzie and no one else for me since we first moved back to Carrick House and she wouldn't kill those baby bats up in the attic. Remember, when we were clearing out to make bedrooms for the others?"

Claire did, only too vividly.

"I knew she was your scout, and already a fighter, and probably far smarter than I, but I saw the gentle side of her that day. And I was never the same after that." He cleared his throat and pretended to check the chart, though St. Moritz was barely off the stern. "You don't know how difficult it's been, watching her turn into a young lady and wondering if she'd fly so high above me that she'd never want to settle for a rope monkey."

"You're not a—"

"I am now. But I won't be forever. That day at her grandparents', in the garden, well ... we settled it then. I know we're too young, but it means a lot that you approve, Lady."

"How could I not approve, dear one?" She left the wheel for a moment to hug him. "Lizzie is a fortunate young woman. And if the two of you are willing to wait until you can afford to establish a home, then that is to your credit. Each of you deserves that respect from the other."

"That's what she says, too." He nodded eagerly. "That's why this mission has got to go well. With Her Majesty watching, it could mean attention in the right quarter, and faster advancement in the Corps than I could hope for otherwise."

She put a hand on his arm. "Do not let the prospect of advancement blind you to finer considerations—such as loyalty to those who gave you your start."

"Oh, I wouldn't leave the captain," he assured her. "He's done more for me than I deserve. But wouldn't you want to see me with a First Engineer's bars some day, even if it's on a different ship?"

"I would indeed." She touched his cheek, delighted with the same deep dimple she found there, in a face that was now a man's. "It would be the proudest day of my life to see you attain your dream."

"That, and my wedding day?"

"Let us not get ahead of ourselves," she said primly. "If there is to be any talk of weddings, it will be the one with which I am most immediately concerned at present."

She could only hope that they would return to take up the preparations for it once again. After the revelations of today and her admission to Alice of her own fear for the girls' safety, she could almost wish she had nothing more urgent to attend to than a dress fitting.

# A LADY OF INTEGRITY

8

"And here I thought I'd managed to weasel my way out
of all this fuss and frippery," Alice grumbled.

As far as Claire was concerned, this fuss and frippery was going a long way toward keeping her fear for
the girls and for Alice herself at bay. If one could concentrate on the sleek line of a cream linen walking skirt,
or upon the delicacy of the cutwork and embroidery
upon one's white waist, one could avoid thinking of ...
oh, dear. There she went again.

"I think you look nice, Alice," Maggie told her.
"What do you think of this spring green skirt?" She
twirled in front of the mirror. "It's the wrong time of
year for it, isn't it?"

"There's a right time of year for green?" Alice asked,
fussing with the supple leather belt about her narrow

waist, and trying to tuck the embroidered front in under it.

"No, dear heart." Claire pulled it out again. "It dips in front like this, so one has the appearance of a pouter pigeon."

"That's attractive?"

"Some gentlemen find it so. Not that we are concerned with such things. We have a higher purpose—and if we must pay the price of vanity to look as though we are fashionable tourists attending the exhibition without a care in the world, then we shall."

"The green is perfect on you, Mags," Lizzie said. "No one would ever guess there is a lightning pistol in your boot."

"Lizzie!" Claire hissed.

"Sorry, Lady," Lizzie whispered.

They were back on good terms again, after Claire's loss of temper the first day of their voyage. She had lifted her chin and lowered her pride, and apologized for speaking to the girls in such a way in front of the gentlemen. Once they understood the source of her anxiety, they had hugged her and assured her they would have "all eyes out for danger, Lady."

Of course they would. They had been scouting since their parents' airship had gone into the Thames when they were only five—an attempt by Lizzie's father to cover up the murder of her mother. Anything less than complete faith in their abilities did them a disservice.

What was wrong with her lately? Claire paid for their disguises and the entire party walked out into the narrow paved lane, their boxes and bags brushing against the walls on either side and now containing the more workaday skirts and blouses they had worn from the airfield on the mainland. She was not prone to fretting and worrying about things she could not control. Andrew was right. It must be because she now knew how much it was possible to lose.

It was true that she had lost everything before. But through her own resources and the efforts of those around her, she had built a life and an estate, for lack of a better word, that anyone might be proud of. And she was determined that the girls might have their share of opportunity and happiness, as well.

They strolled along the Zattere, past the Street of the Incurables where the unfortunates of the city must be, and past the enormous Church of St. Christopher, patron saint of sailors with its enormous rosary made of fishing floats draped across the doors. Claire felt a sense of gratitude flood in, scouring away the fear.

They were a flock. And anyone who threatened the flock would have to deal with all of them. Claire released the last bit of anger at the girls for having disobeyed her, and rejoiced in a sense of thankfulness that they were beside her now. And from that sprang a renewed determination to make their little homemade family whole again with the rescue of Jake.

"We must catch a water taxi here," Andrew said, dapper in a linen suit and boater hat that was so very unlike his usual habiliments that it took Claire a moment to realize who was speaking. He consulted his guidebook and compared it with the name painted over the dock. "Yes, this is the right one."

In moments, a boat steamed up, its stack belching steam and its conductor holding out a hand so that Claire might board.

The art exhibition covered several acres of an area

that Claire understood had once been a convent. But now it was a lovely public park, divided by colonnades and shaded by olive trees, with the Grand Canal visible at one end.

The water taxi let them off on the paved embankment, which Claire was learning was called a *fondamente*. Then, twirling their parasols and as carefree as a flock of frilly birds, she and Alice and the Mopsies accompanied Andrew, Ian, and Tigg into the exhibition grounds.

"I wonder if I will spot Claude first?" Lizzie said, her keen gaze scanning the crowd for her half-brother.

"He won't spot you, that's certain," Tigg said. "I hardly recognize you outside of school uniform or raiding rig."

"I clean up rather nicely, I'll have you know," she told him, her nose in the air. "At least, so I've been told by *other* gentlemen."

"Lewis doesn't count, Liz." Maggie spiked her balloon, earning her a push from her cousin and a rude noise.

"Girls," Claire said, resisting the urge to roll her eyes. "I hope you are merely playing parts; otherwise, Claude will not *want* to recognize you."

"His note said he would meet us here," Lizzie told her, "next to the bell tower. I'm so glad he and his party are still in Venice. I feel as though I want to pinch him to be sure he is all right, after the undersea dirigibles made off with him and we had to spirit him out of France."

Maggie shivered, as if the cold waters of the English Channel could still engulf her, no matter how warm the climate and sunny the day in their present location.

## A LADY OF INTEGRITY

"And there he is!" In a froth of lace and a flash of kidskin boots, Lizzie took off at a run for the bell tower.

From a distance, Claire smiled as Claude Seacombe turned at her call and engulfed her in a hug, whirling her around so that her feet swung out and her skirts belled in the breeze. When they caught up, Lizzie was laughing.

"I can't tell you how glad I am to see you!" With a smacking kiss, she released Claude and took Tigg's hand, pulling him beside her. "Claude, you remember Lieutenant Thomas Terwilliger, who serves aboard *Lady Lucy*? He and Captain Hollys have been granted leave to join us for the exhibition."

Tigg inclined his head in a nod and extended his hand. "Mr. Seacombe, a pleasure to see you again."

"Likewise." Claude's mobile face was still alight with happiness at seeing his half-sister as he turned to acknowledge the other members of their party.

Claire extended her hand and, instead of allowing him to bow over it, drew him in for an embrace and a kiss upon the cheek. "The warm sun of the south suits you, Claude," she said. "You are looking very well."

"Bless old Blighty for providing such a contrast." He mimed looking over his shoulder for eavesdroppers. "The grands aren't with you, are they?"

"Our grandparents? In Venice?" Lizzie snorted. "The closest they will get to sunshine like this is to open a south-facing window."

"Now, you two, enough of disparaging your grandparents," Andrew said firmly. "Tempting as it is, they are still the ones who have amassed the fortune you will inherit one day."

Claude groaned. "And here I'd almost managed to

forget it."

"Forget what?" asked a very pretty girl swanning up just in time to hear. Oh, what was her name? Claire tried to remember, but it was blurred by the events since. Something frivolous, though.

Lizzie and Maggie both stiffened as they were joined by Claude's friends from Paris, all of whom Claire had met, taken the measure of, and likewise forgotten the moment they were out of sight.

If she were forced to admit the truth, she would rather their now large party separated into at least two smaller ones, so she proposed that they meet for tea at four o'clock. Lizzie and Maggie were swept away by the chattering crowd, Tigg pacing with them in his linen suit and straw hat, his spine straight and his alert gaze completely giving him away as an aeronaut of Her Majesty's Corps.

With a feeling of relief, she took Andrew's arm. After a moment, Captain Hollys offered his to Alice.

Her startled glance at Claire said, *What shall I do?*

Claire's discreet nod replied, *Take it, of course. He is a gentleman and you are a lady. In most circles, this is considered to be normal.*

While Andrew's ring and Ian's commitment to finding a different wife posthaste would have made the offer of his arm to her quite safe, Claire was far more satisfied with the situation as it was, thank you. Alice would have to play the part until she was comfortable enough with it to fool those who might be watching.

Under the wide, flattering brim of her hat, heaped with tulle and a lovely cockade of burgundy ribbon to match her skirt, Claire gazed about her with delight. Pavilions held examples of the greatest contemporary art in Europe—and even some very old ones by Venetian masters of the Renaissance.

All the fashionable seemed to be here. There were English ladies who refused to adapt to the heat, sweating in the velvet and wool more appropriate to the northern climate in October. There was a crowd of French ladies, Claire was quite sure, if the dashing cut of their walking suits was any indication. And there, just going into the pavilion of the French Impressionists, was a young lady who must be from the Fifteen Colonies. She was clad in cotton, but what lovely stuff it was, draping so fashionably from box pleats behind that the back of her skirt almost looked like a train. Such an ensemble would have been very expensive. In fact—

Claire's eyes narrowed. "Andrew," she said. "Look at that young lady."

"Which one?" he asked with some humor. "There are hundreds. It is like admiring the flowers at the botanical gardens."

"That one there, in the royal blue skirt and jacket, at the entrance to the Impressionsts' pavilion. Can that possibly be Gloria Meriwether-Astor?"

By now all four members of their party had come to a halt, ostensibly to watch an entertainer on stilts juggle batons.

"I believe it is indeed she," Andrew said thoughtfully as the girl in the lovely suit closed her parasol and strolled into the pavilion for a closer look at its paintings. "Are you going to speak to her?"

"Is that wise?" Alice asked. "I mean, I realize she helped prevent my pa from being hanged in the Canadas, but …"

"But since her father was behind the plot, it is difficult to know if one ought to take up the acquaintance again," Captain Hollys finished.

"One can hardly blame the daughter for the sins of the father," Claire said with some asperity. "If that were so, none of you would be speaking to Lizzie ... or to me, for that matter."

Viscount St. Ives' foolish backing of the combustion engine some years ago had resulted in what the papers had called the Arabian Bubble ... the bursting of which had impoverished its investors and rendered Claire herself homeless and reviled.

"If I met her, I don't remember," Alice said. "I had more urgent things on my mind at the time. But I would like to thank her, if I could and she's of a mind to accept it."

"I think that is most noble of you, Alice," Claire said promptly. "And did you notice one other thing?"

"Other than the fact that she seems to be unescorted?" Ian inquired.

"Her party may simply be in another pavilion. No. Did you not see? She is not wearing mourning. Royal blue is certainly not among the traditional colors. It is far too eye-catching."

It took a moment for this fact to sink in. Andrew was the first to apprehend its significance. "Then Gerald Meriwether-Astor did not die in the sinking of *Neptune's Fury* last month?" His voice was hushed with horror. "I confess I had hoped we had seen the last of him."

"She would not be here if he had, and even if by some error of etiquette she came anyway, she would certainly be in full mourning," Claire said. "Not in fashionable sapphire polished cotton."

"Is it too much to hope that funerary customs are different in the Americas?" Ian said. "Blue is not so far off from black." He could have no fond memories of Gerald Meriwether-Astor, either, having had his ship and crew seized by the man. They had all been at the point of death before Tigg had engineered their escape.

"They're not," Alice said. "I'll do it. I'll speak to her, thank her, and find out where her father is. While I do that, the three of you ought to keep a low profile."

"We are tourists," Claire said. "We have nothing to hide and everything to gain by the acquaintance. You know what they say, Alice."

She met her friend's gaze and Alice finished the thought. "Keep your friends close, but your enemies closer."

9

Alice had consented to wear a hat only because she could stuff her hair up under it without a fuss. Now she settled it more firmly, took a deep breath, and arranged her features into an approximation of pleasant interest.

She was quite sure she looked a complete fool.

Who was she to approach one of the richest heiresses in the Americas and claim acquaintance? With her luck, the girl would look down her perfect nose, then turn it up and deal her the most humiliating set-down in the history of set-downs.

But she had the best of reasons for speaking up—and she'd waited for five years to do it. That alone gave her the courage to stop beside Gloria and look up at the canvas upon which the girl was gazing so raptly.

"It's lovely, isn't it?" she said, doing her best to look

as though the arrangement of dots and splotches on the canvas was something a person might actually buy if they had the coin.

"I love the Impressionists," Gloria sighed. "I cannot for the life of me figure out how it is done, but the overall effect is wonderful." She turned to Alice. "Do you like—"

She stopped. Hesitated. Then subjected Alice to such a stare that the latter felt as though every secret she'd ever tried to conceal was pinned upon her blouse for all to read. She braced herself for the set-down.

"We have met," Gloria said. "I do not remember where, but I will in a moment. You hail from the Texican Territories, don't you?"

"I do. And you're quite right. I saw you go in and approached you hoping you might remember. It was in—"

"The Canadas," Gloria said, clearly pleased that her memory was in good working order. "The Firstwater Mine. You are the daughter of that man who was accused of sabotage."

"Frederick Chalmers. And for the record, he was innocent."

"Yes, of course, or I would not have helped him escape." She examined Alice a little anxiously. "He did escape, did he not? He must have. I remember the to-do very clearly, um …"

"Alice. Alice Chalmers. And you are Gloria, if memory serves."

"I am, and I'm so pleased to meet you properly. The last time, I was fussed about a ball, and then there was an explosion, and I don't remember a single other thing until Claire ran past me and everything changed." The girl beamed, and they shook hands cordially.

"I came over to speak with you for a reason besides simply renewing our acquaintance." The society phrases felt awkward on a tongue more used to plain speaking. "I wanted to thank you. Personally. For helping to save my pa's life."

Surprise mixed with pleasure in Gloria's expression. "I hardly did anything more than have the poor man locked in a closet, along with his friends. It was Claire who saved his life and somehow managed to spirit him to safety. If she succeeded, I am very glad. It makes the month of unpleasantness I suffered afterward quite worthwhile."

"I wondered if you might get into trouble."

"No more or less than usual." She glanced over Alice's shoulder. "Is Lady Claire with you? Have you seen her since that time?"

"She is, and I have. We are here with a party of friends, in fact, for the Exhibition." She touched Gloria's arm, somehow charmed almost against her will by the other girl's artlessness and honesty. And hearing the accents of the Americas after so long in foreign parts was making her homesick. "Come with me. They're just outside, watching a juggler."

Gloria's delight at seeing Claire and the others again puzzled Alice a little—after all, Claire had told her once that upon their meeting at the Firstwater Mine, Gloria had claimed not to remember that the two of them had been classmates at some hoity-toity school in London— or that she had been one of Claire's principal tormentors. But the events at the mine had changed Alice's life and Claire's as well. She shouldn't be surprised that they appeared to have changed Gloria's too.

# A LADY OF INTEGRITY

Her life ... and maybe her attitude toward it.

The little group stood talking so long that the sun moved to the other side of the tower and the bells began to ring all over town.

Claire glanced up. "It is only three. What is all the noise—some special call to worship in all the churches?"

"Brace yourselves," Alice said cheerfully. She, apparently, was the only one of their party who had experienced this before. Not, she supposed, that anyone could get used to it who hadn't grown up with it.

At the end of the colonnade, the bridge that had connected the dock side of the *fondamente* with the exhibition grounds parted in the middle. Each half rose to the vertical, the base on either side clearly on some kind of revolving gear assembly that tipped it the necessary number of degrees.

And suddenly Alice's stomach felt the way it had the first time she'd set foot in a boat. A canoe, to be exact, in a cove on one of the misty islands off the west coast of the Canadas that Davina Dunsmuir had once called home. Her insides swayed and swooped, and a second later, as her body automatically adjusted for weather as though she stood on an airship's deck, she saw the moment when her friends realized what was happening.

"The neighborhoods!" Claire said on a gasp. "They are moving!"

"My word," Andrew said a little unsteadily. "How very disconcerting." He slipped an arm around Claire at once, and she leaned into him as though it were the most natural thing in the world to experience this novelty together. Alice felt a pang within as he pointed to the end of the colonnade, where the sea view was slowly changing before their fascinated eyes, and he and Claire murmured softly together.

*When am I going to have someone to share new things with?*

She shook the brief moment of self-pity away. Claire deserved her happiness, and she would not be so small as to begrudge her even a moment.

Gloria appeared unaffected, simply watching the view as though it were a diorama staged for her entertainment. And Captain Hollys ... well, he had done exactly as Alice had. He stood with his feet braced, his hands clasped behind his back, his gaze fixed with interest upon the sea.

Alice's stomach didn't take long to settle back to normal and she realized that the island in the distance with the tilted tower was no longer traveling slowly across the end of the colonnade. The bridge's two halves met once more in the middle and seated themselves, at which point people began crossing the canal once more.

"Is it over?" Claire asked, and in answer, the bells gave one last peal, as if to sound the all-clear.

Gloria told her, "Once the bridges go down and the bells sound, the neighborhoods are stationary for another day."

"This happens every day?" Claire asked with interest. She and Andrew straightened, though Alice noted that they were still holding hands before she directed her gaze back toward Gloria.

"At least." Gloria nodded. "One never knows. Sometimes it is twelve hours, sometimes twenty-four. Sometimes even two or three days. I have no idea what exactly determines the schedule—if anything does. It could be that Leonardo's clockwork schedules itself by the movement of the moon or the phases of the zodiac ... or the whim of the Doge." She giggled, as if this were somehow amusing. "Claire, I meant to ask you—there is one person here whom I thought to see."

"One of the girls—my wards?" Claire asked. "I am afraid they have gone off with family and friends. But we will be meeting for tea at four so you must come with us."

"I should be delighted. But I didn't mean the girls. I meant that young man who was with you in the Canadas. The very rude one. We spoke at the ball."

"Rude?" Claire's eyebrows went up. "I should hope no young man of my acquaintance would be rude to a lady. He was not of a dark complexion, I hope?"

"No—at the time he would have been fourteen or fifteen, with reddish hair and a chin that I suspect is probably quite fearsome by now."

"Jake?" Alice blurted. "Are you talking about my navigator? I do recall that you and he were talking aboard Count von Zeppelin's ship, just before the explosion."

"Yes, a brief but rather memorable conversation from my point of view. Is he here?"

In the tick of silence following the question, Alice heard seagulls mewing, like the cries of the lost.

"I am afraid not," Claire said smoothly. "We lost him to another field of employment. He and Alice parted ways some time ago."

"Oh, I am sorry to hear that," Gloria said, clearly disappointed. "I had hoped to give a better impression this time."

"I'll be sure to pass the message on if I ever see him again," Alice said. How good they were at telling tall tales. It didn't seem fair, after Gloria had been so kind and so glad to see them all. "Come, we should take in at least a few of these other pictures before we meet the girls and their friends." It was the only sacrifice she could make for Gloria's sake, and she endured looking at picture after picture—some lovely, some utterly puzzling, some she was quite sure a baby could do a better job of with its fingers—until the tower bell struck four.

"Claire, maybe Gloria and Captain Hollys and I could secure a large table in the tea pavilion," Alice suggested. "You and Andrew ought to stay just outside to wave them over."

Claire nodded, then said, "There are so many of them that perhaps the others might take a table of their own. Since our party is now augmented by one, I am sure the girls would appreciate the information." She gave Alice a speaking glance, and suddenly the latter understood.

Gloria's father had, for all intents and purposes, had Maggie imprisoned with every appearance of willingness to let her drown. He had kidnapped young Claude and used him to blackmail the girls' grandparents into allowing a French invasion on the long expanse of their seaward-facing land—until Maggie had foiled it.

Alice had no doubt that without adequate preparation, the girls would mistake Gloria's presence for that of her father, and who knew what might ensue.

Alice wouldn't put it past them to incite a riot.

*

There must on no account be a riot, Claire thought, waving at the Mopsies as the two of them led the way across the square. It would bring them to the attention of the authorities, and that must be avoided at all costs.

In moments she and Andrew were surrounded by what seemed like a flock of birds, all chattering at once, crowding her with their skirts and bumping her hat and—oh, bother, she'd dropped her handbag—

"Lizzie, Maggie, Claude, a moment, if you please," Andrew said with enough authority in his tone that the three of them, at least, stopped talking. "Just to the side, here. We must speak with you before you go in."

"Sounds rather serious," Claude said. "Can't they seat us all together?"

"We don't need to all sit together, like obedient children with the governess," said one of the girls, laughing. "I prefer to be independent."

"You may do as you like," Claire said coolly, taking her handbag from Lizzie with a smile of thanks and dusting it off. Thank goodness she had concealed her own lightning pistol in a slender holster on her boot, under her voluminous skirts. If she had kept it in this velvet bag, the glass globe might have shattered on the pavement. "My business is with the girls and Claude."

"Lizzie's in trouble again," the girl singsonged.

Arabella, that was her name. Arabella de Courcy. "You must have just left your governess, if this is how you behave in public," Claire said in the frosty Belgravia tones that never failed to cut their object down to size. "Perhaps it is a good thing you prefer to sit elsewhere."

Arabella sniffed, took the arms of two of her companions, and swept them into the pavilion.

"Well done, Lady," Maggie said. "It's so exhausting trying to be polite to that girl."

"I've given it up," Lizzie said, clearly not sorry in the least. "The trouble is, no matter how insulting I am, she thinks I'm joking. It never occurs to her that my remarks are perfectly sincere."

"Lizzie, no matter the provocation, a lady does not insult others on purpose."

"But—"

"Talking of sincere," Andrew said hastily, "we have information for you that must be communicated before you go in."

"Have you heard something of—?" Lizzie stopped herself before Jake's name tumbled out and revealed them all as frauds.

"No, of someone else," Claire said. "Maggie, Claude, this affects you particularly. There is a young lady sitting with us whom you girls will remember from the Canadas. Gloria Meriwether-Astor."

"Gloria!" Lizzie repeated. "The one who helped Alice's dad escape?"

"Yes. What a good memory you have."

"Why should that affect us?" Maggie asked, sensing in her own peculiar way that something deeper was afoot. "I shall be glad to see her again. She's handy in a tight spot."

Claude raised one brow. "Are there more tight spots in your chequered past?"

"You have no idea," Maggie assured him.

"And we should like to keep it that way," Claire said. "Claude, I must tell you that she is the daughter of the man responsible for holding you for ransom in France. We believed him to be aboard *Neptune's Fury* when it went down in the Channel, but we observed just now that Gloria is not wearing mourning."

"I shan't complain about that. Never met a girl yet who looked other than a fright in it."

"You are missing the point, brother dearest," Lizzie said fondly. "If she is not wearing mourning, then she still has a father."

Maggie clutched Claire's sleeve. "Lady, he's not here, is he?"

"I do not know. But that must be our primary purpose in asking Gloria to tea, besides the pleasure of her company. We must find out first if he really is alive, and second, where he is."

"I agree," Andrew said. "I am already looking over one shoulder. I should not much like having to look over both."

# 10

"My father?" Gloria repeated rather blankly as Lizzie polished off the last of the little tea cakes and Claude enjoyed his third Burano biscuit. "Forgive me, but are you acquainted?"

"We met in the Canadas, do you not remember?" Claire's tea had gone cold, and she had no appetite for cake. All her concentration was given to making this conversation seem light and friendly and inconsequential. It was hard work. "I hope he is well?"

"I suppose he is. I have not heard that he is not." When Claire showed her surprise, Gloria went on, "We have not been on the best of terms lately. I have been living in Paris at our house there, while he has been doing what Father does—shipping things and making pots of money."

# A LADY OF INTEGRITY

"Is the airship business in the Americas successful?" Andrew asked. "We had heard he had expanded his operations to include the Atlantic shipping routes."

Claire resisted the temptation to step on his foot under the table.

"He tried that," Gloria said, "but it doesn't seem to have been a success. Too many accidents and some ships and crew lost."

"Oh, I am sorry," Maggie said, her sympathy for the crew quite sincere.

"But he wrote me recently to say he would be in Venice on business and wanted to let bygones be bygones," Gloria went on. "That's why I've come for the Exhibition. He will be meeting me this evening at the ball at the Palazzo Viceconte." An idea seemed to strike her, and she touched Claire's arm. "Oh, do come, all of you. I'm so tired of traveling with only a chaperone, and she never wants to do anything interesting. At least if I'm there with you, I might have a chance at actually dancing. And Father will not lecture me on my inability to catch a duke if I am there with a party that includes gentlemen."

"Come to a ball?" Claire repeated. "Uninvited?"

"Oh, I'll send a messenger over with as many invitations as you need. Do come," she begged. "I haven't seen Father in months, but that is no guarantee that all is forgiven and forgotten. He was so angry and disappointed in me that I would love the moral support when I see him again." Her gaze fell to the tablecloth. "He won't cause a scene in public—particularly in the home of his host."

"His host?" Captain Hollys said.

"Yes, the Viceconte di Alba. He is a cousin or something of the Doge and holds some high position in the government. Don't ask me how Father knows him—but if I know Father, it's through business and not pleasure."

Claire and Andrew exchanged a glance, which then widened to include Alice and Captain Hollys.

"Not that I plan to go along, but ... the Viceconte di Alba?" Alice said, as though trying to recall his connections. "Isn't he the Minister of Justice or some such?"

The Minister of Justice! Could he be the man ultimately responsible for Jake's imprisonment—possibly even the man who had sentenced him? How could they walk into his very home, like so many flies dancing along a filament into the spider's web? Of course Alice would not go. It was far too dangerous for her, as there would surely be those in attendance who would recognize her.

"Oh, Lady Claire, do say yes," Claude urged her. "It's just the thing to liven us up."

"Yes, do," Lizzie echoed. "Imagine being invited to a ball in Venice. I can hardly wait to tell Arabella." She shot a wicked glance over at the next table, where the others were laughing and chattering as though there were no connection between the two parties at all.

"It's fancy dress, if that helps," Gloria put in with an air of a gambler sweetening the pot. "There are a thousand costume shops in the city, because of Carnivale. You could come as just about anything."

Fancy dress. With masks.

Perhaps Alice need not be left behind, after all.

Claire's polite smile widened into sincerity. "Masks would be entirely appropriate, though we have no need for a costume—the girls and I, I mean. We have just the thing, don't we, girls?"

# A LADY OF INTEGRITY

*

"This is madness," Captain Hollys muttered for what had to be the tenth time, pacing at Alice's side like a tall, grumpy ... lord.

At least, Alice thought he was a lord. Were baronets considered lords? It did not matter if they were or not—he had been outmaneuvered and out-argued, and here she was, walking to the ball with her very own noble bodyguard.

Whom she was determined to lose at the very first opportunity.

"One slip of the mask and you will be recognized," he said, "and then all Her Majesty's efforts on Jake's behalf will be for naught."

"I'll just have to make sure my mask doesn't slip, then," Alice said cheerfully. "Fortunately, everyone expects Colombina's face to be painted, so it could be torn right off and I'd still be all right."

Ian, dressed as a harlequin, in long bloomers and a silk blouse you could fit both the Mopsies into, glared at her out of his blacked eyes. "If it is torn off, that means you will have been in a fight, and that must not happen under any circumstances."

"Oh, Ian, do give over," Claire said, taking his other arm companionably and patting it. "We must keep a positive attitude. And you must loosen up a little. You move too much like a military man."

"I *am* a military man," Captain Hollys said through his teeth.

"No, tonight you are a harlequin, a trickster," Andrew told him. He and Claire made an odd couple—he as a pirate, and she in her raiding rig. Both wore the elegant gilded masks that were for sale at the base of practically every bridge in town, made of *papier maché* and tied behind with silk ribbons. "Tonight you move loosely, with grace and stealth, not command."

"Alice, too," Lizzie said. "That motley dress is so short you won't have any trouble dancing."

"I won't be dancing," Alice informed her. "I've never shown this much shin in my life, and I certainly don't intend to parade it on the ballroom floor."

"There will be any number of Colombinas," Claire told her in soothing tones that did nothing to calm the butterflies in Alice's stomach. "No one will know. Just remember—we are not going to dance so much as gather information. Mopsies, you are to scout where you should not be, and listen where you are not wanted. Alice, if by some mischance you are recognized, Ian will whisk you out of the *palazzo* and back to our hotel. Tigg and Andrew and I will engage likely guests in conversation and try to learn more about where Jake might be held."

"And not a word to Claude," Maggie reminded her cousin. "He cannot be trusted not to blab, though of course he would never mean to hurt anyone."

"I still don't like abandoning him to Arabella and that lot," Lizzie said, kicking a stone off the pavement with her dancing slipper. It hit the water with a hollow sound and sank with no indication of the canal's real depth. "I don't think they're good for him. Instead of encouraging him to go home and get a start in the business, they keep telling him to come hither and yon with them, frittering away his money and his time."

"They can only give the advice they know to be true

for themselves," Claire said. "But don't fret. Between you and Maggie, he will see the light. Just not tonight. You have work to do."

Below them, a glossy black gondola slipped through the dark water, poled by a man in a loose shirt and trousers. A giggling crowd of girls in filmy white dresses and white face paint, their eyes hollowed out with black, filled it practically to sinking.

"Wilis," Claire said. "You know, the spirits of jilted maidens in *Giselle*, the ballet."

Watching them float away, Lizzie asked, "Is that where that expression comes from—'he gives me the willies'?"

Wherever the word came from, Alice had the willies, well and truly, and the prickly feeling on the back of her neck under Colombina's wig only increased as they presented their invitations, were welcomed into the *palazzo*, and twenty minutes later located Gloria and her chaperone in the ballroom.

"Oh, thank goodness." Gloria practically fell on Alice's and Claire's necks. "Given that Father isn't your favorite person in the world, I thought you might not come."

"I've got nothing against him now," Alice said. "He's paid the debt the government of the Canadas required, and you can't ask for more than that."

The words weren't entirely true, but Alice was glad she'd fibbed when Gloria's face softened with relief. "You're so kind." She turned to Claire and squeezed her hand. "All of you. I'm lucky to have friends like you." The orchestra struck up a waltz, and she clapped her hands. "Listen! It's Strauss—my favorite."

How could such a wicked man have a daughter as

guileless as Gloria? Alice wondered. Or was her approach to life the only way she could survive—the equivalent of hiding one's face behind one's hands?

"Gloria," Claire said, "I believe your father is coming this way. Is he dressed as a Roman emperor?"

"I don't know, but it wouldn't surprise me. He's bound to make comments about my coming alone. Oh, if only I had a partner!"

Alice nudged the captain. "Go on. Ask the girl to dance," she said in a low tone.

"I am not leaving you," he replied stiffly.

"I'll be right here with Claire and Andrew. Quick. You've got a title and you're eligible. You could get her pa off her back for weeks with one dance."

"Great Scott." The captain implored patience of the frescoes on the ceiling. "Very well. Miss Meriwether-Astor, would you honor me?"

Gloria skipped off with him so fast she might not have been there at all, and by the time her father joined them, she and the captain had whirled halfway around the floor.

"Mr. Meriwether-Astor, what a pleasure to see you again," Claire said politely, extending her hand.

Alice would rather simply have shot him, but that wouldn't be polite.

The man peered at Claire from under the leafy excrescence of his laurel crown. "I'm sorry, you have the advantage of me. Did I see you speaking with my daughter?"

"You did. She has procured invitations for us, for which we are most grateful. I was at school with her in London, and met you briefly in the Canadas, in Edmonton at the governor's ball. I am Lady Claire Trevelyan," she said rather grandly, and introduced everyone but Alice, who did her best to melt into the crowd behind them, close enough to hear but far enough away to appear not to be with their party.

So this was the man who had nearly gotten her pa strung up like a criminal. Who had backed the French pretender to the throne in hopes of being the power behind it, and financed an invasion that had only failed because of the quick wits and bravery of the sixteen-year-old girl standing not three feet away. This stout, barrel-shaped man with the red face and the iron eyes was forbidden both European and English skies.

So what was he doing here, pretending to care about his daughter's friends?

"Is that my Gloria there, with that tall harlequin?" he asked as they whirled past.

"She makes a lovely shepherdess, does she not? That tall harlequin is Ian Hollys, baronet," Claire said with her best society smile. "I believe she may well have made a conquest—her first of the evening."

"Is that so? About time she was good for something."

Claire blushed, and even Alice winced at his willingness to shame his daughter behind her back.

"Are you enjoying your time in the Duchy, sir?" Andrew inquired, clearly hoping to deflect the conversation. "Have you been to the Exhibition?"

"I've no time for frippery. I'm here on business, and for Gloria, for her sainted mother's sake. We have not seen one another in some months."

"I understand you take quite an interest in engineering," Andrew went on, "and in fact have achieved great recognition in those circles. Are you working on something presently?"

Meriwether-Astor glanced at him distractedly while he attempted to follow Gloria and her partner around the room. Did he think Ian would abandon her and he would need to tackle the baronet before he got clear away?

"I'm interested in underwater transport," he finally vouchsafed. "Seems like a good place to sell it, don't you agree? Excuse me, I've just seen someone I must say hello to. I've been waiting days to get in to see the Minister of Justice, and there he is in the flesh. Nice to have met you all."

And he hurried off.

As a laurel leaf detached itself from his crown and wafted to the polished floor in the wake of his going, Alice realized he had not been watching his daughter dance, after all. He had been watching for an opportunity to do business.

And now, as they saw him approach a tall, dark-complected man wearing a sword and angel's wings, thanks to him they now knew who the Minister of Justice was.

# A LADY OF INTEGRITY

11

Lizzie rolled her shoulders in irritation, and the wire hoops of her fairy wings bobbed up and down. "This seemed like such a good idea in the costume shop," she said to Tigg, "but so far all I've done is knock against people and irritate everyone within four feet."

"You don't irritate me." His teeth flashed in the slow, lazy grin she loved. If anyone had been designed to wear the costume of an ancient Egyptian pharaoh, it was Tigg. The pleated linen pants and wide jeweled collar—to say nothing of the dress scimitar and the cobra headdress—could have been designed for him. And if she caught any female sneaking glances at his bare chest, she would whip the gaseous capsaicin out of her pocket so fast …

"I'd say take them off and stash them in a potted

palm, but I think they're the point of your costume." He took her hand. "Leave off fretting and come dance with me."

"But the Lady said—"

"I know, and we will. But I must have one dance to remember after all this is over and I'm back aboard ship again."

He swept her onto the floor, and Lizzie really did feel as if she were flying on her gauzy wings, her gossamer skirts floating out behind in a most satisfying way. Equally satisfying were the envious glances of the little cluster of Wilis, who had come without partners and had nearly reached the point of dancing with each other.

"Captain's dancing a second with Miss Meriwether-Astor," Tigg murmured. "Perhaps we ought to take up the watch on Alice?"

"Maggie is with her." Lizzie's sharp eyes picked them out of the crowd. "Come, dance me over behind that man with the angel wings. Meriwether-Astor is heading in that direction, and he's never met me. Remember what the Lady said."

"If we must, though I'd rather dance properly with you."

She smiled up at him. "We have the rest of our lives to dance, and only a short time to find out all we can for Jake."

She felt his hand tighten on her waist as he adjusted their course, and his steps slowed a fraction when they came in sight of Meriwether-Astor and the angel. "It makes me happy to hear you say things like that, Liz," he murmured against her hair, which had been caught up in ribbons and sprinkled with glitter.

"I'm glad," she whispered. "I'm not just saying them to be a flirt, you know. I mean them."

"I've never heard you say a thing you didn't mean." With another smile, he dropped his voice further. "Quiet, now, and we'll listen as the Lady bade us."

Fortunately, the orchestra was playing a slow, dreamy waltz with a pretty melody. If it had been playing a polka, they would never have been able to pull this off. Instead, they took the tiniest steps imaginable and described a lazy circle around the two men, weaving in and out of the other dancers and looking anywhere but at them.

"Minister," they heard Gerald Meriwether-Astor say with a bow. "You are a very difficult man to get an appointment with. Have you been avoiding me?"

The other man gazed down upon him with what Lizzie could only imagine was dislike. "That would be rude. I am a busy man, as my secretaries have told you repeatedly, Signore Meriwether-Astor. Am I to assume you wish to importune me now, in my own home?"

"I need ten minutes, no more. It will be worth your time—if the Duchy is interested in keeping its clockwork going, that is."

"The Duchy is the safest kingdom in the Levant. I hardly think—"

"I understand this particular kingdom has … needs that are not currently being met by its supply."

"I have no time for euphemisms and coy allusions. Speak plainly. My wife, there by the large arrangement of flowers, is beckoning me to dance."

Tigg executed a turn around a couple costumed as lions (how hot they must be!) and came out on the other side of the Minister. Lizzie had never been so glad that good hearing was another of her gifts. It had saved their skins on more than one occasion, and this might prove to be another.

"As you wish," Meriwether-Astor said. "You need more convicts to keep the city moving. I have access to practically unlimited numbers of them, and the means by which to transport them here."

The Minister left off gazing at his wife and focused on the man shifting impatiently from foot to foot in front of him. "Are you referring to ... slaves?"

Tigg tripped. Lizzie clutched him until his steps steadied.

Meriwether-Astor stared. "Good heavens. Of course not. That is illegal."

"Then...?"

"I believe this is best discussed in private, Minister. Do you have an office?"

The minister gazed in despair at his wife, who was very young and had just turned and flounced off into the crowd. "Very well. Come with me."

The two of them left the ballroom, followed by a pair of men in sober monk costumes who did not look as though they were enjoying themselves in the least.

"Come on, Liz," Tigg said. "We can't miss this."

Hand in hand, they slipped through the crowd and out into a corridor, where they could just see four figures passing through a door on the far end. The house was built in a quadrangle, with three floors to a side and rooms opening off a main gallery whose richly draped windows looked out on the central courtyard.

Lizzie slipped off her wings and stashed them under a huge stone urn with an enormous flower arrangement. If she had to run, they would only slow her down. Then she and Tigg entered the other side of the house, where her quick ears soon picked up the sound of footsteps on stone.

"This way," she whispered.

A staircase led up into the family's regions of the house, and another led down to the rooms where business was conducted. Since the ballroom was on the second floor, and it was unlikely the minister would take a guest up to the bedrooms, they had to have descended.

And so it proved to be. A door closed and the two men not in costume took up their stations outside. Tigg pulled Lizzie through another door and into the courtyard they had crossed earlier in the evening. Now servants were hurrying back and forth, and on the far side, a cluster of gondoliers leaned on the walls of an archway leading out to the canal, smoking and gossiping. Beyond them, gondolas bobbed in the current.

"Here," Lizzie whispered. "It's this one."

Quietly, she turned the handle of a French door and, to her gratification, it opened. She only needed a crack.

She leaned against the wall and tugged on Tigg's collar. "Pretend you are taking a liberty," she breathed.

"My pleasure." He leaned into her, and together they listened intently.

"*Bene*, you have ten minutes," the minister said on the other side of the drapes. "Less, since you have already deprived me of three."

"My proposal is one of mutual benefit," Meriwether-Astor said. "I wish to trade in the Levant, from Africa to Byzantium to Rome. You are in need of manpower to keep the city's gears in motion. If you give me a warrant of trade with a guarantee that my ships will be exempt from transfer tax, I will supply you with convicts."

After a moment, the minister said, "And where will you obtain them?"

"From the transport ships going to the Antipodes. With my underwater dirigibles, I can strike, disable, and remove all cargo, human and otherwise, from the ships. For reasons peculiar to the English, they do not send their convicts to the colonies in airships. They send them by sea. This turns out to be to our advantage, for no one will be looking for them once they leave the London side, and on the way to the other side of the world, a thousand things could happen to cause a ship to founder. We will allow enough to pass, of course, to avoid suspicion."

The minister was again silent, while Lizzie fought down the urge to burst through the window, snatch up the first weapon that came to hand, and give Gloria's father what for. How dared he! These were human beings he was discussing as calmly as though they were a hold full of salted cod!

The minister might have been thinking along the same lines, for he said, "And what of these convicts themselves? I cannot imagine they would stand to be re-routed east and put to work underwater."

"They are convicts," Meriwether-Astor said bluntly. "They must serve a sentence for their crimes. I don't imagine it matters much exactly where."

Lizzie's arms went around Tigg, less because she was playing a part than because she needed the comfort. In the old days, she'd known more than one boy transported for thieving a loaf of bread to feed his brothers and sisters. How many alley mice and desert flowers would be aboard those ships, condemned to the underground prison and not allowed even the hope of freedom while they worked off their sentences?

"You are quick to condemn others," the minister observed. "Have you actually seen our prisons, and the way we administer justice?"

"Not up close," the other man admitted. "But I've heard plenty."

"Then perhaps before we come to any agreement, you ought to see the reality of what you speak of so cavalierly. Allow me to arrange a tour of the prison. Would tomorrow suit?"

"The sooner we come to an agreement, the better. But perhaps we ought to disguise our intentions a little. I would be happy to be part of a tour, if my daughter may come along."

"The prisons of the Duchy are no place for a woman."

"My daughter needs to experience the hard-headed reality of my business if she is to run it after I am gone. I say it is exactly the place for her. Will you send a conveyance—say, at two o'clock?"

"Very well. A gondola bearing no colors will wait at the Hotel Exelsior's moorage. The gondolier will wear a red ribbon tied around his arm. I do not wish this excursion associated with me in any way. I will leave word with the Master of Prisons that you and your party are to be admitted."

"Understood. I will be in touch afterward." Meriwether-Astor paused. "And after today, I do not expect to be kept waiting by your lackeys."

The minister murmured a reply—but Lizzie did not hear him, for Tigg was whispering, "We have to tell the Lady."

"Of course. What a horrible, horrible plan!" Lizzie whispered directly into his ear. "How can one man be so evil? As soon as one of his plans is scotched, he immediately concocts another, each more deplorable than the last!"

"Liz, we have to be on that gondola."

She choked back a startled sound. "I'm not going to the wretched prison."

"Oh, yes you are, and I am going with you. Don't you see? Once we get in there, we can scout all the ways to get out. Perhaps we might even see Jake—or at the very least, find a way to get a message to him. It's of utmost importance, Lizzie. He must know he is not forgotten."

Lizzie had overcome many of her deepest fears, but she had no idea what might happen if she deliberately went into a place that was dark, enclosed, and full of water. One thing at a time she could manage, but all three?

"Who's there?" The drapes were wrenched back. The Minister of Justice pulled open the French door and glared at them.

Instead of playacting the part of lovers, in her surprise Lizzie lost her head. She grabbed Tigg's hand and ran, across the courtyard to the open door through which a small crowd of waiters had just gone.

"You there! What were you doing? Stop! Guards!"

# A LADY OF INTEGRITY

12

"This way!" Lizzie skidded around the corner and yanked on Tigg's hand.

"Back to the ballroom!" he said.

"No time—quick—through here."

They couldn't go up, because the running footsteps of the two monks were nearly upon them. Thank heavens the door under the staircase was unlocked. They tumbled through it and nearly fell down the stone steps. Tigg hauled back on Lizzie's arm and she found her footing, then both ran down as lightly as they could.

Above them, the door opened, and they heard a shout.

"Stop or they'll hear us!" Tigg held her, both of them breathing hard and hoping against hope that no one would investigate further. The stone felt cold under

Lizzie's thin dancing slippers.

A brief consultation occurred in the Venetian language, and then the door slammed with a hollow echo.

A lock grated into place.

Oh, dear. She must not give way to hysterics. She must be calm.

"Liz? Are you all right? You're shaking."

"It's c-cold."

"Right. Well, we can't go up, so we've no choice but to go down."

"I don't want to."

He wrapped his arms around her and spoke into her hair. "It's all right, Lizzie-love. We're together, and we aren't out of options yet. Come on, now. Breathe."

She did her best. The air smelled of cold stone and dust and ... "I wonder if this goes down to the water line. I smell weed."

"Seaweed?"

"Yes. Damp and green and salty and ... weedy."

"Let's hope so, then. I've still got my invitation. We can come in the front again and lose ourselves in the crowd."

A plan. A hope. Lizzie took a firm grip on her courage.

They ventured farther down the staircase, which, instead of being lit by the usual ribbon of electricks along the ceiling, was illuminated by old-fashioned oil lamps set at intervals in niches in the wall. At the bottom they passed through a wooden door so old and heavy they could barely push it open. As they emerged onto a stone landing, Lizzie heard the water lapping against it and wasn't sure whether to sigh with relief or take an apprehensive breath. Here again were all three things she didn't like. "I can't see."

"One shake." Tigg left her, and in a moment returned with one of the lamps. He held it up and it took a moment for both of them to realize what they were looking at.

"Great Caesar's ghost," Tigg said on a long breath.

The area might once have been a cellar extending under the house, but it was filled with seawater now. They stood on a stone pier similar to the one in the cave below her grandparents' house, but there the resemblance ended. Thick columns jutted up out of the black water, holding up the house, but the floor was submerged to such a depth they couldn't see the bottom. The expanse of restless water, flashing in the lamp's light, had been divided up into smaller areas by iron grates.

Cages.

"Is it a menagerie?" Lizzie asked. "Like the one we stole into at the Tower of London when we were children?"

Over the top of one iron divider, a long tentacle curled up and out of the water, as though it had sensed the light and was feeling its way toward it. Lizzie sucked in a breath of alarm—the tentacle was as big around as she was. How big could the creature be to which it belonged?

But it did not seem threatening. It seemed to be ... appealing to them.

It couldn't be. She was being fanciful.

There was a splash to one side and Tigg lifted the lantern to reveal a smooth, smiling snout and a black, intelligent eye bobbing in the cage closest to them. "It's a dolphin!" she exclaimed.

"Down here in the dark? That's criminal, is what it is. Look, there are more. Half a dozen, at least."

The light seemed to have excited them, and the first one began to bump its nose against the iron grate that held it. One, two three …

"The poor thing. It will injure itself," she said softly.

"What else is he keeping down here?" Tigg's tone was moving from wonder into indignation. "Isn't being in charge of putting people in prison enough for this man—does he have to put creatures in, too?"

Something spouted on the other side, but the light wasn't strong enough to reach. The tentacley creature had more of its legs—arms?—wrapped around the grate that held it in. The iron shook but did not give. And now a second one, with smaller, more spidery arms, began to thrash about in its cage, as though the light were agitating it. In a cage beyond the dolphins, a smooth, gleaming loop of scales rose and slipped beneath the surface, then rose again to reveal a wedge-shaped head. A forked tongue tested the air in their direction.

"This is awful," Lizzie said, shivering now from more than cold. "These poor creatures. Tigg, we must find a way out. I can't bear it."

"I imagine they feel the same. But it doesn't look as though there is a way out. He comes down here to play with his toys and goes back up by the same stair."

"He had to get them in here, didn't he?"

Tigg held the lantern so the golden glow fell on her face. "Are you planning to swim out? That might attract some notice when we go in to dance—unless you're planning to tell people you're Undine?"

But Lizzie did not answer. Her near-panicked gaze had fallen on an ironwork in the wall that seemed to be connected to a frame on the ceiling. "Tigg, hold the lantern up. Look, just there, and tell me what your engineer's eyes see."

It did not take long for him to reach a conclusion. "It appears that those levers control the walls of the cages. They can be made larger or smaller by dropping in a grate or removing it altogether."

"If you were a dolphin, say, and you remembered how you were brought in here, would you be able to find your way out again?"

He left off his perusal of the mechanism to gaze into her eyes. "Are you planning to use a dolphin as your guide?"

"I'm planning to let them all go," she said with grim resolve. "There is no way out of here, and the minister will just come down when it's convenient and feed us to the snake—or that thing with the tentacles. Or lock us up in prison. We can't swim past all these cages, so we'll just winch them up and free everyone, leave the dolphins for last, and swim out with them."

"He saw both of us, Liz. He'll know we did it."

"He'll see neither of us again, then. It will prevent our going on the jaunt to the prison, and don't think I'm not happy about that."

"You'd rather face a grotto full of tentacles than a tour of the prison?" Tigg's voice held teasing, but his gaze was absolutely serious.

"I would." Lizzie nodded firmly. "You pulled me out of the Thames when I was five. I'm quite confident that you'll do the same now if I need it. Can you see any other course of action we might take?"

Silently, his gaze moving from pulleys to levers to the increasingly agitated splashing in the cages, Tigg shook his head. "No time like the present, I suppose. Hold the lamp."

With one final moment of study that seemed to set the working of it in his mind, he hauled on a lever. In the far reaches of the grotto, metal screeched and rattled, and the splashing of many—what? Flippers? Legs? Fins?—was the result.

Tigg pulled on the next, and the snake flowed under the grate and out the other side, thrashing and sliding in the light. One more lever, and the two tentacled creatures released their grip on the grate just before it cleared the water. Time seemed to stop as the larger creature's baleful gaze met those of Lizzie and Tigg—it took them in—seemed to understand. Its many tentacles released the grate and it fell into the water with a loose, messy splash. The water mounded up over its body with the speed of its departure, following the snake, until it was lost to sight in the darkness.

By now the dolphins were making curious conversational noises, swimming in tight circles, bumping the grates impatiently with fluke and nose.

"Hang on just a minute," Lizzie told them. The words were barely out of her mouth when the boom of the door above startled her nearly off the edge of the landing. "Tigg, someone's coming!" she hissed in alarm.

Tigg rammed the final lever forward, and the last of the grates lifted, dripping with seawater, weed, and the remnants of whatever the minister had tossed in for food. The dolphins surged in the direction the other creatures had gone.

The pounding sound of boots on stone echoed in the stairwell.

"Now, Liz!" Tigg grabbed her around the waist and

together they leaped off the landing. Lizzie had just enough time to gasp in a big breath before they plunged into the cold, dark unknown.

*

"I cannot think what has become of Tigg and Lizzie." Claire gazed anxiously around the crowded ballroom. The whirling color and movement, to say nothing of too-brilliant lights and the crush of bodies, were beginning to give her a headache.

"They were following Meriwether-Astor," Andrew murmured, "but he returned some time ago and is standing there, by the punch."

"And what of the Minister of Justice?"

"No sign of him. And since we have had no real success with our other efforts, I am hoping Lizzie will have had better luck."

This was not like Lizzie—or Tigg, for that matter. The point of scouting was to come back and report what one had seen, not to vanish with one's young man and find a private corner in which to spoon.

"Do you want me to look for her, Lady?" Maggie asked.

"No, darling. It is not safe for you to scout alone. Wouldn't you rather dance?"

"I danced with Claude and Mr. Malvern."

"But there are several other young gentlemen among Claude's friends, are there not?" Arabella de Courcy, dressed as a medieval maiden in the style of Waterhouse, floated past in the arms of Adolphus von Stade, who had borrowed an aeronaut's uniform. How original.

"Perhaps, but I don't much fancy them."

Claire sighed. "I cannot blame you. I don't much fancy them, either. I wonder if everyone at the Sorbonne is so odious?" She rose on tiptoe and scanned the ballroom once again. "Andrew, do you think perhaps she and Tigg have gone into the courtyard? Or even outside, to walk along the canal?"

"It is possible. Shall we check?"

"Could we? The very thought of a bit of starry sky and some air is a relief."

Maggie hesitated, clearly uncertain about whether she might be intruding. "Shall I come with you?"

"No, you wait here. When Captain Hollys returns with Alice from the polka, ask them to meet us outside, at the canal. I'm sure we shall see Lizzie and Tigg out there."

"Neither of them are ballroom people," Maggie agreed. "I like it in moderation, but this is ... too much."

"Venice does tend to strike one that way," Andrew murmured as they crossed the floor, winding between the couples until they reached the central courtyard. But other than servants hurrying this way and that, and a cluster of gondoliers talking among themselves, there were no other guests visible.

"The street door is here." Andrew nodded at the gatekeeper and the two of them emerged onto the *fondamente* with a sense of having escaped out the end of a kaleidoscope.

Claire walked to the pavement's edge, where the water seemed disturbed, though no gondola or one of the slender rowing boats that ordinary people used was visible. "Andrew, does the water level look higher to you?"

# A LADY OF INTEGRITY

He peered over the edge. "I cannot tell. But it does seem rather rough—Claire! Get back!"

For in the canal was a most astonishing sight. The water roiled with the force of a large creature's passing—a creature with many legs, swimming with speed and power by means of flexing its body in and out like a bellows.

"Andrew—can that be a—*kraken?*"

"If it is, it is a very small one—but still large enough to swamp a gondola without much trouble. Look, there it goes, into the Grand Canal. Great Scott! I hope it will find its way out to sea. That is not a sight one wishes to encounter when going to visit St. Mark's in a boat."

"It must be lost. My word, Andrew—look there!" She pointed at an enormous snake, rolling along the canal in sinuous S-curves, its wedgelike head breaking the surface with such force that a small wave purled before its chin. "Please tell me it is not hunting the kraken."

"Please tell *me* the canals of this city are not routinely infested with creatures born of a nightmare. For if they are, it is becoming more urgent by the moment that we free our young friend."

Claire shuddered. There were places where she must not allow her imagination to go, or she would fall to her knees screaming and be of no use to anyone.

A sound rather like laughter now rose from the restless waters, and she could not help it. With wondering eyes, she leaned cautiously over the edge to see the smooth, satiny bodies of dolphins, rising and falling in a rocking-horse motion as they rode the waters. It almost looked as though they were pursuing the kraken and the snake—which made no sense whatsoever.

"There are no dolphins in the canals of Venice," Andrew said flatly. "I could believe a kraken might live down there—or a snake—but dolphins, absolutely not. Something is definitely out of the natural balance here."

And there was that peal of laughter again.

One she knew very well.

Claire's mouth dropped open as a drenched figure, its long blond hair clinging wetly to its head and shoulders, broke the surface of the canal. It clung to the dorsal fin of a dolphin—and behind it was another, larger figure, equally soaked and covered with weed.

"Steps!" the first figure called, and released her mount. "Thank you!" she told it. The dolphin chattered, rolled, and dove, following its fellows to the Grand Canal visible at the end of this smaller tributary.

The larger figure, naked to the waist, hoisted the smaller one up the first several stairs and the two of them crawled on all fours to the top, as if they'd forgotten how to use their legs—or were too weak to manage it.

They heaved themselves up onto the pavement in a wave of canal water, practically at Claire's and Andrew's feet, and Lizzie rolled onto her back, gasping and laughing in equal measure.

And then she realized who was gaping down at her. "Lady," she managed, and went into a coughing fit. "Oh, thank heaven. I believe there is a sardine in my hair."

# A LADY OF INTEGRITY

13

The polka, Alice was quite sure, had been invented by a snob to separate those who belonged from those who did not.

"Right foot, Captain Chalmers. A lady always starts on the right foot." Ian Hollys corrected her course and turned her the opposite way. This particular version was called the "traveling polka," and involved galloping sideways for three counts, then turning to face the other direction for one count, then galloping again. Making the turn in one beat was physically impossible, since the music was so fast. Captain Hollys had been reduced to taking her into the center of the crowd presently leaping around the ballroom, and describing much slower, shorter steps.

And the center of the floor, as everyone knew, was

where the incompetent were penned, so they would not get in the way.

"Please take me back, and dance with someone else," she begged for the third time.

"Nonsense." His tone was bracing, as though she were a midshipman learning the ropes. "The trouble is that you are trying to lead. If you leave that to me, both mind and body will accept the step easily."

Alice, whose opinions about the leadership of men had been formed in the unforgiving desert and rocks of Resolution, tightened her lips and did her best to do as he asked, but it wasn't easy. If he had been a terrible dancer, her feelings would have been different. But as it was, any woman in her right mind would have been delighted to let him take the lead. Why did she have to be the one woman who objected?

"You'd do better asking Gloria. At least she knows what she's doing."

"I have already danced two dances with Gloria. If I am to do my duty, I must dance an equal number with you. To the right, please."

*Thanks ever so much.* His *duty* was to keep her from being recognized. She didn't appreciate in the least being reminded that, to that end, it was also his duty to dance with her so that they blended more completely into the crowd.

"Captain? Alice?" The voice at her elbow made Alice miss her step, and she and the captain came to an ungraceful halt. Maggie stood there in her fairy costume, her face as pale as her own silvery skirts. "The Lady asks that you come. We are returning to the hotel."

Thank goodness.

"Maggie, are you quite all right?" the captain asked, examining her keenly. "Has something happened?"

"Lizzie—"

"She has news," Alice told him with sudden understanding. "I must let Gloria know we are leaving."

"Allow me," the captain said. Did he have to sound quite so eager?

"We will both go."

Gloria made no secret of her disappointment at their departure. "But you've barely been here two hours. Do you not want to stay for the fireworks?"

Ian said, "It would give us great pleasure, but young Miss Seacombe has been taken ill."

"Oh, such a shame. I hope she will be better tomorrow. Oh!" Gloria's blue eyes widened. "I almost forgot. Father is dragging me along on some dreadful tour of the prisons and gearworks in the morning. Please come—I know it's awful, and not the sort of exhibition we are all here to enjoy, but I would so like the company of congenial people." Her face clouded. "The combination of my father and a prison would be enough to make anybody ill. We can help keep one another's spirits up."

"I shall be honored to accompany you," Captain Hollys said gallantly. "I am afraid Alice and some of the young ladies will be unable to, but we shall certainly convey your invitation to Lady Claire and Mr. Malvern."

As they hurried out of the *palazzo*, Alice said, "That was a little high-handed, Captain. I'm quite capable of accepting or declining my own invitations."

"I will not allow you anywhere near the prison."

*"Allow—"*

"I should hope not," Maggie said, following so closely she was practically clutching Alice's arm. "If anyone should recognize you, it's hardly the work of a moment to clap you in an underwater cell."

Well, fine. There was that. But he could have put it a different way.

Out on the pavement they were treated to the astonishing sight of Lizzie and Tigg, drenched to the skin and reeking of effluvium and seaweed. They closed ranks and hustled the pair along the canal to a water taxi. It wasn't until they had both bathed and changed into their normal clothes that they all gathered in the sitting room of the suite that Lady Claire had taken to hear the tale.

And what a tale it was.

"Lizzie, dearling, you have a positive genius for getting into scrapes that no one else would ever dream of," Alice said when Lizzie and Tigg, holding hands as they sat side by side on the settee, had finished.

"I am only thankful she has an equal genius for getting out of them," Claire said. "Did it never occur to either of you to return to the ballroom and seek safety in numbers with us?"

"It did," Tigg said, "but there wasn't time. They'd have caught us. And the good thing is, we were able to free the creatures." His face clouded. "It was awful, Lady. The poor kraken, used to being the king of the sea, and there it was, reaching out a tentacle like it were pleading for help."

"Seeing if it could reach its dinner, more like," Maggie corrected, hanging over the back of the settee, close to her cousin.

"No, it wasn't like that," Lizzie said. "It *looked* at

us, like an intelligent being. If it wanted to have us for dinner, it certainly could have waited in the canal and had us, and any number of dolphins for dessert. But it seemed to understand we were all in the same boat, with only one chance of escape."

"For which the minister will not thank you," Claire told her. "You are going to have to lie very low now. In fact, I would suggest that you and Tigg return to *Athena* on the mainland if it were not for the fact that you must be chaperoned."

Lizzie blushed scarlet and even Tigg cleared his throat in embarrassment.

"Aside from kraken and cages," Andrew said, "what disturbs me most is this dreadful plan of Meriwether-Astor's. Waylaying the convict transports and kidnapping the occupants! Is there no depth to which he will not sink?"

"Every time we plumb the depths of his wickedness we find something new," Claire agreed. "Even his affection for his daughter is tainted by it."

"She has asked for our help tomorrow," Alice said, recollecting the message they had been asked to deliver. "No sooner did Lizzie overhear Meriwether-Astor browbeat the minister into a tour of the prison and the gearworks than he must have sought out Gloria to tell her she was going along."

"I accepted on your behalf, Claire," Captain Hollys said. "The poor girl was quite distraught at the thought of braving the place in only her father's company."

"As well she might be," Claire said.

"And I have made it clear to Alice that she will not be accompanying us, and she has agreed it would be far too dangerous."

"Have you?" Claire raised an eyebrow in Alice's direction.

"I have," Alice said. No point in going into detail and giving Ian Hollys the opportunity to rub it in a second time.

"Lizzie and Tigg cannot go, of course," he went on. "It is a shame. Tigg, I would have been glad of your support."

"Sorry, Captain. I lost my head and—"

"No need for apology. Your duty was to protect Lizzie, and while your methods were unorthodox, they were also effective. Claire, I believe that leaves you and Mr. Malvern to make up our party."

"And me," Maggie said quietly.

"Maggie, I do not think—" Claire began.

"If you need a scout, Lady, it will have to be me. Luckily, I can swim."

"We could scout around the outside of the place, Lady," Lizzie suggested. "We wouldn't have to go in."

Claire shook her head. "It is entirely too dangerous. In fact, a thought has just occurred to me. Alice, you must also remain concealed from prying eyes. I think it would be most practical if you were to return to *Athena* with Lizzie and Tigg. That way, you will all three be safe, and if we must make a quick exit once we have Jake in hand, it would be very helpful if the ship already possessed a captain and an engineer on board. Do you not agree?"

Of course it was a practical plan.

It made all the sense in the world.

And as Alice exchanged glances with Lizzie and Tigg, it was clear that the three of them would sooner be captured than allow it.

# A LADY OF INTEGRITY

14

Claire's cream linen dress, ruffled parasol, and pinwheel hat loaded with tulle and a large green satin bow created such a contrast with her surroundings that it felt almost obscene—as though one were laughing in a cemetery.

She and Andrew followed Meriwether-Astor, Gloria, Maggie, and Ian from the majestic, marble-inlaid Hall of Justice down a stone ramp to what lay below the surface of pavement and canal. Claire wished she had worn raiding rig. Anything else seemed like snapping one's fingers in the face of fate.

They were escorted by two men—the Master of Prisons and an assistant, one ahead and one behind, presumably so none of them wandered away, never to be seen again. Maggie was finding this particularly irksome. The damp seeped through Claire's linen jacket, rendering the crisp fabric limp and every bit as dispirited as she herself was becoming.

Gloria clung to Captain Hollys's arm, and Claire did not miss the occasional glance of satisfaction bestowed on them by her father, who otherwise treated her as though she were a featherhead. As though his training of her to manage his affairs was a burden, and he didn't hold out much hope of success. In Claire's opinion, this was doing Gloria a grave injustice. As Maggie had so accurately pointed out, Gloria could be very handy in a pinch, being possessed of both intelligence and a most unladylike willingness to take a risk.

From the outside, the building's façade was of white marble, and at the water level, they had seen the mighty arches holding it up. Through these passed the boats bearing the condemned or their families and lawyers, passing from sunshine into deep shadow where even the wavering reflections of the water did not penetrate.

"Here are the piers where the accused disembark," their guide intoned. From where they stood, Claire could see the aforesaid arches framing the busy canal outside—the last glimpse of the familiar world that many of these poor people would ever see. "Come along. The cells are at water level. To go below that, we will need to enter a diving bell."

"Oh, Lady," Maggie whispered. "I don't want to go below the water."

"Do not be afraid, darling," she whispered back. "We will be with you every moment." She did not particularly want to go, either, but what if they caught a glimpse of Jake? "We must learn as much as we can in order to be useful."

*For Jake*, was her unspoken message.

Maggie took a deep breath and nodded. "I don't suppose they would leave me alone on the landing, anyway," she said.

"Certainly not," said the man bringing up the rear. "No uncondemned person may pass the water gates unescorted."

"Is there any other way into the prison and the gearworks?" Andrew inquired.

This brought a tightening of the man's facial muscles that might pass for a smile. "Not many wish to come in. Plenty wish to go out, however."

"That is well understood. But in answer...?"

"Yes, of course. The mighty gearworks that support the city are accessible by anyone with a diving bell."

"Then you must have had to deal with misguided persons attempting to free their relatives and associates?"

Claire squeezed his arm in appreciation. She would never have dared to ask such a question, but his reputation as an engineer had preceded him even to this benighted place. The Master of Prisons fancied himself an aficionado of mechanics, and had read every monograph Andrew had ever published.

The master turned now to provide an answer himself. "There have been attempts, but none have succeeded. Several factors must be in place, you see."

"Factors? Do go on." Andrew's face held interest.

The Master of Prisons expanded like a flower under the opportunity to give information to a man of such a reputation in the world. "First, one must possess a diving bell and the accompanying hoses and engines which produce air. These, you may imagine, are strictly regulated. Possession by unauthorized persons is illegal and punishable by imprisonment."

"And who may be authorized?"

"Employees of the Ministry, naturally."

"Ah," said Andrew. "And another factor?"

"The position of the great arms and cogs of the gearworks." They passed through a set of oak doors so thick that they might have come from a medieval castle. The men who held them open cranked them closed behind the little party, and Claire felt the *boom!* and the change in air pressure in her very bones.

Now they were trapped and at the mercy of inhospitable forces. She shivered the dread away. They were in no danger. She was being fanciful.

"How might the position of the gears affect a rescue attempt?" Andrew inquired.

"Ah, but this factor is best illustrated by demonstration, not explanation, in true scientific fashion." The Master of Prisons beamed. "In a moment you will see for yourselves. The third factor, of course, is the kraken."

"The what?" Gloria squeaked, clutching Captain Hollys's arm more tightly, as though she expected a tentacled arm to rise out of the water below them and wrap itself around her ankle.

"Perhaps you are not aware that kraken are immensely intelligent," the master went on indulgently. "A well-trained hound or even a horse is no comparison to one of these. If they are captured young and trained by the methods we have developed, they become the vicious equivalent of guard dogs. The diving bells then serve two purposes—they provide air in the first instance, and protection in the second."

"The kraken attack the diving bells?" Andrew asked.

Claire's spirits began to waver as the magnitude of their task made itself clear.

"Oh yes. They attack anything—except the gear-works, of course, for which they have a healthy—and, it seems, hereditary—respect."

"And these training methods?" Claire asked, willing her voice to its normal smooth civility. "What do they involve?"

"Ah, but that is no subject for a gently reared lady's ears," the master said with a plump-cheeked smile. "I will tell you, however, that our own Minister of Justice has some expertise in this area. He has studied the kraken for many years in experiments with both living and dead animals, and is considered an authority among biologists—perhaps the equal of yourself, sir—" He nodded at Andrew. "—in the corresponding field of mechanical sciences. The animals trained by him are particularly effective at protecting the citizens of Venice from the condemned below."

Claire exchanged a speaking glance with Andrew, the memory of that creature swimming as fast as it could down the canal in search of escape vivid in both their memories. Lizzie had said that it had looked pathetic, almost pleading. To what tortures had the poor creature been subjected?

The fact that she could feel pity for a kraken, of all things, was perhaps the strangest of all the strange moments she had experienced thus far in this peculiar city.

"Come," the Master of Prisons said as a lackey opened another thick door for them. "Let us enter a diving bell so that you may see for yourselves Leonardo da Vinci's master work."

*

The Lady had entrusted the chaperonage of herself and Tigg to Alice, but in Lizzie's mind, a resourceful young woman halfway to seventeen and a young man of nineteen already well established in a respectable career had no need of it. But Alice did not seemed inclined to hire a water taxi to take them back to the mainland and *Athena*, which was why they were presently dressed in holiday style, strolling around the environs of the Ministry of Justice as though it were one of the sights recommended in Baedeker.

If anyone questioned it, they could always say they were lost.

Her half-brother Claude had turned up at the hotel while they were at breakfast, and had lounged along with them when they'd set out. Lizzie herself was torn about how much of their purpose here she could reveal to him. While he knew the broad outlines of the plot to hold him for ransom in France a few weeks ago, he did not know that Gerald Meriwether-Astor had been behind it. He labored under the delusion that Lady Claire's party was here on holiday, much like his own, and had questioned their activities no further. But how long would they be able to keep up the pretense?

It dismayed her to keep anything from the dear boy, whom she liked immensely and who, she had always believed, was similar to Goria Meriwether-Astor in that the people who had been closest to him underestimated him rather badly.

But still ... they were here on a matter of life and death. How much risk would she incur for Jake if she confided in Claude? Or was she just as guilty of under-estimating him as their grandparents were?

Now he looked from the arches on which the build-ing rose, to the roofline far above. "This isn't a church," he said. "Aren't we meant to be going to San Marco to see the gilded interior?"

"Oh, are we?" Lizzie said innocently. "I suppose we must find our way around this building, then. Good-ness, how big it is."

"Lizzie, old girl, it's a government building. Justice, I think—it's a temple, sure enough, but filled with law-yers instead of priests. Prayers won't do a man much good here, either, from what I understand."

"So I've heard," Tigg said. He led them along the pavement on one side. Here, toward the rear of the building, they climbed a stair where the embankment had been built up and the arches filled in, giving what was left of the apertures the effect of windows at the street level.

A sound filled the air, like the calling of gulls. Cry-ing. Weeping. Coming from some distance below them.

Alice drew in a breath. "Is that—?"

Now it appeared the occupants had realized someone was standing outside, blocking the light far above. Cries for help, for mercy issued thinly from between iron bars. Weak voices begged that they take a message to wife, to sweetheart, to solicitor. Others merely implored God to end their misery.

Alice's face turned white under the shade of her lacy parasol. Claude looked as though he might be ill.

Behind them, a rough voice demanded something in

the Venetian tongue, and their four horrified gazes swung upward. A man in a blue tunic and a military cap snapped a command that Lizzie had no doubt was the equivalent of one she'd known well: "Move along, there! This is no place for the likes of you."

He was going to chase them off and they had no recourse but to go. But she could do one thing. Flinging herself to her knees, she wrapped her fingers around the bars. "Jake!" she screamed into the dark abyss of the dungeon. "Jake!"

The soldier snapped another command and seized Lizzie's arm, but not before her keen hearing clearly detected a voice far away. "Lizzie? Maggie?"

She shrieked his name once more in a paroxysm of relief and fear, and wrenched herself from the soldier's grip. If she were detained, she might be tossed in the clink—or worse, taken before that nasty Minister, who would do the job himself. Without thinking further, her instincts once again took over and she took to her heels, hauling up her skirts and dodging between buildings, down an alley so narrow her elbows brushed it on both sides, and out along a broad waterway she recognized as the Grand Canal.

No, too visible. She plunged into a cobbled street that ran between the grand palaces that fronted the canal. Slumping against a railing that separated a garden from this narrow street, she caught her breath, only to be startled half out of her skin by a feminine voice above her.

"Really, Miss Seacombe, are you so fond of our company that you must run all the way here in this precipitate fashion?"

Arabella de Courcy was draped over the balcony

overlooking the garden, gazing down at her in amusement. Lizzie suddenly realized where she was—at the *palazzo* rented by Arabella's family for their daughter's stay with her friends. Apparently the elder de Courcys were also here, though Lizzie had never seen them yet and did not expect to.

"I believed myself lost, but you have proven me wrong," she told the girl in what she hoped was a flippant tone.

"Are you unescorted?"

"Of course not. I took a wrong turn. Claude and Lieutenant Terwilliger are just behind me, no doubt looking for me."

"No doubt." Arabella gazed at her, and it seemed civility finally forced her to say, "Would you care for some refreshment?"

After what she'd just seen and heard, if she tried to swallow anything, it would likely come back up again. "No, thank you. I will rejoin my party."

"When you see Claude and Miss Meriwether-Astor, do tell them we are planning to attend the opera this evening. It is *Die Fledermaus*. We should adore Miss Meriwether-Astor's company."

"I am sure she would adore yours, too, but she is too much engaged with Captain Hollys at present to have time for schoolgirls such as we."

Arabella's face fell, and Lizzie felt a most unkind moment of triumph. She waved farewell in the satisfaction of having had the last word, when Arabella recovered herself and called, "Oh, Miss Seacombe, a moment. A messenger came this morning bearing a warning of the *acqua alta*. In case you are not staying in a hotel that might warrant such an attention, I am passing it on to you. It comes with the full moon, two days off."

Not for worlds would Lizzie admit she had no idea what the *acqua alta* was. "Thanks ever so," she said, and walked in as ladylike a fashion as she could back down the street to the canal.

She could only hope that the others had got away clean. Now all she had to do was find them.

# A LADY OF INTEGRITY

15

"It is quite safe, *signorina*," the Master of Prisons said to Claire. He held out a hand, and she was forced to draw upon four centuries of breeding and self-confidence in order to put her gloved hand in his and step inside the diving bell.

It did not look safe at all.

It was made of glass, and from a structure in the apex hung a web of harnesses and the kind of narrow platform favored by the brave souls who washed the windows of churches for their living. The bell, large enough to contain their party, stood upon a platform that was winched down into the water.

"The bell is maneuvered by a man we call the *campanaro*, in this chamber here." He pointed to the apex, separated from the harnessed individuals below by a brass cage. "He also controls the air hoses and the propulsion. The wonders of steam power have allowed us to create a system unique in the world." He beamed at Andrew. "I am honored to be the one to introduce you to it."

"Fascinating," Andrew murmured, gripping Claire's hand in his.

They were soon separated, however, and buckled into the swinging harnesses. Claire was familiar with the principles of physics that allowed the bell to be submerged and yet not fill with seawater. But familiarity was no help as the dark water closed over their heads outside the membrane of glass and they began to sink into the depths under the city.

Maggie whimpered, swaying in her harness, feet dangling a yard above the water that swirled in to contain them completely.

If her molars had not been clenched together so tightly, Claire might have whimpered herself.

They descended into the Stygian depths and a lamp was lit on the bell's apex, so powerful that they could see the wavering weed and schools of fish around them. And then Andrew drew in a breath.

"You may well be amazed," the Master of Prisons said proudly. "This—unseen, unknown outside of the Levant—is the real source of our Duchy's success. No one has matched it, and no one ever will."

The enormous arms of Leonardo da Vinci's masterwork became visible in the gloom. They were the size of a building—no, the size of the cliffs above Resolution. Only at a distance could one apprehend the revolving gears and massive cogs that powered the movement of the neighborhoods above.

# A LADY OF INTEGRITY

"This gearworks has kept the Doge safe for centuries," the master went on. "Who can locate him when his palace may be here one day and gone the next? There is a pattern to the movement, of course, but only the true Venetian, who has felt it in his blood and flesh his entire life, can tell what it is."

"And the task of the convict?" Gloria seemed to force the words from her throat in order to appear brave and insouciant before her father. Such was Claire's impression, at least.

"You shall see for yourself." The master said something in the Venetian tongue to the *campanaro*, and the bell changed its course a few degrees, approaching a massive joint in one of the enormous arms. "This arm we call *Zattere*," he said.

"Why, that is where our hotel is located," Maggie managed to say, clearly taking her example from Gloria and Claire.

"Then you will appreciate the skill and commitment of the prisoners who labor for you," the master said complacently, as though the poor devils had volunteered for their terrifying duty. "Observe."

Along the massive arm that supported the neighborhood, diving bells like their own clung like tiny bubbles. As they steamed closer, Claire observed men inside, hanging from harnesses, but sloshing in the water up to their waists, scrubbing the algae off the moving parts, dancing free so as not to be caught and dragged into the mechanism. When one crew finished scrubbing, another bell floated into place.

"What are they applying?" Andrew asked, squinting through the gloom. "Could that be grease?"

"You are very astute," the master said, clearly

pleased with the engagement and interest of his guests. "Each part of the gearworks is greased annually. It takes an entire year for the convicts to make their way over the entire mechanism." He turned to Gerald Meriwether-Astor, who had not said a word since they had left the lobby of the Ministry of Justice far above. "While one of course deplores that part of human nature which embraces lawlessness, one must admit that the frequency with which it happens enables the work to go faster."

"Quite so," Meriwether-Astor said, tight-lipped.

Perhaps he was afraid of water. But that could not be. He had crossed the Atlantic in an undersea dirigible called *Neptune's Fury*, had he not? And planned to continue his business now in some other vessel, in order to deliver more convicts to this dreadful penance.

"Those with life sentences have the opportunity to rise in the ranks," the master continued. "Grease men are esteemed more highly than scrubbers. Each crew possesses a master. Highest of all are the *campanari*. But sadly, the life expectancy is such that rising to that rank is difficult. We are often forced to hire men."

Claire swallowed. "What most affects their life expectancy?"

"Pneumonia, *signorina*," he said sadly. "That and the kraken. For of course the condemned regularly attempt to save themselves by escaping the harness and swimming for the surface."

"Oh," she whispered.

How were they to free Jake? Could they somehow commandeer a diving bell, comb the arms of the gearworks until they located the one in which he labored, transfer him, and escape, all without detection? It did not seem possible.

And yet, not to make the attempt was unthinkable.

"Do all the convicts labor for life?" she asked. "Are there circumstances under which they might be freed?"

"Certainly." The Master of Prisons signaled to the *campanaro*, and the bell began to move away from the gearworks. "If they survive until their trials, in some cases they can be declared innocent. In other cases, if it is a civil matter, a fine may be paid. But these are rare, you understand. Our Minister of Justice has tuned the system like a fine instrument. If one is so unlucky as to be imprisoned, it is usually because such a punishment is well deserved."

There was, of course, no rebuttal to this official line of nonsense, which no one in her right mind would believe. "And in the case of—"

*"Maestro!"* came a voice from above. *"Attentione!"*

A brief exchange in the Venetian tongue ensued, and the Master of Prisons pointed to the far end of the arm, just before the joint that rose under a neighborhood. "Observe," he said. "Escapes are most often attempted at this point on each arm, where the water is comparatively shallow and one might hope to reach the surface. Sadly," he said, shaking his head, "one so rarely does."

Far above, silhouetted against the light filtering down from the midday sun, a figure thrashed frantically for the surface.

Diving bells detached from the arm and rose in pursuit, filled by men waving their arms and swinging. Were they cheering the man in his attempt to win his freedom? Or were they warning of some—

On the *campanaro*'s shout, the master found what he was looking for, and pointed. "There."

Out of the depths rose a creature that even Claire's nightmares had never conjured. Seeing one in a biological publication—even seeing the small one briefly in the canal the night before—had not prepared her for the reality. Swimming with a terrible speed and a motion like a bellows, its tentacles trailing for more than thrice the length of a diving bell, came a kraken.

The man thrashed and swam with energy born of fear, but to no avail. The kraken reached—engulfed— hugged. The man's body disappeared in a welter of tentacles and suckers, and the kraken swam back down into the depths, stealthily clutching its prize. But from out of the gloom came two or three more, and a fight over the prey ensued. By this time, any hope the man might have had to escape while they were thus occupied was extinguished. No one could survive so long without air.

"They will attempt it," the master said sadly, "though they are all aware of the consequences."

*I am going to be sick. Violently sick.*

But she must not. Instead, she reached for Andrew's hand on the one side and Maggie's on the other. They gripped hers so hard that she could feel the bones grind.

*How are we to save him? And in the attempt, how are we to save ourselves?*

\*

Venice lay basking in the sun, the breeze toying with the lacy drapes inside open windows. Somewhere down one of the waterways, a gondolier sang a plaintive melody.

"This is what comes of allowing women and children

to interfere with one's duty." Captain Hollys stalked along the pavement as though he would beat Lizzie's location out of the recalcitrant stones. "I should never have permitted it."

"I don't recall that you had a choice in the matter," Alice told him mildly, her gaze combing walls and alleys for any sign that either Lizzie or Tigg had passed this way.

"It has been nothing but chaos and confusion and the unnecessary involvement of others since the moment we landed."

"I believe that was the plan. We're to look like tourists, aren't we? The best way to do that is to join a party of people who really are tourists—and while I have never been one before this week, I understand that some confusion is inevitable."

This logic had no effect on him. "And now we have lost Lizzie. What possesses her to draw attention to herself in this irresponsible manner?"

"Her irrepressible spirits and warm heart?" It had worked, hadn't it? "Thanks to her calling through that grate, we have information now that we didn't before." When he did not deign to reply, she said, "Captain, we're not going to find them. I think we had better return to the hotel. Lizzie will find her way back to report to Claire, never fear."

"It is not a matter of fear," he said stiffly. "It is a matter of discipline."

"I'll be happy to watch you explain that to Lizzie, then, since *discipline* isn't a word we usually associate with her or Maggie."

He eyed her, his shoulders stiff and his bearing upright. "Surely you do not condone her behavior?"

"She's a young woman who has come through worse than a brush with the local militia. It's not my job to worry about her behavior, anyway. It's Claire's."

"If it had been mine——" But he cut himself off.

Alice saw where the course of his thoughts had been set before he altered it. If Claire had accepted his offer of marriage, the remainder of the Mopsies' upbringing might have been laid at his door. She did her best not to smile at the thought, to no avail.

"Do you find something amusing, Miss Chalmers?"

"Captain Chalmers," she corrected him. "I'm sorry. I did have an amusing thought, but it's none of my business."

"Do tell."

"You won't like it."

"There are any number of things about this mission I do not like, but I bear them with what equanimity I can."

Goodness. Did all baronets talk like a dictionary, or just this one? "I was just thinking you've had a narrow escape. If things had been different, you would have been standing in a father's place with the girls now, and that would have been even more trying for you."

He stopped altogether, in the shade of a shop awning. "That is absolutely none of your business."

"I said so, didn't I? And I told you that you wouldn't like it."

"I had no idea—save me from your impertinence." He stalked on.

Blast her big mouth. She had meant to needle him out of his stuffiness, and all she had done was tear the scab off a wound that was not yet healed. The poor man was striking out in pain, not arrogance. "Forgive me, Captain," she said softly, tucking a conciliatory hand into the crook of his elbow as they strolled along together. Well, she was strolling. May as well pretend to be a fine lady while she tried to reef in the rope she'd already hung herself with. "I didn't mean to offend you and I'm sorry I hurt your feelings."

He cleared his throat, but instead of shaking off her hand, he allowed it to stay on his sleeve. "For us to speak of Lady Claire in this way dishonors her … and me. She has made her choice, and I am happy for her."

"And you? What of your choices?"

"I have chosen my duty, of course."

Of course. "But there is more to life than duty, and flying, and the sound of the wind in the ropes."

"I might make this same observation to you, Captain."

He must have forgiven her if he remembered to use her title. "That's because we have more in common than you know." The words fell out of her mouth before her mind realized it.

It took a moment for his understanding to catch up, and by then it was too late. "I see," he said at last, in a tone of discovery. "You had entertained a similar hope, only to have it similarly dashed?"

"If you laugh at me, I swear I will push you in the canal," she said fiercely, and tightened her hand on his arm as though she meant business.

But he did not laugh. "Believe me, affairs of the heart are no laughing matter. One puts on a smile if one can, and if one cannot—"

"One tears up the ballrooms of London?"

"Quite. Or the skies over the Atlantic."

"Any success in that quarter? Mayfair, I mean?"

"None I wish to admit to. And yourself?"

"None at all. I'd admit to an opportunity if I had it, but I haven't, darn it." Which was a humiliating confession if ever there was one. "What about Miss Meriwether-Astor? I think you can admit to some success there, can't you?"

"I hardly know the young lady well enough to say so."

"Be careful, Ian. Using her for a screen is one thing, but her pa has his eye on you. I saw him watching at the ball last night. And you don't want to hurt her, either."

"I have no intention of hurting her."

What did that mean? That he actually meant to court her? Or that he was going to be friendly and partner her for waltzes, but nothing more?

But Alice didn't have the courage to ask him to elaborate. She really didn't think she wanted to know the answer, anyhow.

"Here's the hotel," she said with some relief. "Let's go in and see if Lizzie has come back."

As they climbed the steps, her hand slipped from his arm, and with a sense of shock, she realized that a moment before, she had called him by his first name.

And he had allowed it.

16

"I must go somewhere cheerful," Gloria Meriwether-Astor had said the moment they descended the ministry's steps, her face as white as the Brussels lace on her blouse. "In the sun, where it is warm, and I cannot see the water."

"Don't be ridiculous," her father had replied in a tone that would have crushed any other young lady. "One cannot be anywhere in Venice out of sight of the water. I am due at the minister's offices in half an hour. Are you coming?"

Claire had been quick to offer an invitation to take tea in her sunny sitting room. "Thank you," Gloria said with relief—though whether this came from the thought of tea or of ridding herself of her parent, it was difficult to determine.

They had found the other members of their party already in the suite, sitting down to tea themselves.

Or almost all.

"Alice, I distinctly remember your departing with Tigg and Lizzie for *Athena* this morning," Claire said. "Why have you returned and they have not?"

"We became separated," Alice said with maddening brevity. "But that can wait until later."

Granted, they could not very well speak of their true purpose in Venice in front of Gloria, lest it get back to her father and subsequently to the Minister of Justice, but were one or two salient details too much to ask? Add to this the fact that no good ever came of being separated, and Claire wondered if perhaps she ought to drag Alice off into one of the bedrooms and grill her like a fish.

"Very well," she said instead, taking a biscuit she was unable to eat. Her stomach pitched with anxiety. "Are Tigg and Claude with her?"

"We split up into search parties, and I haven't seen them. Claire, you'll just have to wait for her to come back. Because you know she will."

*I do not know that at all.* So many dangers lurked in this city that looked so beautiful and serene on the surface, like a water lily, and underneath was so utterly terrifying.

"Would you like me to go look for them, Lady Claire?" Maggie asked. The use of her title told Claire that Maggie was aware both of the need for secrecy, and the fact that something might have gone dreadfully wrong.

"No need," Ian Hollys said before Claire could reply. "Captain Chalmers and I had a good look round, but could turn up no sign of her."

Gloria's gaze took in Ian and Alice, sitting on either end of the sofa with Maggie like a flower in the middle. She seemed to relax a little, and waved a hand. "Don't worry, Claire. Your Lizzie is a spirited young lady. Ten to one she is flirting with a Venetian boy on a bridge somewhere."

"Tigg would have something to say about that," Maggie observed. "They are keeping company."

"Is that so?" Gloria's eyes took on a sparkle of interest. "I do love a good romance. Is that why they ran away on you at the minister's ball, too? To be alone?"

Goodness. There was nothing wrong with Gloria's powers of observation. "I'm sure it was," Claire said. "She received quite a lecture afterward about it, however—which, as you see, has done no good."

The sound of rapid footsteps came from the corridor, and in a moment the object of their concern burst through the door, Tigg and Claude right behind her.

Lizzie's green eyes were wide with urgency as she bounded into the room. "We heard Jake, Lady. In the prison. He's alive!"

Claire's relief washed through her like a tingle in the blood. Here at last was the proof they had been craving that he was not yet dead. But she must stem the tide of Lizzie's words, quickly, before Gloria realized the sense of them. "Lizzie—"

"He recognized my voice—at least, he called my name, and Maggie's," Lizzie rushed on in her excitement. "He knows we're here, so he knows we'll be getting him out. I only hope we can do it before—" Belatedly, she realized that their number had been augmented by one. One, moreover, who was sitting in the wing chair, her cup of tea arrested in the air as she listened with interest. "Miss Meriwether-Astor," Lizzie finished lamely. "How nice to see you."

"You have been getting into a scrape, haven't you?" Gloria said. "Springing people from gaol? Here? Are you mad?"

"Of course she is not," Claire said hastily. "Mad, that is. She is simply speaking of—of one of her brother's friends, who was not permitted to join them at the exhibition today. She was simply exaggerating for effect. A deplorable trait, is it not?"

Gloria gave her such a pitying look that Claire felt the blood of sheer chagrin flood her cheeks. "Claire, do not mistake me for one of those silly schoolgirls you and I once knew. I remember Jake vividly. I am particularly interested in his welfare, the young scamp. He is Captain Chalmers's navigator, is he not?"

"Yes," Alice said.

"What has happened to him?"

Claire exchanged agonized glances with Alice, with Andrew, with Ian. Wouldn't someone speak? What could they say?

"I see," Gloria said, her interested expression fading, like a flower that folds up when the sun goes down. "Of course your affairs—and his—are none of my business. But since we have met again, I thought that— Never mind. I was wrong, that's all." She set her cup and saucer on the low table and rose, shaking her pretty van-dyked skirts so that they fell more perfectly.

Claire could not bear to see the life fade out of her eyes, leaving her resembling the little doll her father imagined her to be. "Gloria, you don't mean to go?"

"I'm afraid I must. I do not wish to intrude."

## A LADY OF INTEGRITY

Claire might have given in and regretted the circumstances forever if she had not heard the tremor in Gloria's voice. A tremor that made her suspect that Gloria had held the same hope of friendship that Claire herself possessed. A friendship that might nurture a lonely young woman—that might change the course of the future.

Claire saw that Alice had also risen, and in one of those moments of perfect agreement, realized that her friend's thoughts aligned with her own. A flicker of her lashes was all it took to signal her thoughts. Alice touched Gloria's wrist to stop her.

"Please don't. We want to hear what happened at the Ministry of Justice. Let me tell you why." In brief but pithy sentences, Alice outlined the circumstances that had brought herself and Jake to Venice. Claire took up the tale, leaving out Ian's and Tigg's purpose for being there, but making it clear what the intentions of the party in general were. And, since it appeared Claude had been taken into Lizzie's confidence, she included him as she related the facts.

As she spoke, Gloria sank back into the chair as though her knees could not bear her up. "Do you mean to tell me," she said when Claire finished, "that you honestly believe you can free him? After what we saw today?"

"What did you see?" Tigg asked. "We've told you what we saw and heard—now you must return the favor."

Claire and Maggie tried, but in the end it was Gloria and Captain Hollys who filled in the most horrifying details, and brought them up to the present moment. Lizzie covered her mouth with her hands, her face turning pale, and could not speak.

Even Tigg's good humor deserted him, and Claude looked utterly ill. "It's bad luck all round, old chap," he said to Tigg, clearly doing his best to bear up. "But if anyone is to succeed, it will be you lot. If you have one tenth the ability of my sister, you won't be able to help it."

Lizzie gripped his hand in silent thanks, and Tigg nodded. "Jake's me mate, and has been since I was a little tyke, turned out on the streets by the madam when my mother died. He saved my hide enough times that I'm not going to give up easily. He never gave up on me, even when circumstances looked bleak."

"Or me," said Maggie.

"Or me," echoed Lizzie.

"Well, then," Gloria said, picking up her cup and saucer once more, "how can I help?"

"You already have," Ian said with some warmth. "If you had not invited us along on that dreadful excursion this morning, we should still have been sitting here trying to plan a strategy for seeing the prison ourselves. We are extremely grateful to you."

Gloria blushed, and Alice looked away. "That was sheer cowardice. It *was* utterly dreadful—but imagine how much more it might have been with only Father for company."

"Are you ... not close to your father, then?" Alice asked diffidently, as though she expected Gloria to snap at her and tell her it was none of her business.

But Gloria only shook her head. "I was not born a boy, and twenty-three years later he still cannot forgive me. He has no choice but to treat me as his heir, but he hates every moment of it. I never used to care about his business affairs, but after I met you all in the Canadas..." A smile flickered on her lips. "Your young navigator changed my way of looking at the world—and at myself. If he is imprisoned, I must help to free him, even if it's only to thank him face to face."

"Do you know about the convict plan?" Lizzie asked. When Claire hushed her, the girl protested, "Well, she knows everything else—she ought to know the whole."

"Convict plan?" Gloria repeated. "What do you mean?"

"Your dad plans to help the Minister of Justice with his shortage of convicts by capturing the ships transporting them to the Antipodes, and bringing them here," Lizzie said.

"Lizzie, really," Claire sighed. "Poor Gloria has quite enough to deal with already, don't you think?"

"It's all right," Gloria said, her prettily coifed head drooping. "I didn't know the details, but I knew he was up to something. All the undersea dirigibles that have been plying the Mediterranean have for some reason been ordered *en masse* into the Adriatic. It's as if they're waiting for orders. Pigeons are flying back and forth with messages—most of which I've managed to read while he was busy elsewhere."

"How many vessels?" Ian asked.

"Half a dozen, I would say. A few are the large transatlantic ones, and the rest are smaller ones that don't have that kind of staying power for long voyages."

"Manned and crewed?"

"Oh, yes. Each has a crew of nearly fifty, and the big ones well over two hundred."

"Like a private navy," Maggie murmured. "Just like before."

"He has no shortage of men wanting to serve," Gloria told them. "He must pay very well, though I don't know how. I've seen the accounts."

"But this is not getting Jake out of gaol," Alice said, clearly impatient with a discussion of Gerald Meriwether-Astor's resources. "Now that we know exactly what we are up against, what are we going to *do?*"

# A LADY OF INTEGRITY

17

"Captain Chalmers is quite right," Ian Hollys said. "We must act. I have been considering a number of strategies, but I must caution you once again that each of them holds its dangers."

"Not as many dangers as Jake is facing," Lizzie pointed out.

"On the contrary," Ian told her. "The ultimate price any of us will pay if we do not succeed is to join him. Mr. Malvern, Lady Claire tasked you with the invention of a device that might aid us. Have you made any progress?"

"I had, in fact." Andrew opened a drawer in the sideboard where one might expect to find linens, and withdrew instead a large sheet of engineering paper. "Maggie's adventures in the English Channel gave me the idea. I had thought that, instead of constructing a rudimentary *chaloupe* manned by one or two people, one might devise a helmet of a similar shape to fit over the head, so that one might breathe. With a few modifications to the rocket rucksacks in *Athena*'s emergency equipment, one could swim to Jake's assistance."

Claire saw the flaw in this otherwise brilliant plan at once. "But—"

Andrew nodded sadly. "But the kraken put paid to that idea. Even if we were able somehow to swim undetected to Jake's location on the gearworks, we could not assist him to freedom. The kraken seem to be attracted to movement near the surface. I have no doubt that the Minister of Justice's 'training' includes this unnatural behavior, for surely kraken prefer to hunt in the depths, where they have cover."

"Wretched, cruel man," Lizzie muttered. "Those poor creatures."

"Quite so," Ian said. "Mr. Malvern, have you an alternate plan?"

"Not that I have conceived in the hour since our return from the tour, no."

"Then I am convinced that military strategies must prevail, if those of science have failed us," Ian said.

"Now, wait just a moment—" Andrew began.

"They have not *failed*," Claire said in Andrew's defense, with no little indignation.

"What military strategies, Captain?" Tigg inquired, his deepening voice having the effect of a bell in an enclosed tower. "How do you suggest that we proceed?"

"Simply this—that we go to the Master of Prisons and propose an exchange. How much was the transfer tax, Captain Chalmers?"

"Half the value of the cargo. So, about three hundred pounds."

"Good. I am sure I am worth three hundred pounds, so it ought to be convincing."

"I beg your pardon?" Claire exclaimed. "You cannot mean to exchange *yourself?* What good would that possibly do?"

"Captain, I don't understand," Tigg said. "We'd just be trying to figure out how to spring you, not Jake."

"Let me explain," the captain said, the corners of his lips curled in amusement at their consternation. "I propose we strike a deal: myself and the certainty of ransom money from the family in exchange for Jake's freedom. This way the corrupt government saves face— they let Jake go quietly, and I am a guest of the state until the money is just as quietly delivered. Her Majesty is not involved, since neither politics nor commercial interests come into it. Here in the Levant, ransom is a business not only lucrative, but socially acceptable. I am a gentleman, whom they would not dare to imprison below the water. There must be some accommodation for those in the upper echelons of society who have offended the government."

They had best revisit the *chaloupe* idea, for this was ridiculous.

"Then," Ian went on, "at the moment of the exchange, Tigg exercises the—er—" He glanced at Gloria, who was struggling with her horror, too, at this mad idea. "—the orders he has from his commander. We take Jake and make a quick escape. Mission accomplished."

"I would lay better odds on the kraken," Andrew said bluntly.

"Your odds would play out as well as others' have before you, as we saw this morning," Ian said just as bluntly. "I do not see that we have an option."

"And if anything goes wrong, we lose you and Jake both, and likely Tigg as well," Alice pointed out. "No, we must think of something else."

"There is nothing else, because if there were, the minds in this room would have put it forward," Ian told her. "No, we must play on their greed and exercise subterfuge."

"And if you are wrong, and they treat a gentleman no better than the *canaille*—the riff-raff that loiter on the banks of the canals?" Gloria asked. "What then?"

"Then I shall endure as best I can until the ransom is paid by the Dunsmuirs," Ian said.

He could not be serious. Claire would sooner see him married to—to Catherine Montrose than allow such a crack-brained scheme. "Ian, you seem to be placing a great deal of faith in the rules of gentlemanly behavior," she said in as calm a tone as she could muster. "But I have not seen much evidence that the rules in the society we have been exposed to are the same as they might be at home. Not," she said modestly, "that I know so much of what goes on among gentlemen. But I do not believe that—"

"Claire, forgive me for saying so, but you are quite right. You do not know what goes on among gentlemen. Trust me when I say that you must leave Jake's rescue to me. I have seen much of this world and I have a fairly accurate estimation of what it takes to get the job done successfully."

If he had struck her, she would have been no less surprised—and hurt. She stared at him, speechless with the affront not only to her intelligence and experience, but to their friendship as well.

She did not miss the way Lizzie's and Maggie's eyes widened. They would expect her to deal him a set-down he would not soon forget ... but she could not. Any disagreements among them could only harm, not help, Jake's chances. So she bit back the icy words on her tongue.

"You will need reinforcements," Alice said. "My Remington is in my room, and I brought extra bullets for just this kind of situation."

"I will indeed need reinforcements, but with your permission, Captain, not from you."

"I beg your pardon?" Alice's voice rose in just the way Claire's might have a moment ago had she allowed herself to speak.

"You have forgotten that there is a price on your head," Ian reminded her. "You have taken enough risks. One glimpse of you by anyone connected with Jake's incarceration and your days above the water are ended, too. No, I will take only two with me—Lieutenant Terwilliger and Mr. Malvern."

"Impossible," Claire burst out. "You cannot—"

"Claire," Andrew said gently, "he is right. It is far too dangerous. This is no task for ladies."

"It is no task for any person with an ounce of sense or integrity!" she cried. They planned a bait and switch—and the murder of any witnesses. Surely it need not come to that, if the plan were managed properly. "You will need scouts—lookouts—we must all assist in order to *reduce* the danger."

"On the contrary, Lady, if you'll forgive me," Tigg said. "With fewer men we attract less notice."

"To say nothing of the need to protect you," Ian added.

"I can protect myself!" Had he learned nothing during their adventures in the Canadas? Had he not seen the proof of his own eyes that some women, at least, had every advantage in intellect and resources that men possessed? How dared he cut herself, Alice, and the girls out of an opportunity to assist one of their own simply on the basis of their sex?

"I am sure you can, in any circumstances but these," Ian replied, which did not exactly pour cool water on the fire of her temper. "However, the four of you are needed on another front. Once we have Jake secured, we must depart these skies with all possible speed. Your task will be to have *Athena* ready to lift on a moment's notice."

"Oh, thank you very much," Claire said waspishly.

"What about the *Stalwart Lass*?" Alice wanted to know. "Once I have my navigator safely returned to me, I can't leave without my ship."

"There's a task for us," Gloria said brightly, as if cheering on a horse at the races. "We can steal your ship back. I can help—it will be just like helping you get away at the Firstwater Mine."

Claire and Alice both stared at her, ready to leap like cats on this betrayal of their arguments. And then Claire saw something in Gloria's face that she had never seen before. It was excitement—and hope—and once again, the longing of someone outside the circle for the warmth and camaraderie within.

To be a part of something, no matter the risk.

Gloria had proven to be an able ally once before. And if she displeased her father by her actions, well, she appeared well able to bear up under the burden. Gloria might not know it, but she had an ace up her sleeve. And Claire would bet her stock in the Zeppelin Airship Works that she would throw in her hand with them when Claire told her what had been simmering in her mind for some minutes now.

This would be a high-stakes game for ladies only ... since the gentlemen so bullheadedly insisted.

*

Alice found herself stricken silent with shock when Claire took a sip of her cooling tea and said, "Very well, Ian. You must do as you think best. We will assist you in any way we can, and if that means being ready to pull up ropes, then that is what we will do."

It was almost funny, the way the menfolk goggled at her. Clearly they'd expected her to put up a fight, and when she didn't, all the gas was sucked out of their balloon.

Claire raised her gaze over the rim of the teacup to meet Gloria's. "Are you familiar with the area where Alice's ship is impounded?"

"No," Gloria admitted, as though there had been no silence and they were simply carrying on with the discussion. "But I know it's on the island they call the Lido. It's a long, skinny sandbar out in the lagoon that forms a barrier between the city and the open ocean. Bathers are allowed on the landward part of it, but the rest is fenced off."

"Ah," Maggie said with satisfaction. "I have always wanted to sea-bathe in the Adriatic. Especially in October."

"As have I," Lizzie agreed. "Claude, what about you?"

"Never fancied it," he said, then, when Lizzie's elbow met his ribs, blurted, "but I suppose there's a first time for everything."

"Excellent." Claire beamed at them. "Except I am sorry to disappoint you. You three will ready *Athena* for lift while Gloria, Alice and I manage the *Stalwart Lass*—and the sea-bathing."

"But Lady, that's not fair," Lizzie protested. "*You're* the captain of *Athena*. Anybody can steal a ship. It doesn't have to be you."

Alice could see Lizzie's point of view to a point. But she could also see the value of the youngest members of their party staying somewhere safe while everybody else risked their lives on one front or another.

"That is precisely why I must go," Claire said pleasantly. "I have experience in stealing ships. You have experience in disabling them—which is highly useful in many situations, but not, I am afraid, in this one."

Her brows drawn down in displeasure, Lizzie subsided ... but only until, Alice was quite sure, she could sneak up on an argument from another angle.

"When have you stolen a ship, Claire?" Gloria leaned forward with interest, pouring herself another cup of tea.

Mr. Malvern's brows rose, and the Mopsies looked at each other. Maggie stifled a giggle—but only just.

"I stole *Athena* from your father," Claire said with no shame whatsoever. "Or at least, from the Meriwether-Astor Munitions Works, when she was a cargo ship running illegal arms into the Canadas. I do hope you do not mind?"

Gloria paused, as though it took her a moment to digest this information, then waved away the idea as though it were a fly. "Think nothing of it. I have no illusions about him, believe me. If I knew how to fly, I'd steal one myself and head for Edmonton or somewhere, just to get away. I'm glad she's filling a useful purpose now—or at the very least, an honest one."

"Right, then." Captain Hollys clapped his hands upon his knees and rose. "We need to make preparations, and send a message to the Master of Prisons. I must also send a pigeon to John and Davina apprising them of our plans, so that they do not become anxious when the ransom demand arrives. Lieutenant, Mr. Malvern, if you are ready, we must begin."

"I should like a moment alone with my fiancée, Captain," Andrew said.

"And I with Elizabeth," Tigg added, whereupon Lizzie blushed scarlet—stood—and sat down again in a fluster.

"Very well," Ian said. "I will meet you in the lobby of the hotel in half an hour."

In the ensuing bustle, Alice took the opportunity to slip out the door and follow the captain down the corridor. "Captain Hollys, if you please," she said as he stepped inside his room.

He held the door as she slipped in ahead of him. "This is most irregular, Alice. What if someone should see you?"

"I've been seen in worse places," she said bluntly. "Ian, please don't do this."

"I am afraid it is already decided."

"But you don't know—" She stopped. What was she thinking of? A feminine glance exchanged over a teacup

... a discussion of sea-bathing. These were not exactly the kinds of proofs that would make a man change his mind. Not a man who was authorized by Her Majesty to use deadly force.

"What don't I know?" he prodded. "I do not have much time, Alice. I must see to my arms and send that message."

"Claire is up to something," she said desperately. "More than simply stealing my ship back. Don't do this. Talk to her. She's only taking the bit in her teeth because you were high-handed with her. You need to work together, not against one another."

"I understood we *were* working together. It is a good plan. And it will work, I promise you, if we all do our part."

"That may be, but meanwhile—"

"Alice." He was standing very close, so close that Alice was forced to tilt up her chin in order to look him in the eyes. They were the color of a storm at altitude— gray and powerful. "Why this sudden anxiety?"

"I—I don't like the two of you at odds, that's all."

"We are not at odds. I am relieved at her willingness to see sense and cooperate."

"But that's just it. She isn't. She's faking it."

"Lady Claire?" He chuckled, and in the sound was a hint of bitterness. "Believe me, if ever a woman was brutally honest and open, it is she. No, I am fixed in my purpose ... sure of her cooperation ... and touched by your concern."

"But—"

He took her by the shoulders and gave her a gentle push out the door. "I will send a message both to *Athena* and here to the hotel when we have a meeting time and place. Be ready to lift by sunset."

"Ian, please—"

"It will be all right," he said. "Thank you for coming to me. It was the act of a true friend."

So swiftly that she hardly believed it had happened, he leaned in and kissed her cheek. And the door closed, leaving her standing in the corridor, her fingers touching the place where his lips had been.

18

"You must not allow them to continue on this fool's errand," Claire said urgently. Andrew stood with her in the turning of the staircase, where three windows arched in the Moorish fashion looked out upon the Giudecca Canal and its busy boat traffic. She gripped his hands with a strength that seemed half pleading, half preventing his departure. "I cannot believe that a culture so blasé about the despicable practice of ransom has not already experienced every possible double cross, and will take all of them into account."

"That may be true," Andrew said, "but we will be alert and ready for them." What else could he say, when those beloved gray eyes held such anxiety?

"Please, Andrew," she begged. "I believe there is another way—one that will incorporate your breathing globes without attracting the attention of the kraken."

"Claire, dearest, believe me, I have applied every spare ounce of brain power to that problem, and come up with nothing. Our resources are simply too limited in this foreign place to come up with a better plan."

"But with Gloria we can—"

He stopped her with a kiss. Time was short, and they had much to do. "I will not say goodbye, but only 'until we meet again.' Which, I hope, will be shortly after sunset, aboard *Athena.*"

"Oh, Andrew—"

The pain in her voice nearly undid him, and it was only the thought of her joy when they returned with Jake, whole and unharmed, that allowed him to walk away and return alone to his room. There, he collected the lightning pistol that she had made for him with her own hands. It had not exactly been an engagement gift, but to him it was as precious as the pearl ring that had not left her finger since he had slipped it on. The pistol held her confidence in him, and her concern for his safety, as well as gears and rods, barrel and grip ... and the power cell that gave it life.

He could not take her with him, thank God. But he could take the weapon she had made him, and use it wisely.

Into his boot he slipped the knife that Mr. Bowie had made for him in the Texican Territories, and slipped one or two devices of his own manufacture into the pockets of his tweed coat and those of his trousers. They were small, about the size of a walnut, but if one but pulled a pin, they produced a flash and a bang that could disorient even the most seasoned soldier.

When he was ready, he found Tigg and the captain

waiting in the guest parlor off the hotel's lobby. Though not half an hour had passed since they had parted ways, Captain Hollys had just received a reply from the Master of Prisons. Andrew scanned it quickly.

*My dear Sir Ian,*

*I am honored that you solicit my help in such a delicate matter, and if you will permit me, perceived you to be a man of integrity and moral fortitude during our tour today. I will proffer your proposal to his lordship the Minister of Justice, whose unhappy duty it is to oversee these matters, and will convey his reply to you personally.*

*Please meet me at the door of the church of San Barnaba at sunset. There is a particularly fine painting there of the Holy Family by Veronese that would be worth a moment of your time. You will, of course, come unarmed, and unaccompanied by the delightful young ladies and gentlemen of your acquaintance.*

*I remain, sir, your servant,*
*Paolo de Luca, Master of Prisons*

Andrew looked up as he folded the letter. "Do you think they will actually go through with it? Bring Jake to trade for you?"

"They are fools if they do not." Ian Hollys pocketed the letter, then sighted down the barrel of his pistol and broke it to check there were no bullets inside, before he handed it and his ordnance bag to Tigg.

"Sir—" Tigg began in some surprise.

# A LADY OF INTEGRITY

"I am not unarmed. My Smith and Wesson thirty-eight is in my rib holster, and there is a Scots *sgean dhu* that belonged to my grandfather in my stocking. Come. It wants an hour to sunset, and I wish you both to take up your positions as soon as possible."

Casually, affecting interest in the scenery around them, the three men strolled along the canal and then zigzagged down several narrow lanes. When the alley would have decanted them into the large square in front of the church of Saint Barnabas, Ian leaned against the wall, looking over his shoulder and around the corner to scan it for signs of ambush.

"If you are to meet on the steps, any attack would likely come from outside," Andrew suggested. "There is no cover in the church's immediate vicinity, but one could lie in wait in the surrounding alleys, as we are doing right now."

"But why ask me to go in, ostensibly to look at a painting?" Ian mused. "Unless the rules of sanctuary apply here as they do in England, making it a safe place to perform an exchange."

"I'm sure that's it," Andrew agreed. "Though I am not inclined to observe the rules at the moment."

"You can't kill someone in a church, sir," Tigg murmured, sounding a little shocked.

"We are *authorized* to kill, Lieutenant," Ian said. "That does not mean we shall do so. I should prefer to disable instead, if at all possible. But in self-defense, one must do as one must." He gazed out at the square, where families strolled and where the umbrellas of cheerful cafes sheltered tables in colorful groups, where people were drinking tea and stronger beverages at the end of the day. "I do not think it wise to post one of you inside. There is too much risk of discovery. But I believe they will come from the direction of the Ministry, which would put their arrival in that quarter." He pointed to the corner behind the church. "If one of you takes a seat at that café and the other conceals himself behind the wall opposite, you will both be within hearing. We can stage our own attack in that alley, acting as though we are being set upon and robbed."

"Dibs on the café," Tigg said. "Begging your pardon, Mr. Andrew, but the Master of Prisons has already seen you with Captain Hollys. Unless he was at that ball, too, he hasn't seen me."

In Andrew's mind, the young man was far too happy about engaging in all this skullduggery. Nevertheless, he allowed the younger man to boost him up the wall, where he squeezed between iron railings that were clearly meant more for decoration than protection, and took up his post.

Tigg took a seat outside the café and ordered lemonade. He had barely taken the first sip when footsteps echoed in the alley. Two people. Andrew risked a glance over the bricks and his shoulders sagged in relief at the sight that met his gaze.

And immediately, compassion welled in his heart.

Jake looked dreadful. His skin was white, and in the few weeks he had been incarcerated, he had lost weight, to the point where his cheekbones looked sharp and his elbows stuck out under his rolled-up shirtsleeves. His cotton pants were soggy and green at the bottom, and he was barefoot. Bruises discolored what Andrew could see of his ankles, and his eyes—

Jake's gaze met that of Tigg with a sense of recognition like a shock, and the boy stiffened. His head moving as though on ball bearings, Tigg looked away, pretending interest in a flock of pigeons landing upon the cistern in the middle of the square. He took another sip of his lemonade.

The Master of Prisons yanked Jake back into step, and Andrew distinctly heard the clink of a fine-gauge chain, though none was visible. Had the poor boy been tethered to his captor to prevent his breaking and running? It seemed likely. It would make their task somewhat more complicated, but would not deter them in the least.

On the other side of the square, a pair of men who had not been there a moment ago lounged against the same wall where Ian had reconnoitered the scene. A third had put his boot up on the church steps, adjusting its laces. And there, another held the door for the Master of Prisons and Jake, and followed them inside.

Three—and a half, if you counted a starved and barefoot young man—against five. Andrew supposed the odds could be worse. He cleared his throat and Tigg cleared his in return.

They had nothing to do but wait.

And wait.

Tigg paid the bill and got uneasily to his feet. From his cramped position on the ledge, Andrew could hardly contain himself a moment longer. How long did it take to release one prisoner and take another into captivity? The church steps were empty, and there were fewer people in the square, mothers and fathers having taken their children home with the deepening of twilight.

The bells began to ring, a cacophony of warning, and the bridge behind him rose with agonizing slowness. Again Andrew felt the disorienting sensation of the ground moving—but the feeling in his stomach was entirely eclipsed by his increasing unease.

Something had gone wrong.

"I believe I shall visit this lovely church," Tigg said to the garden wall, and strolled across the square and up the church steps. Andrew swung down with much more grace than he had scrambled up. They were merely tourists, he thought as he joined Tigg. If their quarry were in the midst of negotiations, they would simply conceal their faces by inspecting the nearest painting, and take their leave.

Inside, twin sets of pillars marched down the nave, sheltering a number of old ladies in black kneeling on the marble in prayer. The benches for the Sunday service had not been put out on a weekday, leaving the great open expanse of the transept in clear view.

There was no sound except for the murmuring of the ladies, and, leaving Tigg admiring a Madonna set into a niche next to the door, Andrew walked the perimeter and checked each chapel, expecting every moment to surprise his quarry. When he reached the front doors again, he found Tigg shifting his weight from foot to foot. "I don't like this."

Andrew nodded, his jaw tense. "They're not here. Did anyone pass you?"

"No one, sir. I don't understand it. Those miscreants in the alley the way we came were gone by the time I crossed the square, but the two at the church went inside. How can five men disappear?"

"Let us search again."

But a second search revealed nothing but the priest, who emerged from the confessional with yet another old lady, who joined her companions in prayer.

"May I be of some assistance?" he said in heavily accented English, perceiving them to be from foreign parts.

"We were to have met some friends here, *monsignore*, but we cannot find them," Andrew said with an ease he did not feel. "Have you seen a military man in the company of a boy of about eighteen, with reddish hair?"

The priest shook his head, clearly sorry to have to disappoint them. "We will be singing vespers soon, so I must go. Perhaps they have found their way into the crypt? We have the finger bone of San Barnaba enshrined there—it might interest you to see it."

Andrew and Tigg looked at one another. If one were to have a secret meeting, a crypt sounded like a capital place to do it. Following the priest's directions, they went around to the back of the altar and down a staircase beneath, lit by lamps set into niches.

The finger bone of Saint Barnabas may have been there, lying in state, but Captain Hollys and Jake were not. Andrew stood in the cramped, cold space in front of the elaborately decorated altar that held the casket, his flesh nearly creeping on his bones. "Where could they have gone?" he asked the saint.

From above could be heard the sounds of singing, something in the construction of the spiral staircase filtering and transporting the old ladies' voices into a sound that was almost celestial.

"Sir, over here," Tigg said. "Round the back. Bring a lamp."

Behind the casket's resting place Tigg knelt on the stone, his keen eyes having seen in the thick shadows what Andrew would likely have missed. Andrew raised the lamp.

A metal ring as thick as his thumb was set into the stone. "Help me lift it," Tigg said.

When the trap door was hefted back, they peered into the abyss to see the flicker and shine of the lamp's flame on water, moving restlessly at the base of a ladder some six or eight feet below.

"Oh, no," Andrew breathed.

# A LADY OF INTEGRITY

19

"Elizabeth Seacombe, now is not the time for an unseemly display of misplaced independence." Claire leveled her best Belgravia stare on her ward, which had no effect whatsoever on the green eyes flashing with temper.

They had not yet left the hotel—a fact that was grating on Claire's nerves enough without Lizzie's rebellion added to the roiling in her stomach. She had promised herself that she would not bring Gloria in to rescue Jake unless they had no other choice. Hence, their efforts were to be concentrated on stealing the *Stalwart Lass* from the impound field while they counted on the success of Ian's mission.

But one did not need six people to steal an airship.

"I am sixteen years old, Lady—too old to be treated

like a child and sent to my room."

"Preparing *Athena* for lift is hardly the equivalent of being sent to one's room," Claire snapped. "It is a vital part of this rescue."

"It's you getting me and Maggie and Claude out of the way."

"Nothing wrong with that, old girl," Claude put in. "I'm all for getting out of here with skin intact. Place has gone cold on me, rather."

"Claude is right," Alice said, to Claire's relief. "Claire is responsible for your safety. This is the best way to ensure it and to make a quick getaway, too."

But Lizzie was beyond logic. "If you don't let us help, I'll take a water taxi over to the Lido and come anyway."

Goodness. What had come over her?

Lizzie flounced away to the window and stood looking out over the water, her arms crossed and her fingers nervously tapping her elbows.

And then Claire knew.

"Darling, we are all worried for their safety," she said quietly, crossing the room and slipping an arm around Lizzie's waist. "But Tigg is an aeronaut now, fully trained and capable of defending himself. You need have no fear on his account."

Lizzie's lips trembled, but she was not willing to give in and concede that their dispute had an underlying cause unrelated to who was performing what duties.

"And while it distresses me that Captain Hollys was unwilling to hear my suggestions, he is also very capable. If anyone should be worrying, it is I. Andrew can hold his own, and has done so many times, but he is a man designed for thought, not action."

# A LADY OF INTEGRITY

It was some small comfort that Andrew was in the company of two of the most resourceful, brave, and intelligent men of her acquaintance. Surely among the three of them, they would be able to prevent disaster— or at the very least, escape from it.

"Be fair, Claire," Alice said, pacing from window to door for at least the fiftieth time. "Mr. Malvern's quick thinking saved your hide when you were swinging from the bow line during your escape from the mine, if what you told me once is true."

"It is quite true." Claire shuddered at the memory. "And I must trust that his quick thinking will aid in their present mission as well."

"Are you really so worried for him, Lady?" Lizzie asked, searching Claire's face.

"I am," she confessed. "What woman does not worry for the man she loves? But I must say that I have given him far more cause for concern than he has given me. And as for you—" She brushed Lizzie's blond hair back, attempting without success to tuck the ends into their chignon. "I fear that Tigg will share the same fate as Andrew, as will the fortunate young man who wins our Maggie's affections." When Lizzie smiled at that, and Maggie blushed, Claire went on, "In fact, the only person who will not experience such anxiety is the future Lady Hollys, whoever that complacent and rather dull creature may turn out to be."

Lizzie giggled, but Alice turned so sharply at the end of her circuit of the room that the corner of the carpet flipped over. "If you girls are done making jokes, I think we should get on with it," she said. "It's after sunset. We won't be able to fake sea-bathing, but we could pretend an interest in astronomy, if anyone can lay hands on a telescope."

"There is one on *Athena*," Maggie began, only to stop abruptly at the sound of footsteps coming rapidly down the corridor.

Claire's knees went weak as Andrew and Tigg pushed open the door. Without a sound, Lizzie left her side and walked into Tigg's arms—and, throwing propriety to the winds, Claire flung herself likewise into Andrew's embrace. How blessedly warm he was, how solid, how alive! His arms went around her, tightly, as though she had been the one to put herself in danger, not he. But they only had a matter of seconds in which to indulge their emotions before Alice's voice came from near the door.

"Where is Captain Hollys? And Jake? What happened?"

With an exhalation of breath, Andrew set Claire slightly away from him, at which point she saw the pallor of his skin and the despair in his eyes. Her heart seemed to stop in her chest.

"Andrew—they're not—"

"Not dead, no. Not as far as we know. But they have been taken."

"Taken?" Alice repeated, as if she'd never heard the word before. "Taken how? And where? By whom?"

The facts he proceeded to relate were simple. And damning. Each word brought home to them all exactly what they were up against.

Claire had to sit down.

Andrew poured a shot of brandy from the decanter on the sideboard and gave it to Tigg, then poured another for himself. "I am at a loss," he said baldly once he had recovered from the first gulp. "We went in believing that we had out-thought them, that we had a foolproof plan. Captain Hollys was to have surrendered himself, and then Tigg and I would assist him in overpowering them all in the alley, leaving the captain and Jake both free. But they have bolted into a hole like the foxes they are, and I fear our resources may not extend to faking a ransom a second time."

"Certainly not," Claire managed from the corner of the sofa, where she had curled up, her arms wrapped around her knees while she did her best not to break down completely. "I am the only one who can claim a connection to the peerage—and no one is going to pay a ransom for me."

This sad fact had been borne in upon her once already, in a locked room in Resolution, a town on the other side of the world. While her mother, Lady St. Ives, might have married into some semblance of security for herself, this happy state of affairs did not extend to her daughter. The estate simply did not have the funds for ransom. And while Claire's means had improved markedly since that day in the Texican Territory, she doubted very much that, even if she offered these rascals everything she had, it would be enough to satisfy them.

"Count von Zeppelin might," Maggie offered.

"Not after she scarpered in the night, against his wishes," Lizzie reminded her, her voice muffled in Tigg's shirt.

"Then the Dunsmuirs would," Maggie persisted, her optimistic nature unwilling to concede defeat.

"They will not even receive Ian's pigeon about his own ransom for days yet," Claire said. "And even if they send it, I doubt the Minister of Justice will free him. He will simply make him disappear in the most permanent way possible, and either deny all knowledge of such a person, or send his condolences to the family."

"Well, we have to do something," Alice said. "We just have to do what you always say, Claire ... catalog our resources and come up with the best plan we can."

"If ... I might offer a suggestion?"

For a moment Claire could not place who was speaking, but with a flush of embarrassment, she unfolded herself and turned to Gloria, who was standing near the window and had hardly said a word all afternoon. Claire was ashamed of herself. Here she had planned to ask Gloria an enormous favor—to put herself in danger for their sakes—and for the past ten minutes she had completely forgotten the girl was in the room.

"Please do," she said, her voice only wobbling a little. "I shall be glad of any suggestions at all."

"It seems to me that the first thing we must do is find out if Captain Hollys is to be imprisoned like a gentleman, or merely tossed into the dungeons with Jake," Gloria said.

"He seemed convinced he would be treated like a gentleman," Alice said, "but our enemies are not behaving as well as all that. I wouldn't bet cash money on anything, at this point."

"Even if you are right, Alice, how would we discover this?" Andrew asked. "I cannot very well walk in there and ask what they've done with him—I'd likely be clapped in the dungeons myself, simply for being an associate of his. I place no trust in the Master of Prisons, bowing and scraping to a man one day and abducting him the next."

"That is why I should go," Gloria said. "The Minister is in negotiations with Father, and even though Signore de Luca knows that I was with your party, I do have Father's protection."

"Absolutely not," Andrew said.

"Agreed." Tigg spoke quietly. He had not yet let go of Lizzie, but Claire did not have the strength to remonstrate with him. There were more urgent matters to be dealt with.

Gloria merely waited for someone else to offer an idea. When none was forthcoming, she said, "Very well, then. I shall go in the morning."

"Why not tonight, if you're going to go?" Alice demanded. "Does anyone want to see the captain imprisoned for even a single night—and poor Jake for more?"

"No, but it is possible that she will get in to see the Minister of Justice tomorrow," Claire said slowly. "I should think it likely he keeps bankers' hours. We can do no more tonight, other than allow them to think they have outwitted us. In the meantime, I believe we have an airship to recover, do we not?"

"We do," Alice said. "Though the timing might be tricky. It's one thing to liberate the *Lass*. It's another thing altogether to be floating around in the sky waiting for the rescue of my navigator without being spotted or even shot down."

"Alice is right," Andrew said thoughtfully. "Any rescue must happen concurrently with the flight of the *Lass* and the lifting of *Athena* with all its occupants safely on board."

"I don't see a problem with the airships," Tigg said. "But the rescue has us back at square one. We are no better off than when we first arrived—in fact, our situation is twice as bad."

"At least we know what the gearworks look like," Maggie told him. "We didn't know that before."

"And there is more," Claire said slowly. Now was the time to speak, before they all lost hope and sank under the weight of the impossible. "I believe there may be a way to launch a rescue attempt, once we know whether or not Captain Hollys will be sent out to the gearworks. And Gloria, I believe you must be a part of it."

"I?" Gloria's eyebrows rose right up under the wispy fringe that framed her eyes. "How can I be of any help? You all sound so dashing and determined ... and I've been sitting here like a bump on a log all afternoon wondering how it's possible for anyone to be so brave. I was quite serious before—please let me help steal the airship back." Her voice took on a note of pleading. "I'm quite willing to get dirty, you know, and I can run like a deer. I took all the ribbons at school."

"You may be called upon to demonstrate both those qualities," Claire told her with a smile. "But perhaps not on the beaches of the Lido. No ... Gloria ... what I propose is that you steal not an airship, but one of your father's undersea dirigibles."

*

The profound silence that met this extraordinary suggestion told Alice that the stress had knocked Claire clean off her keel once and for all. And no wonder. Alice knew from hard experience that sometimes hope was all that kept you going—and when that was finally taken away, the mind did its best to stave off the inevitable conclusion that you weren't going to win by substituting all kinds of crazy plans.

Which was clearly what was happening here.

No one had told Claire this yet, though, and Alice wasn't going to be the one to do it. Other than bombing the whole prison to kingdom come and knocking the entire city into the ocean, Alice didn't see how on earth they were going to succeed. But there had to be a way. Because the only other point on which nobody could concede was that Ian and Jake had to be rescued. And, she supposed, they would stay right here in this awful place until somebody figured out a way to do it or they died of old age, whichever came first.

"Steal … a dirigible," Gloria repeated, as if she couldn't possibly have heard correctly. "One of Father's, out there in the Adriatic."

"Yes," Claire said, clearly pleased that the girl was following. "We will liberate the *Stalwart Lass*, to be sure. But before we do that, we send a message to the dirigible fleet saying that your father has requested you have the use of one—the smallest one—for maneuverability around the gearworks. Then you tell its captain that you wish to see the gearworks from the bridge of his vessel. While you do that, Andrew and I will come out of concealment and swim to Jake's and Ian's rescue."

She smiled at them all, like a gambler who has just laid down a royal flush and is about to rake in the pot.

"Swim?" Andrew repeated. "From the dirigible, under how many feet of water?"

"Not more than a hundred," his fiancée told him. "We will do as you proposed in the beginning, Andrew, and use the glass breathing globes and our rocket rucksacks. We free our friends and swim to safety, where

Alice will collect us."

Andrew stared at her as if she had gone mad. "Darling, I realize you have spent some amount of time thinking this through, but I must tell you that there are one or two tiny holes in your plan."

"One big enough to swim a kraken through, begging your pardon, Lady," Tigg said.

"But you said yourself that it appears the kraken have been trained to attack escapees at the surface. We shall effect our rescue in the depths, and return secretly to the Meriwether-Astor dirigible."

"But we will be the only two with a breathing apparatus," Andrew said. "How will Jake and Ian manage?"

"We will of course return to the dirigible as fast as our rucksacks can take us," Claire assured him. "One can hold one's breath for thirty seconds, if necessary."

"And what happens afterward?" he asked. "With five on board where there should only be three?"

"We shall conceal our friends, and even if we are taken out to sea, the *Lass* can rescue us as we rescued Maggie in the English Channel not so long ago. I am sure Gloria would assist us there, as well."

"Certainly," Gloria said with no little irony. "I could say my friends were doing a little sea-bathing and of course the crew would believe me." She crossed the room to Claire. "The kraken aside, dear heart, how are you going to locate your friends in the first place? You saw the size and the extent of the gearworks. There must be miles of cogs and track and moving parts."

For the first time Claire seemed to hesitate. "I have not quite worked that out yet. But you do agree that it could be possible? You are, at the very least, willing to try?"

"Of course I'm willing to try," Gloria told her, but not until a few tense moments had passed.

Alice found with some surprise that her chest was tight, as though she'd been holding her breath waiting for the answer. She exhaled, and it was like releasing her despair. When she drew in her next breath, it seemed to come fortified with new hope. With determination. And clarity.

"I think it could work," she said, and even Maggie looked surprised. "We would need to coordinate the timing carefully—and needless to say, we can't do it at night. If you're going undersea bathing, you need to be able to see. The water is unusually clear, but we still need light—especially when you surface."

"How will we do that?" Lizzie asked. "How can we send one another messages if some are in the air and some under the water and some goodness knows where else?"

"I can modify the pigeons." Tigg released her and took a piece of paper from the sideboard. He began to sketch as he spoke. "They don't need to be as big as they are. Just the bare minimum of gears, and short-range propulsion rather than the usual long-range. If I remove the container, all we would need is some means of securing a message to its structure."

"Not a pigeon, then," Maggie said, coming over to look. "A hummingbird."

"Exactly," Tigg told her with a smile.

Alice's gaze met that of Gloria, whose face had gone a little pale at the thought of what she'd just agreed to do, but whose eyes had regained their sparkle. "Looks like our friends' lives might just depend on you," she said.

She should be glad they had even a whisper of a chance thanks to this girl. And even then, Alice wasn't completely sure Gloria wouldn't blab to her pa about exactly who she was keeping company with, and what they were up to. But worst of all was the prospect of Captain Hollys owing his gratitude to her, after she'd made no secret of her pleasure in hanging on his arm and dancing with him. That fact most of all was what stuck in Alice's craw.

Which made her so annoyed with herself that it was all she could do to be civil when supper came.

# A LADY OF INTEGRITY

20

Gloria and her father were staying at a different hotel, much closer to the Piazza San Marco and consequently much more expensive. When Gloria came down the steps in her most elaborate walking costume yet, Lizzie heard Maggie sigh with envy. Gloria had brains, it was clear. If a lady were going to a gaol to inquire after a gentleman, Lizzie mused, it was best to look as dainty and harmless as possible.

The yellow skirt was split up the back and trimmed with big black bows that held the two halves together. Spilling out from underneath was a modest fishtail train—just enough to sway attractively with her motion but not enough for people to step on. Her matching yellow jacket sported a black silk bow across the bosom, and her black hat was trimmed with a profusion of yellow and blue and green ribbon.

"Some day I'm going to dress like that," Maggie whispered after Gloria had gone inside the forbidding doors of the Ministry.

"You'll have to fall in love with a rich man, then," Lizzie told her. They were concealed under an arch next to a church because Lizzie wasn't going any closer to that building than she could help. All they needed was to run into the same guardsman and have him recognize her.

Maggie made a rude noise, softly. "I shall be rich myself, and not depend upon a man to buy my things for me. I shall be like the Lady."

Lizzie had to admit this was probably the wiser course. While Mr. Andrew was famous the world over in engineering circles, it could not be said that he was rolling in gold guineas. After all, he still lived above his laboratory, and Lizzie knew for a fact that, while comfortable, his quarters were not posh.

Not like Carrick House, which the Lady had inherited, lost, and bought again with her own money, firmly tied down with legal documents prepared by her solicitor, so that no one would be able to take it from her ever again.

Gloria had not seen the girls as they trailed her to the Ministry, nor did she notice them fall in behind her when she came out half an hour later. It was just short of eleven o'clock in the morning and the bridges had all just settled into their places again when it became clear she was going straight to their hotel.

Lizzie and Maggie joined her as she was mounting the front steps. "Good morning, girls." She smiled at them on either side of her. "Did you enjoy your morning constitutional?"

"Yes, we did, thank you." Maggie smiled back, innocent as a rose.

"I have news. I assume everyone is in Claire's suite?"

Indeed they were, watching with varying degrees of tension as the three of them came in. Wordlessly, the Lady offered Gloria tea and watched her like a hen watches a bee until she had drained half the cup.

"The Minister of Justice was unable to see me," she said at last, "but he referred me to our friend the Master of Prisons, who was only too delighted to entertain me in his office."

"Dear me," Claire said faintly. "I hope it was not too onerous."

"Onerous enough. I haven't flirted and fluttered so much since my come-out ball in Philadelphia, and that was some time ago. But in the end I did what any woman would do who was not getting what she wanted."

"What was that?" Alice asked, rather tersely.

"I burst into tears."

"Well done, Gloria," Claire said with approval. "Did it work?"

"It always does, you know," Gloria confided. "Even with Father, who should be wise to my tricks by now. In any case, Signore de Luca finally spat up the one fact I wanted, which is that Captain Hollys is *not* being housed in the dry cells. He is being treated, not like a gentleman, but like any common criminal off the streets."

Lizzie and Maggie looked at one another, eyes widening in horror.

Gloria went on, "I was there ostensibly as the captain's intended—and the odious man told me with a show of crocodile tears as good as my own that the captain and Jake have been assigned to the same work crew, since it was clear they knew each other. And since Jake has been … difficult … their assignment is in the lowest levels of the gearworks. Where somehow their duties involve … skeletons … and the cleaning of dead creatures out of the works."

Maggie's face crumpled in a grimace of distaste. Lizzie's stomach rolled uncomfortably.

"His intended?" Alice asked, but no one seemed to notice.

"Gloria," the Lady said, "you are a true friend, to endure such a man in such a place."

The girl blushed, and her color deepend further as she said, "I want to see them freed. Captain Hollys has been lovely to me, and Jake—well, I still want my chance to shake his hand and say thank you. In order to do that, I must throw *my* hand in where it is needed."

"And we are grateful," Mr. Malvern told her warmly, but the poor girl couldn't get any redder, so she merely sat on the sofa next to Maggie, dipping her head so that the ribbons and plumes concealed much of her face.

"Our course seems to be clear, then," the Lady said. "Andrew, how soon can you have the breathing globes prepared?"

"I understand there is an island in the lagoon that specializes in glass. I shall take the specifications and hopefully have what I need this afternoon. Then, I will join Tigg on *Athena* and while he modifies the pigeons, I will build the breathing apparatus. We should be able to launch our effort shortly after sunrise tomorrow."

Lizzie knew in her bones that the Lady's next words would relegate her and Maggie to the role of assistants on *Athena*, handing the gentlemen wrenches and staying out of the way. But even as Claire opened her mouth, Alice said, "If Gloria is going with Claire and Andrew, I'm going to need help at the impound yard—help that comes with sharp ears and sharp eyes. Lizzie or Maggie, I'd like one of you to come with me."

Lizzie could have hugged her. Instead, she concealed her excitement and she and her cousin looked to the Lady, wordlessly asking permission.

"If Alice needs one of you, then I believe Maggie ought to go," she said, and Maggie straightened in surprise. "Though you must do exactly as she instructs you. I will not have any more of the people I care for sent to prison on the bottom of the lagoon to pick through skeletons, of that you may be sure."

"And what of me?" Lizzie asked. Surely the Lady would not punish her now for her unbridled temper earlier. Would she?

"If Mr. Malvern, Gloria, and I are out in the lagoon, that leaves Tigg, Claude and you to provide a rescue should something go wrong. Tigg can fly the ship, and Claude can operate the basket, but Lizzie, if it comes to dropping gaseous capsaicin or any of the other bombs we have made, we will be relying on your keen eye and excellent aim."

Well, that put a different complexion on the entire exercise. Lizzie nodded, as sober as a soldier receiving instructions from his sergeant. It would never do to let the Lady know that inside, she was doing handsprings of joy.

21

The next morning, before the sun had even risen above the roofs of the churches, Alice and Maggie were on their way to the *fondamente* along the Giudecca Canal to rent a boat. They were dressed in the absolute minimum required to maintain public decency, but the contents of their bags told a different story.

Where one might be expected to go sea-bathing in a modest costume of wool, trimmed with cotton ribbon, perhaps, they carried instead their raiding rig—or in Alice's case, a sensible pair of pants and a shirt. Where normally a beach-goer carried a parasol, a novel, or perhaps a stool on which to paint in watercolors *en plein air*, they carried a selection of bombs constructed by Claire and Alice herself the previous day. The only concession Alice was willing to make to everyday tourist behavior was the packing of a substantial lunch.

"After all," she told Maggie as they changed shoulders yet again under their heavy bags, "we don't know where our next meal is coming from. For all I know, the next time we moor, it'll be in France, or Switzerland."

At the dock, they had a surprising amount of difficulty in finding someone to take them out to the Lido. One grizzled boatman stared them up and down, and Alice was about to ask him where in the Sam Hill his manners were, when he said, "It is not safe in the lagoon today. Do you not know about the *acqua alta?*"

Alice shook her head. "*Aqua* what?"

He pointed to the edge of the stone pier upon which they stood. "You see how high is the water? It has risen at least a foot overnight. It is the full moon, *signorina*, and the high tide. We shall be flooded by sunset."

"Flooded?" Maggie sounded worried, and Alice couldn't blame her. "How high does the water go?"

Wordlessly, he pointed at the row of buildings, painted a cheerful salmon and yellow and blue, down the nearest canal. "You see? There, below the windows?"

With a sinking feeling, Alice saw that the paint had been stained a darker shade all the way up—at least eight feet above the current level. And now that she thought about it, the pavement on the way here had been wet, too, the water in the canals slopping over the edges and creating puddles. She had naively thought it had rained in the night. But clearly there were greater forces at work here in this strange city than mere weather.

"Do you think it will go that high tonight?" she asked the boatman.

He shrugged in the Venetian manner, bringing an ear down to one shoulder. "I have lived on this canal all my life, and my bones tell me that it will."

"But not before we go sea-bathing," Maggie said. "Please, *signore*, it will not rise before we have a chance to do that, will it?"

He gazed at her soberly. Perhaps he was thinking that if Maggie were his daughter, he'd have her safely installed on an upper floor, not galloping about on such a frivolous quest. "I offer a suggestion merely ... that you return by noon. The beaches are shallow and the water rises quickly. You will have nowhere to go, and the Doge's men will not allow you through the palisade to higher ground."

"I understand that there is quite a large area fenced off," Alice said. "Are the guards so fierce that they would not allow two young ladies in to find safety?" She tried to look young and defenseless, but wasn't sure how well she pulled it off.

"They are Justice men," he said, as if this was all the information anyone needed.

So the impound yard was guarded by men from the Ministry. They had quite the respect for justice around here, didn't they? Where were the representatives of the Ministry of Fishing, or the Ministry of Culture?

"Sister, please," Maggie begged. "I so want to go sea-bathing. I promise I will be ready to come back before noon."

"If you do so, I will take you," the boatman said, and spat over the side.

They would be well airborne before then, with any luck. "I promise, too," Alice told him, and the two of them climbed aboard.

## A LADY OF INTEGRITY

The little boat's triangular sail caught the wind, and within the hour the boatman beached on the Lido's silvery sands on the landward side. He jumped out and pulled it up so they could disembark without getting their feet wet, and Alice paid him.

"Noon," he said. "When you hear the bell on the watchtower strike, you must come down here. I will take you back."

"No, you don't have to do that. We can find our way back ourselves."

He gazed at her. "No one comes today." He gestured to the landing, and to the grassy banks and inlets of the island. "Do you see other foolish ladies here?"

"Well … no." Clearly they had been frightened up onto that upper floor back in the city.

He grasped the bow of his boat and pushed it down the slope, then jumped in, splashing his canvas trousers to the knees. "Noon," he said, and set the sail. He was soon out of sight.

"I feel badly about bringing him back out here on a fool's errand," Maggie said, picking up her bag and hefting it over her shoulder.

"It can't be helped," Alice told her. "Come on. Let's find a tree and get out of these dresses before we blow away like kites."

The breeze was downright sprightly even in the lee of the island, blowing across as it did from the open sea. It wouldn't bother the *Lass*, though, unless it turned into a proper gale. But it was enough to make wearing a dress inconvenient, wrapping cotton around calves and blowing one's hat clean off.

"Let it go," Alice said, when Maggie took two steps after the little straw and ribbon confection. "I'll never wear it again after today anyway."

"I'd have worn it." But Maggie let it go, and turned away.

After they'd changed in the shelter of a scrubby tree, it soon became apparent that locating the *Lass* would be more difficult than they'd first thought. "All the high ground is behind the wall," Alice complained. "And what fool called this a fence? The boatman was right. It's a palisade."

There was a gate every hundred feet or so, facing the beach where presumably sea-bathers would frolic. And each was guarded by a man in uniform. "This is no good," Maggie said from where they were concealed behind a thick, plumy tussock of sea-grass. "It's one thing to walk the beach when you're one of hundreds. But we'll be stopped and questioned for sure if we attempt it today."

"We're going to have to go in on the windward side, where there are no beaches," Alice told her. "Come on."

The palisade might be an impressive wooden barrier when it had to keep out ladies and children, but as they climbed over the rocks at the tip of the island, they discovered that it degenerated after several hundred feet into barbed wire on posts, which wouldn't keep out anything smaller than a cow. In the act of holding the barbed strands apart for Maggie, Alice saw something in a tidal pool below. Spilling out of it, rather, like a huge tangle of weed.

"Maggie, what is that?"

It was gray and white, and motionless, and some twenty feet long. It was also quite dead, if the ravens inspecting it were any indication.

Maggie inhaled in sudden realization. "It's a

kraken!" she exclaimed. A flock of egrets rose, startled, out of a copse of trees, and Alice instinctively hunched down.

When no alarm seemed to have been raised, she raised her head and indicated that Maggie should climb through the fence. "Poor thing. I wonder what killed it?"

But there was no satisfying her curiosity on that point. She followed Maggie through the fence and continued forward until the trees thinned, and they were high enough to be able to see some way off.

"So many ships!" Maggie breathed.

So many it was difficult to count them from this distance. Single, double, and even a couple with the old-fashioned stacked fuselages, airships were neatly lined up and tied to black mooring masts. The fuselages moved restlessly in the sea breeze, bobbing like guilty children shifting from one foot to another.

"How many people crewed all these ships?" Alice wondered aloud. "Are they all imprisoned and working underwater, like Jake and the captain?"

"It's shocking," Maggie murmured, her eyes wide. "I wonder how long some of them have been here. If their crews have … died."

It was a distinct possibility. For if the entire crew were under water, it left no one to do as they were doing—stealing one's ship back. "Maybe they sell them when everyone is dead. How horrible."

"Can you see the *Lass*?"

"Not from here. Come on. Let's see if we can move to the west a little, and get a better view."

Moving in fits and starts, they zigzagged from tussock to tree, staying low until they were close enough to one creaky old dame of a ship to see the lettering on her gondola. Alice had a good look all around them. "We'll make a run for it across this open stretch, and hide under that old bucket there. I'm pretty sure the *Lass* is two rows away, about halfway across the field. The color of her fuselage is pretty distinctive, because of the waterproofing we use in the Territories."

"I wish it were dark," Maggie said.

"So do I. But ours is the least dangerous job. Think of what the others are enduring at this moment. Ready? Let's go."

Hunched over, bags on their backs, they ran for the old airship. Alice dove under her gondola, hearing the wood groan as the breeze tugged on her ropes.

Maggie settled into place next to her, breathing hard. "Were we spotted?"

"I hope not," Alice whispered. "I haven't seen a guard yet on this side. They must concentrate all their men on the beach side to keep the ladies and children out."

Maggie grinned, and then as her gaze swept the field, it faded. "Let me go first."

"Hardly. We go together."

But Maggie shook her head. "It's what me and Lizzie do, Alice," she said, sounding less like the educated young lady she was than the street sparrow she had once been. "You let me scout, and I'll call like a robin with the all-clear."

It was what she had counted on Maggie for, wasn't it? So Alice nodded, and the girl took off, as silent as the breeze and nearly as fast. When a robin twittered, Alice followed, and, taking ship by ship and row by row, they hopscotched toward their goal.

## A LADY OF INTEGRITY

Crouched under the blue fuselage of what might once have been a military vessel, Alice caught up with her and followed the direction of her gaze. "It's the *Lass*," she said on a long breath of relief. "Not sure what I would've done if she hadn't been on this field."

"Stolen another," Maggie said with practical brevity. "Can you tell if she's damaged?"

"Her gas bags haven't been deflated, at least, and there are no holes stove in her hull."

Some of the ships had sustained awful damage before they'd come to this graveyard, sitting forlornly on the gravel with their bags in heaps on their gondolas, looking abandoned and alone. A serving airship never touched the ground, not really, unless it was in a hangar somewhere for repairs. To see a hull tilted on the ground was unnatural, like seeing that kraken cast up and drying out on the rocks, any beauty it might once have possessed gone with the absence of its natural element.

"Let me have a look round," Maggie whispered. "Back in a tick."

If Alice, who was watching with every sense on alert, couldn't see her making a circuit of the *Lass*, then she dared to hope that no one else would either. When Maggie returned, she nodded in answer to Alice's silent question.

"Looks all right. Boarding will be tricky, though. There's a direct sight line to the westernmost tower on the palisade."

"We'll stay close to the ground—in fact, look." One of the derelicts had spilled its innards, and a piece of ancient canvas flapped, caught on a stanchion. Moving quickly, Alice pulled it free and carried it over to their hiding place. "We'll crawl to it under this. It's close enough to the color of the gravel that maybe they won't notice."

The canvas stank to high heaven, as though a hundred years of mildew had been growing under it since its ship had been impounded. But Alice just held her breath until they had crossed the short expanse to the *Lass*'s gondola and the hatch directly into the engine compartment.

She heaved Maggie up inside, tossed their bags in after her, and then hoisted herself up past the engine to the deck, kicking the canvas free.

Home.

Alice couldn't help herself—she put a hand to the battered engine casing that had once been an automaton called Four, and which now cradled Claire's energy cell. "All right, old girl?" she asked it, gazing around her. The casing was cold, and the interior smelled of dust and gear grease and a faint whiff of whatever she and Jake had last cooked in the galley before everything had gone to Hades in a handbasket. But the ship looked sound. Nothing appeared to have been disconnected or sabotaged.

A quick check of the cargo hold, however, confirmed what she'd suspected all along. "They've taken the furs."

"You didn't really think they would leave them here, did you?"

"No, I don't suppose I did. I wonder where they hold the valuables they seize?"

"I don't know, but I suspect the Minister's young and pretty wife will have received a new mink stole."

Alice swallowed her bitterness at the probable truth

of this, and they returned to the gondola. "Maggie, have you piloted a ship before?"

"Of course. The Lady taught us all, and to read charts. The only thing I don't know how to do is repair an engine, but Tigg said he'd show both me and Lizzie a few common repairs on his next land leave."

"Good. I'm going to fire her up. You take the tiller. The automaton intelligence system has Twelve back here on Claire's cell, and Thirteen controls the vanes."

"Aren't you going to captain her?" Maggie asked, for the first time sounding a little unsure of herself. "It's not my place if you're aboard."

"That's why I asked you if you'd had any experience. I want to keep an eye on the engine. Sometimes when she's been standing for a while like this, she needs a little tuning."

Maggie nodded at last and went forward, taking the bags with her.

Alice pulled the lever that set the movable truss in motion, and then heard Maggie say, "Twelve, prepare for lift. Thirteen, vanes full vertical."

Obediently, the lamp lit on the console, indicating that Twelve had activated the power cell, and in a moment the familiar smooth purr of the engines vibrated the deck under her feet.

"Good girl," she said fondly, adjusting current and checking the pistons' motion with the familiarity of long practice. "Nobody's going to hurt you as long as I'm here." She hollered through the portal, "I'll cast off."

Dropping lightly to the ground, she ran to the bow and climbed the ladder to the mooring rope like a monkey. This was the tricky part. The Ministry men up in that tower might not have seen them board, and the wind was too loud for them to hear the engine, but a woman swaying on a mooring mast? It would be hard to miss that.

She untied the rope and scrambled down. The ships only seemed to be anchored at bow and stern, so all she had to do was cast off the second rope, jump back in the engine compartment's hatch, and tell Maggie to lift.

A report like a hunting rifle sounded in the distance, and something whistled over the fuselage of the neighboring ship. The stern rope still in her hand, she turned. What—

Another report. A fraction of a second later, the *Lass*'s starboard fuselage bobbed and rocked. Another report. And then Alice realized what was happening.

"Maggie!" she screamed, running like hellfire for the engine hatch. "They're shooting at us! Get her in the air!"

*Crack. Crack.* The other ships gave the port fuselage some cover, but at this rate frequency would trump accuracy, if the shots were coming from that tower.

And then Alice heard the sound that she never wanted to hear again—the one she had first heard in the Canadas, when they had crashed in the Idaho Territory. The shrill, forlorn whistle of gas escaping from the fuselage. More than one whistle. Three—four—it sounded like a regular choir of hopelessness.

"Maggie, lift!" Alice heaved herself into the engine compartment and slammed the hatch closed, turning immediately to kick the auxiliary engine's throttle to full ahead. Thank the good Lord that Claire's cell wasn't powered by steam or they'd be full of bullets long before the engine was ready to fly.

"The gas in the starboard fuselage is below the red

line!" Maggie shouted.

"Tell Eleven to disable it. We can still fly under one."

"Eleven, disable starboard fuselage. Thirteen, full lift vertical. Up ship!"

As soon as they left the ground, the deck tilted drunkenly, off balance without the second fuselage to hold the gondola level as it hung between them. Everything that wasn't tied down slid to the opposite wall, and if Alice hadn't been hanging on to a safety rope, she might have gone clear out the exhaust well.

"Alice!" Maggie shrieked.

"Are you hit? Did you fall?" With one foot on the deck and one braced against the wall, Alice struggled forward. She had no sooner gained a handhold on one of the lamp cornices that she heard the *ping!* of a bullet striking metal. And another. And a third. Behind her, Four groaned like a man taking a fatal blow.

"No!" Alice shouted. "No! Not my engine!"

A bloom of flame curled up from beneath Four's thorax and with a blast that would have killed her had she still been standing beside it, the engine exploded. Alice was thrown the length of the corridor and into the navigation room.

"Alice! Oh, Alice, don't be dead. Please don't be dead." Maggie's voice came from a long way away.

*I'm not dead,* she tried to say, but her head seemed to have expanded to the size of the remaining fuselage.

Fuselage.

Gas.

*Fire.*

She opened her eyes with an effort of sheer will. There was no way on this green earth that she was going to stand in front of Claire and explain how she had let Maggie be killed. Not after what those two had been through in the English Channel. She struggled up.

"Gas," she croaked. "Abandon ship."

But the *Lass* was already rolling, its controls gone, poor Twelve and Thirteen helpless to make the engine obey their pilot's commands. The corridor was already on fire—she could feel the heat of it from here, and the poor old girl was so old that her teak was dry as tinder. They'd burn right out of the sky unless they jumped, fast.

"Jump!" she ordered. "I'll try and bring her close enough to one of the other ships that it won't be too bad."

"What are you talking about?" Maggie snapped. "If I go, you go."

"Maggie, no—"

The auxiliary engine exploded and Alice realized they might not even have time to jump. Maggie had already flung on their two bags, crossing them over her chest, but now she grabbed Alice in a hug. Then she rolled them both right down the gangway and out the main hatch.

If they were going to die, let it be together, Alice thought as the sky whirled around her. Then the breath was knocked clean out of her as they landed. On something solid but giving. That smelled like canvas and warm pitch.

"Alice! Grab hold, quick, before we roll off!"

It was all she could do to close her fist around one of the ropes that formed a grid over whatever ship's fuselage they had landed on, and lie flat on her back, gasping for air. Above them and about fifty feet to starboard, the *Stalwart Lass* rolled sickeningly as the flames leaped up the ropes and consumed the gondola with blazing speed. The second fuselage caught and there was a mighty *boom* as the gas exploded in a fireball that felt as though it singed the very eyebrows off her face.

What was left of Alice's ship—her home—her way of making her living in the world—plunged to earth with a heartrending crash, and all that marked the grave of her captain's hopes and dreams was the plume of black smoke rising slowly into the air.

## 22

"Do you think the captain of the vessel will ask permission of your father first, before he takes us aboard?"

Claire couldn't help her anxiety—the spectre of Gerald Meriwether-Astor discovering their purpose and realizing that it would likely jeopardize all his plans hung over them all. Add to this the fact that she had been separated from the Mopsies and from Alice, and it was a wonder she could stand here so calmly on the stone pier, instead of snatching up the lightning rifle and plunging off to make sure they were all right.

"I don't see why he would," Gloria replied, looking fresh as a daisy in a white linen walking suit trimmed in royal-blue grosgrain ribbon. "My message simply said that Father wished me to come aboard *Neptune's Fancy* until the *acqua alta* has receded. I did not actually men-

tion the two of you, but it is not likely anyone will
question that, either. I go about frequently with large
parties, though ..." Her tone turned pensive. "I cannot
really say that any of them are friends."

"Well, we are," Andrew said in bracing tones. "No
matter what happens, we are here for you as you have
been for us."

Gloria's face softened and Claire squeezed Andrew's
arm in thanks for saying exactly the right thing.

They had settled up their bill at the hotel earlier,
with an air of people taking a step from which there
could be no return. Their trunks had gone to *Athena*
with Tigg, Lizzie, and Claude. Her lightning rifle, sadly,
was in Tigg's possession as her second, and already she
missed its comforting presence. At their feet, damp from
the puddles on the pier caused by the ever higher lapping of the waves, sat their valises.

Claire imagined that Gloria's actually contained a
change of clothes and her brushes and combs, but hers
and Andrew's did not. They bulged instead with the
rocket rucksacks, a glass breathing globe each, and a
quantity of hose connected to a small engine.

"We will not have much time," Andrew had cau-
tioned her earlier as he divided the equipment between
their two cases. "The rucksack will propel us into the
depths, but not back again. The breathing engine will
produce air for about fifteen minutes, if the monograph
I read on its experiments is correct, so we must surface
well before then."

Fifteen minutes did not seem to Claire much time to
locate their friends, free them, and swim back to *Neptune's Fancy*, where Gloria would conveniently find
them in the stern should anyone have noticed their ab-

sence and mounted a search in the meanwhile.

But it would have to be enough. With the dismal failure of Ian's Plan A, they did not have a Plan C.

"Here they are," Gloria said suddenly, and raised a gloved hand to point at the wavering shadow that had appeared thirty feet off the pier, under the water.

Claire watched in awe as the undersea zeppelin caused the surface of the sea to distend in a dome the size of a cottage, then break free of the water to rise above it, sheets of seawater cascading from its sides like the gleaming, moving walls of a mermaid's castle.

When the viewing ports were clear, the vessel floated slowly to the pier. It was a good thing they were some six feet above the water, for it washed ahead of the sides of the vessel in a wave that crashed over the top, making them step hastily back.

Though why they should have done this when they were shortly to be as wet as it was possible for human beings to be was a puzzle. Instinct, Claire supposed.

A hatch lifted on the side of the vessel and a gangway tilted out and down. An officer in a neat blue uniform appeared and strode down it, removing his cap in the presence of his employer's daughter. "Miss Meriwether-Astor, it is a great pleasure to meet you. I am Captain Barnaby Hayes."

He quite reminded one of poor Captain Hollys, with his direct gaze and upright bearing. But he was somewhat younger, and Claire wondered if his ship had been caught in the debacle that was to have been the French invasion not so many weeks ago. She hoped not. He looked too nice to have been a misguided criminal.

"I am deeply grateful to you, Captain Hayes." Gloria's china-plate eyes had never been used to greater effect, and her hand lay in his like a confiding dove. "Father is concerned for my safety during the *acqua alta*, but *I* am concerned that looking after me is taking you away from your duties."

"Not at all," he said gallantly. "We are on standby awaiting orders. Nothing will give us more pleasure than to act as host to you ... and your friends?" He turned to Claire and Andrew.

"Doctor Andrew Malvern," Gloria said. Andrew shook hands and indicated Claire. "This is my fiancée, Lady Claire Trevelyan. Miss Meriwether-Astor has been kind enough to offer us refuge. It seems our hotel is rather unprepared for the water levels, and we made the mistake of hiring first-floor rooms."

"Space is tight aboard ship—the *Fancy*, as you see, is not as large as many in the fleet—but we will find accommodations for you. Come along. Do watch your step."

He guided Gloria across the gangway and waited as Claire crossed, then Andrew. A short ladder extended into the interior from the hatch, and he proved he was a gentleman by looking the other way when Claire and Gloria climbed down, both having to tuck their skirts into their belts in order to leave their hands free.

Andrew could not very well drop the valises down with the glass breathing globes inside, so he was forced to slip the handles of both bags over his arms and descend carefully without being able to see where he was putting his feet.

"Do leave your luggage here," the captain said, showing Claire and Gloria into a cabin with two metal beds one above the other that had clearly been recently vacated and freshly made up. "Doctor Malvern, if you will follow me, I hope you will accept a cot in my cabin." Andrew handed both valises to Claire and she stowed them under the lowermost bunk until they should be needed.

At length they were shown into a salon and introduced to the other officers. "Our journey back out into the Adriatic will take about two hours," Captain Hayes said. "Please make yourselves comfortable next to a viewing port. We may be fortunate enough to see dolphins, or even a kraken."

At Gloria's gasp, he smiled. "Do not be alarmed. They feed on mollusks and fish, not dirigibles."

"It is not that," Gloria said. "Did not Father tell you? I should like to see the gearworks before we go."

The smile on the captain's face was replaced by confusion. "The gearworks? Under Venice? Whatever for?"

"I am afraid her enthusiasm for the sight is my fault," Andrew said, smiling in his self-deprecating way. "I am deeply interested in their operation, and prevailed upon Miss Meriwether-Astor to include a look at them in our brief journey. I do hope this will not incommode you?"

"Well ... Doctor Malvern ... certainly not. We will be honored to assist in the process of scientific research."

Claire felt almost ashamed to have to deceive the poor man, he looked so delighted to have his ship chosen for the privilege. But deceive him they must, and soon.

The captain gave orders to submerge, and the three of them stood next to a wide viewing port, the urgency of their mission eclipsed momentarily at the awe-inspiring sight of the water racing up the sides of the vessel and then closing over the bridge. They plunged into the green gloom of the lagoon, leaving the pier behind and sinking into the depths with a motion that could hardly be felt.

"There to port, ladies, you may see the arm of the gearworks that holds up Zattere and your hotel."

Since this had been the location of the unfortunate convict's untimely death, it was all Claire could do not to shudder and find somewhere else to look. "Is there any danger of the arms moving while we are down here?" she asked instead. "I should not like to think we might be hit."

"The watch is on deck," the captain said in reassuring tones. "And the gears move so slowly that with our greater maneuverability, we shall be able to get out of the way in time."

"I am happy to hear it," Claire told him, hoping her eyes and warm smile were at least as effective as Gloria's. "How is this vessel propelled? I have just graduated this summer with an engineering degree, you see, so the gearworks hold only part of my interest. Transportation was the focus of my studies."

"Ah, then perhaps once you have seen the gearworks, our chief engineer might give you a tour of the engine room."

"I should like that very much," Claire said, hoping devoutly that she would return to take him up on this generous offer. "Thank you."

"Suffice it to say that the Meriwether-Astor submersible steam engine is the power that enables us to cross entire oceans in comfort. The technology is such that our two steam engines put out twice the thrust of the original models."

"And is the vessel armed against attack?" Claire asked.

"Oh yes. That is only practical in any transoceanic endeavor—though if the truth be told, the only thing we have fired upon so far is a rather large kraken who became enamored of the vessel and would not let go of it."

"Dear me," Gloria said, fanning herself with one gloved hand. "How terrifying."

"Fortunately it clung to the stern, and the aft torpedoes—which carry an eighteen-pound charge—gave it a fatal stomach complaint. Have no fear, Miss Meriwether-Astor. We will let nothing keep you from a reunion with your father once the water levels in the city recede."

Claire exchanged a glance with Andrew. He had theorized that the best way for them to leave the vessel undetected was through the hatch where either refuse or weapons were released. With a nod, he confirmed that the torpedo tubes would be their goal.

*Neptune's Fancy* sank even lower, and lamps came on to illuminate their way through the gloom. The lagoon was much deeper than it appeared—though she had heard there were ancient channels scored in the seabed that had provided a defense for the early inhabitants. Only mariners aware of the channels could bring a ship close to the city. All others wrecked on the shoals.

"There." Gloria pointed. "What is that?"

"You have a good eye. That is the base of the gearworks, my dear young lady," the captain confirmed. "Leonardo da Vinci's masterpiece—though I suppose few but the convicts have seen it."

Glinting in the lamps of the dirigible, the base on which the gearworks depended was massive—so vast that the mind could hardly take it in. Buckingham Palace was not half so large, and how far into the distance did it extend? Part circular track, part clockwork, the incomprehensibly complex system of cogs and wheels and balancing weights moved slowly yet inexorably on its appointed rounds. Not even a typhoon could move it down here on the seabed—though Claire supposed an earthquake might.

Slowly, their own vessel dwarfed to inconsequence by even the smallest of the cogs, they began to circle the gearworks. While the captain and Andrew discussed the miracle of its operation after five hundred years, Claire peered through the gloom for any sign of a diving bell.

Then— "Captain, my goodness, what is that?" she asked, pointing.

He joined her at the glass and squinted. "That, Lady Claire, is a diving bell containing convicted men. You are familiar with the justice system in Venice."

"I am, yes. Dear me. Are those … skeletons caught in the track? Might we go a little closer?"

"What do you hope to see?" His gaze was curious. Too curious.

She must not give them away, not when they were so close. "I do apologize. That must have sounded positively ghoulish. I am only interested in the propulsion in the diving bell. One would not imagine it to be so sophisticated as to be able to transport men down to these depths."

"There your guess is as good as mine—and probably better," he said gallantly. "This is my first visit to the gearworks, as well. All my knowledge heretofore has been the result of my own study. Let us go a little closer. Perhaps we might be able to satisfy our joint curiosity."

With relief, Claire watched him cross the room to give the order to the helmsman, before her gaze was drawn back to the diving bell. Could this be the one in which Jake and Ian were working? How many were there, laboring so deep under the water where everywhere they looked they saw only hopeless imprisonment and the impossibility of rescue?

Slowly, the engines cut nearly to an idle, the *Fancy* drifted closer. In the powerful glow of its forward lamps, Claire could clearly see the moment when the men within realized that they were being observed. There were five, not including the *campanaro*, and three seemed to be occupied in an effort to extract an enormous bone from between a cog and its toothed track.

The other two were pressed to the glass sides of the bell, watching the approaching vessel.

One was tall, with dark hair and a wondering gaze. And the other was shorter—thin and wiry—with reddish hair plastered to his skull, as though he'd been sent out into the water with no breathing globe to reconnoiter whatever problem the bone was causing.

Relief and joy swamped her in a wave as strong as any the city's piers had ever seen. With a moan, she slumped to the deck in a pool of skirts, one hand outflung in an unconscious plea.

"Claire!" Andrew leaped to her side and gathered her tenderly into his arms. Standing, with Claire's skirts hanging nearly to the floor, he said to the captain, "The sight of those unfortunates has overcome her. I will take her to her cabin."

"Let me help," Gloria said. "She may need ... feminine assistance."

The bathynauts who had moved to help checked at this unforeseen prospect. "Of course," the captain said, his tone worried. "We have no medic aboard, but I will send for one."

"That will not be necessary," Gloria said quickly. "Claire is of a delicate constitution and is prone to being overcome, particularly at such a grisly sight as this."

The unconscious form in Andrew's arms twitched slightly.

"We will prepare to join the fleet, then, in case one is needed."

"I am sure she will come around as soon as I administer my smelling salts," Gloria assured him. "I would like just a few moments more of taking in the gearworks. Please hold the vessel here until I return. I will only be a moment, until I am assured she is recovered."

Andrew carried Claire down the arched passage to the room she and Gloria had been assigned, and as soon as the door closed behind them, tipped Claire onto her feet.

"Well done, both of you," Claire said breathlessly, patting her hair. "Jake and Ian are in that bell, and we haven't much time." She began to unbutton her walking skirt.

"Claire!" Gloria whispered, raising scandalized brows. "You are removing your clothing in the presence of a gentleman!"

"Not all of it," Claire assured her. "But we would have more room if you were to step outside and stand watch. I am sure you will have no trouble at all providing a distraction—especially if Captain Hayes should happen to come to check on me."

"You're a very convincing fainter," Gloria told her, slipping out the door. Then she said through the crack, "You'll have to show me how you do it sometime."

Under her skirt Claire wore a pair of Alice's trousers and her leather corselet and blouse. "Should I remove my boots?" she asked Andrew anxiously.

But he did not reply immediately. Gazing at her, he said, "Dearest, I must ask you one last time to reconsider."

There was no doubt as to what he meant. She shook her head. "I will not let you risk your life alone."

"But Claire, think. If I take a breathing globe and a rucksack, then I can give it to one of them. That will leave only one man to face the uncertainty of holding his breath all the way back to the *Fancy*. And with the knowledge that you are safely inside, I may focus my resources on my task without distraction."

"But if something goes wrong, you will have no means of help. No, Andrew. My purpose is fixed. If you are to risk your life for our friends, then I will, too. And if by some dreadful mischance we are meant to lose our lives today, I would rather that we were together." She paused, and her throat thickened with emotion. "I do not think I could bear it if I were left behind to grieve you."

"Nor I you," he said softly.

He took her in his arms, and in his kiss she felt his fear for her—and also his gratitude for her refusal to allow him to face this alone. When he at last released her, he cleared his throat and returned to the more prosaic subject of boots.

"I believe we both ought to keep our boots on. You might need to use your feet to cushion your arrival at the gearworks. The propulsion of the rucksack is easily controlled in the air, but I am not certain of the effects of my adjustments for underwater travel. I should not like you to be injured."

He helped her on with the rucksack and then the breathing globe, running its hose under the strap so it would not be caught on an errant piece of metal or entangle her arms. All sound was then silenced except for that of her own breathing.

Andrew outfitted himself likewise, and then they opened the door.

"Good luck," Gloria said, her words muffled and coming from a great distance, as though Claire were already under water.

It was indeed a stroke of luck that the tiny cabin was in the stern, and that their side trip to view the gearworks was as fascinating to the crew as it had been to Claire and Andrew. The men had all gone forward to the viewing ports, so they made their way unaccosted back to the defense station in the stern, and thence to the pressurized chamber containing the torpedo tubes.

Fortunately, since the *Fancy* had been safely in the midst of a fleet of its fellow dirigibles for several days now, the tubes were not armed. Claire gazed down into the dark well, where water lapped restlessly.

Andrew took her hand and indicated he would go first. When he would have crouched to slip into the water, she did not let go, instead tugging on his hand until he looked up.

*I love you*, she mouthed.

His face softened in a smile, and in his eyes she saw his response even before his lips moved. *And I love you. Come. We go together.*

Claire's instinct was to hold her breath as she slipped into the dark well and swam down the short tunnel, her feet and hands brushing the sides. But the small engine that Andrew had rigged to produce oxygen in the breathing globe seemed to be performing. Regulating her breath under stress, if anything, seemed the greater difficulty to be overcome.

*Neptune's Fancy* appeared to have turned away to investigate something a little farther along the cog track, probably due to Gloria's timely request. They did not have much time. Gloria would keep the crew busy for the fifteen minutes allotted before they were forced to return. If they did not succeed in that time, well ... Claire shook away the discouraging thought.

Ahead of her, a plume of bubbles jetting upward in an arc told her that Andrew had activated the rocket rucksack. She pulled the cord on her own, and found herself powering through the water much as she had on her one and only safety exercise with the rucksack in the air, years ago. It was not an experience one was likely to forget, however. The drag of the water had the added benefit of increasing her ability to control her direction. She resisted the urge to whoop with excitement and trepidation—it would use oxygen unnecessarily—but it did not stop a high note of exhilaration escaping her lips, similar to one's scream at reaching the apex of the Ferris wheel and going over the top.

Fish dodged out of their way as they careened toward the diving bell. If only two of the convicts had seen the *Fancy*, they all had now observed the curious pair weaving toward them like dolphins. Jake leaned against the curved wall of the bell with his hands cupped on either side of his eyes, like a child at a shop window, before he was dragged roughly aside and another of the convicts took his place.

Andrew tilted his body in the water so the stream of bubbles from the rucksack acted as its own braking system, extended his legs like an eagle landing in a tree, and grasped the nearest extrusion of metal to bring himself to a stop close to the diving bell. Claire attempted to do the same, and succeeded merely in doing a graceful backward flip before she recovered her ability to judge the speed and angle of the jet.

She did, however, succeed in getting even closer to the bell—so close that if she had not dodged to one side, she would have been plastered flat against it in an echo of Jake's own stance a moment ago.

Their friends had recognized them.

Jake's mouth opened in a shout, and he grabbed Ian's arm and shook it vigorously. Ian merely stared.

Claire hoped that in all his travels, Jake had seen a pantomime, because there was no other way to communicate. Swiftly, as Andrew made his way down the cog track to join them, she mimed their taking a deep breath, dipping down and under the rim of the bell, then clinging to each of their rescuers as they swam away.

Jake gave her the thumbs-up, and grabbed the buckle across Ian's chest, shaking it. Ian seemed to come out of whatever stupor held him captive, and his face lost its slack expression. He began to unbuckle himself while Jake shrugged out of his harness, landing with a splash in the water. But at the same time, their companions woke to what was about to happen.

As one man, they flung off their harnesses, each desperate to escape and seeing immediately that only two were going to be successful.

But Jake, thin and starving as he was, had not amassed a reputation as a dab hand on the streets of London without cause. He snatched up what appeared to be a scraping iron and gave the closest man an almighty wallop. Since their quarters were cramped, that man took down the one behind him. Jake heaved on the captain's harness and when he fell out of it, gave him less than a second to gulp a lungful of air, and stuffed him under the water and hence under the rim of the bell.

Andrew swooped down and caught him under the arms, then, proceeding much more slowly than he had arrived, swam in the direction of the glow of the *Fancy*'s lamps.

If Claire could have shrieked a warning, she would have, for two men, enraged at the escape of someone who was not either of themselves, leaped upon Jake. Instead, bobbing against the bell's cowling, she was forced to watch the frenzied splashing in the bottom of the bell. Jake came up, sucked in a breath, and in a moment a skinny leg thrashed under the glass lip.

That was all Claire needed.

With the force of the jet behind her, she dove for his pitiful white foot, grasped it in both hands, and pulled.

Jake came out of the bell as though he had been greased. Once they were clear, she did another backflip, grasped him around the chest, and followed as fast as her rucksack would take her in Andrew's wake.

Jake's arms went around her back and, though she was quite sure he had had his eighteenth birthday some time ago, he tucked his head against the straps on her chest like a small child and hung on for dear life.

# A LADY OF INTEGRITY

The trail of bubbles led her to a great curving orb that likely locked into a larger gear above, where Andrew swam back and forth, the captain's body dangling from his arms. What was he waiting for? They had less than thirty seconds to jet back to *Neptune's Fancy* before both their friends drowned!

And then she realized what was missing.

Light.

The lamps of the undersea dirigible illuminated its way for at least fifty feet. But not even a glimmer was to be seen. No light.

No ship.

No Gloria.

Where in the name of all she held holy had they gone?

But there was no time to waste. Jake's cheeks were already puffed in an effort to keep as much oxygen within as possible. She had no choice. They must return to the diving bell or the boy would drown right here in her arms.

She gestured to Andrew and he followed her, his greater speed telling her that the captain was close to expiring as well. When they reached the position where the bell had been, her eyes bugged out in horror.

It was gone.

Jake bumped the breathing globe with his head, forcing her to look up, and there she saw it, ascending as fast as it could, where no doubt they would report the escape and soldiers would be sent down to capture them.

Not if she could help it.

She had no idea how much propulsion was left in her rucksack, but there was not a second to waste. She jetted upward—stuffed Jake up under the lip of the bell as she passed—then swam up to the apex of it.

The eyes of the *campanero* were desperate as they met hers. Still, she shook her head and threw the lever on the cable, forcing it into the closed position with both hands. The bell shuddered to a stop, the occupants thrashing in their harnesses, kicking at Jake as he gasped for air.

Andrew rose up inside it, still hauling the captain, and before the latter could so much as inhale, two of the harnessed men released their latches and dropped on Andrew. Claire clung to the outside of the bell, watching helplessly as they hauled the breathing globe from Andrew's head, tore the rucksack from him, and swung the scraping iron. He ducked, but it caught him a glancing blow and the impact was enough to render him so dizzy that he fell back into the water. If Jake, treading water below, had not managed to keep his head above the surface, he would have sunk, insensible.

And now the *campanero* scrambled off his perch and down the short metal ladder. He leaped on the men clinging to the one wearing the rucksack, and without another wasted second, they all plunged into the water, swam out from under the lip of the bell, and jetted off into the marine gloom, four sets of legs dangling and twisting like those of a species of kraken.

She hoped that was exactly what their fate would be, the wretches. Swiftly, she swam down the side of the immobilized bell and up inside it. Surfacing, she trod water and struggled to remove the breathing globe.

"Andrew!" she gasped when she finally got it off. "Is everyone all right? Andrew, dearest, speak to me."

"I'm all right," Andrew mumbled, one hand pressed

to the side of his head. He brought it away smeared with blood. "Stings like the devil."

A quick examination ascertained that the edge of the scraper had grazed his scalp and, while bleeding rather alarmingly, the cut was not deep. "That is the salt water, dearest. It will help more than harm, if you can bear it."

Captain Hollys said nothing, merely gazed at the bubbles of his erstwhile companions' jet as they rose lazily through the water to the surface.

Jake's eyes, hollow and yet fiercely alight, met Claire's as she turned to him and laid a hand briefly to his cheek, as if even the evidence of her own eyes might have deceived her. "Hullo, Lady," he said, still breathing hard as water ran in rivulets down his temples. "We've got a wee bit of a problem, it seems."

While she could also take three men to safety, there was nowhere now to go. They could not rise on the diving bell's normal trajectory, for nothing awaited them at the top but Ministry men. They could not jet away, for their sanctuary had inexplicably gone. And they could not rise to the surface like so many bubbles and hope for the best, as the convicts had been willing to do, because she had no idea where they might come up, and an attack by the kraken was almost certain.

All that their attempts at rescue had netted them was that first one, then two, and now four were imprisoned deep below the city, with all hope of help denied.

"Oh, dear," Claire said on a long breath of despair.

23

"Holly! Ivy! You rascals, this is no time to take a flyer—Claude, Mr. Stringfellow—help me."

Obligingly, Claude and the young middy loped down the gangway and took up positions to left and right. "Like this?"

"Yes," Lizzie said. "Move slowly. The object is to herd them back up the ramp."

But the two little hens had been penned in their aviary aboard *Athena* for far too long, and when Lizzie had made the mistake of leaving the door open while she filled their water container, they had taken advantage of her inattention and made a bid for freedom.

Now they ran about on the grassy field where visiting airships moored, yanking worms from the ground and snatching at blades of grass, neatly evading every effort to catch them.

"You'll have to provide them a better reason to be in than out," Tigg called from the hatch. "Try this."

He tossed out a cold prawn from the collation the hotel had provided when they left, and, necks stretched out with curiosity, Holly and Ivy ran to investigate.

With relief, Lizzie threw it ahead of them up the ramp and Mr. Stringfellow closed the hatch behind them. "You're a bad lot," she told them affectionately as they tortured the succulent pink flesh. "But it's my own fault for giving you the chance. I wouldn't like being cooped up for most of a week, either."

Claude joined them in the salon, where they helped themselves to the remainder of the sandwiches. It was nearly noon, and the fact that they'd had not a word from anyone was beginning to gnaw at the edges of Lizzie's composure.

"We ought to have heard from someone by now." Tigg checked the communications cage even though he'd only done so ten minutes before. "I hope nothing's gone wrong."

"The Lady would find a way to tell us if she were in danger."

"How?" Claude asked around his lunch, honestly curious. "She's on the bottom of the lagoon with kraken and convicts and goodness knows what else."

"And Mr. Malvern and Gloria," Lizzie pointed out. "The dirigibles have a communications system, too. Even if she had to steal something, she wouldn't let us worry."

A sound in the stern made Tigg jump to his feet. "There it is. The hummingbird we sent to Alice has come back."

The young middy brought it in so they could all see Alice's message, and unrolled the piece of paper tucked in the tube Tigg had rigged. Then he frowned and showed it to them. "This isn't right. It's the message we sent her, not a reply."

"It came back without delivering its message?" Claude said, as though to clarify. "They're not supposed to do that, are they?"

"The Lady's pigeons always get where they're supposed to go, because we have special ones that fly just among the flock's ships," Lizzie explained. "Tigg, it didn't pick up a fault somehow when you took it apart?"

He shook his head. "Couldn't have. The automaton itself is unchanged. I only removed the carrier and the long-range engine. No, there's only one explanation—it couldn't find the *Stalwart Lass.*"

"Impossible," Lizzie said flatly. "All our pigeons have been to the *Lass* at least once. They found her in Scotland—in the Canadas—even in the West Indies that one time."

"You don't suppose something happened to Alice's ship, do you?" Claude voiced the fear that had been niggling in Lizzie's insides but that she hadn't wanted to acknowledge.

"That's the only conclusion I can come to," Tigg said slowly. "I think we had better lift and have a look ourselves."

"The Lady told us to stay put until she and Gloria signaled us from the dirigible," Lizzie objected. "We can't very well go floating about over Venice."

"Why not? The tourists do," Claude said. "Ripping good fun."

"Yes, but not in cargo ships. We're five times bigger than the sightseeing balloons."

"We'll just say we're lost and looking for the airfield," Claude suggested. "After all, what can they do? Shoot us down with a cannon?"

"Yes, I think that's exactly what they might do, if they knew what we were up to," Tigg told him. "But I don't see that we have a choice. It's too strange for the hummingbird to come back without delivering its message. Alice and Maggie might need help."

While Tigg told the automaton intelligence system and Mr. Stringfellow to prepare for lift, Lizzie and Claude ran down and released the ropes. When they were safely back aboard, he called "Up ship!" and *Athena* rose gracefully into the sky. She turned to the south and flew over the lagoon, Tigg keeping her well clear of the church towers and the tourist traffic over most of the city.

It pleased Lizzie no end to watch him pilot the ship. He stood at the tiller and kept her on her heading with one hand, so familiar with the mechanics of flying that he might almost be a part of the ship itself. He was a lieutenant now, but it would not surprise Lizzie if he had his captain's bars by the time he reached his majority at twenty-one.

And then? Would he ask her to marry him?

Lizzie shivered with delight at the thought. Though they were both young, the Lady had approved his courting her. Not that Tigg needed anyone to give him permission to do what he thought was right, but all the same, if Claire had not approved, he would have felt honor bound to respect her wishes, no matter how Lizzie felt about the matter.

She could only be glad that such was not the situation. That the Lady trusted them both. And that they were together here in this strange place, where nothing seemed to go as you might expect and everything was twice as dangerous as you planned for.

"I'm going to take her higher so we can get a look at the impound yard on the Lido and stay out of firing range," Tigg said, sounding every inch an aeronaut of Her Majesty's Corps.

"I say, old man, I wasn't really serious about that cannon," Claude said from the viewing port.

"I am," Tigg said, "and I'm not willing to take chances."

The earth receded a little, until Venice laid itself out beneath them, all pink and cream and frills above, and rot and weed and death below. Lizzie recognized the ornate bubble shape of Saint Mark's Cathedral, and then the exhibition grounds where only a handful of days ago she had paraded in the sun in her new dress. Then they were crossing the lagoon and the long, narrow shape of the Lido floated beneath them, cradling the city in its protective embrace.

"That's odd," Claude said. "I could swear that's where my lot and I were swimming the other week, and the beach is quite … gone."

"Can the water really come up so far?" Lizzie craned to see. "What a lucky thing we're up here and not down there."

"Let's hope Alice and Maggie aren't down there, either," Tigg said. "I'm going to bring her round and take a pass over the impound yard. Keep your eyes peeled, as Snouts used to say, for the *Lass*'s double fuselage, Lizzie my girl."

Lizzie smiled at the reminder. Except, as they both knew, Snouts had never called her "Lizzie my girl." He was usually somewhat more terse and to the point.

Rapidly, she scanned the rows of impounded ships. Goodness, what a lot of them there were. Well, she could discount all the single fuselages, which left not all that many, and if you narrowed it down to the burnished bronzy-brown of the *Lass*'s canvas, you'd be left with …

"Tigg?"

"Out with it, love."

"The *Lass* isn't there. Is there more than one field?"

"No idea. Are you quite sure?"

"Quite sure, unless Alice has changed the coating she puts on her canvas. There's nothing down there except something on fire, toward the middle."

"On fire?"

Something in his grim tone penetrated straight to Lizzie's heart, and she actually pressed a hand to her chest, as if to protect that sensitive organ. "You don't think—surely—"

"I'll bring her around once more, but we'd best be ready for a scarper—this place has guard towers and you know what that means."

Lizzie certainly did. And when Tigg brought *Athena* around again, she barely had enough time for a glimpse at the burning wreckage before something pinged off the bottom of the gondola with a whine like a mosquito.

"Tigg!" Claude exclaimed. "That was a shot! Take us up!"

"Seven, vanes full vertical. Nine, full lift!"

The deck pressed against Lizzie's boot soles as the ship gained altitude so fast that her ears popped, too.

And then Tigg spun the wheel and brought *Athena* into full retreat northward, heading for the city at twice the speed with which she had approached.

"That was close," he said at last, clearly forcing himself to speak casually. But Lizzie wasn't one bit fooled.

"It's a good thing we were expecting trouble," she said. "One bullet through the fuselage might not hurt us, but one straight into the engine would."

"Did you see anything of that wreck? Could you identify it?" Tigg asked.

In her mind's eye, she saw it again, and now that they were safely out of range, her brain finally acknowledged what her sick stomach had known for long moments already. "It was the *Lass*," she said. "That poor old gondola was nearly all gone, but Four's chest and the Lady's power cell were both burning merrily. It looked dreadful—sad and horrible and—" She choked, unable to go on.

Claude slid an arm around her waist and squeezed. "She'll be all right, old girl. We know our Maggie has resources. She and Alice will turn up, you'll see."

But there had been no sign of two female figures anywhere on that deserted graveyard of a field. There had been no sign of life at all save for the men shooting at them and a lone boatman on the narrowing beach, standing as though waiting for someone.

*Maggie*, her heart cried. *What happened? Where are you?*

But her only answer was the singing of the wind in the ropes as they floated once again over the city.

She choked back tears and squeezed Claude in thanks, then did her best to sound like a grown-up instead of a little girl they had to soothe and protect. "Maggie and Alice unaccounted for ... the Lady and Mr. Malvern still underwater ... what are our options, then? I don't much relish going back to the airfield and waiting when it's clear we're needed."

"We simply have to figure out who needs us the most, and where they are," Tigg agreed. "You don't suppose that undersea dirigible has run back out to sea, do you, and taken the Lady and the others with it?"

"It's going to eventually," Claude pointed out. "Pity those hummingbirds of yours don't operate underwater."

"There's no reason they couldn't, if they—"

"Tigg! Claude!" Lizzie, standing at the forward viewing port, beckoned rapidly with one hand. "Come look. What on earth is that?"

"Not a burning airship, I hope," Tigg muttered as he and Claude joined her. "Nine, decrease speed by half and hold our course."

The three of them gazed down as *Athena* floated lazily past a church spire and over the Giudecca Canal, the wide one close to where they had been staying. A little tourist balloon scudded out of their way, its cheerful round fuselage narrowly missing a bump by *Athena*'s shabby but majestic nose.

Down in the canal, something was disturbing the water—not quite a whirlpool, but not quite a waterspout, either.

"That dirigible we were just speaking of," Claude murmured. "It wouldn't be surfacing there, would it?"

"No—not a dirigible—my goodness! Look!"

Out of the thrashing, frothing water came a long tentacle, fast as a whip, curling and plunging and sending up a plume ten feet high.

"Kraken!" Tigg exclaimed. "A ruddy great kraken—and those are men, trying to escape!"

Then, out of the maelstrom shot a figure—straight up—up—

"It's Mr. Malvern!" Lizzie shrieked. "Quick! We must—"

"No, it isn't." Tigg grabbed her. "That bloke's got prison togs on. But that's the breathing globe Mr. Malvern was wearing—and the rocket rucksack."

"What's it doing on a convict? Where's Mr. Malvern and the Lady?"

"Never mind—get back to the basket and we'll grab him," Tigg ordered. "I want some answers."

But before they could move, or even tell *Athena* to drop her altitude, the rocket rucksack seemed to reach the apex of its mad vertical flight. The convict flailed in the air, clearly trying to stay aloft, but alas, the rucksack had done all it could. As his fall back to the water began, a lazy, curling tentacle reached up, wrapped itself around the man's leg, and yanked him out of the sky. Water erupted as he fought the creature—tentacles writhed—and with a splash that wet the fronts of the nearest houses, the creature sank into the canal, its prey secure.

Lizzie whirled, staggered into the galley, and was violently sick into the washing-up basin.

"Nine, circle this spot on a tight radius. Claude, keep an eye out for Ministry men." Tigg came in, wet a cloth, and tenderly wiped Lizzie's face. "All right, Lizzie-love? I'm so sorry you had to see that."

She would not be a mewling baby. She would not force Tigg to look after her when she was perfectly capable of cleaning up her own messes. "Yes," she said, doing her best to straighten her spine. "That poor man. We don't know what he's done, but no one deserves to come to his end like that." Swiftly, she rinsed out the basin and her mouth, and took Tigg's hand. "But I've just thought of something."

At the viewing port, she pointed to where the kraken had gone under, the water still roiling and waves crashing over the *fondamente* and into people's little gardens. "That man had to have stolen Mr. Malvern's rig. He also had to have been in a diving bell. So one minus one equals—"

"Mr. Malvern and the Lady in a diving bell, somewhere under there," Tigg said, his eyes aglow with admiration.

"Which helps us how, exactly?" Claude wanted to know. "Or helps them, I suppose I should say?"

"We have to let them know we're here," Lizzie said urgently. "If the Lady is alone—or if by some miracle Jake and Captain Hollys are with her—she'll be able to do something if only she knows she has help."

"Can you shoot the kraken if she does a flyer?" Claude asked with interest.

"I have the lightning rifle," Tigg reminded him. "I can shoot anything that would harm a hair on her head, kraken and Ministry men included."

"Oh, I say, well said," Claude said with admiration. "So then how will you tell her you're up here?"

Tigg and Lizzie looked at each other.

"Bombs," they both said at once.

# 24

Alice's lungs inflated after what seemed like an age of agony, and, flat on her back, she dragged in breath after breath of blessed air. If this was how the crushing burden of no oxygen felt after only a few moments, how must those poor devils in the diving bells feel? How could you bear it—the cramped space, never being dry, the knowledge that your air came at the whim of your captors, with fathoms of water between yourself and freedom?

She wished she'd never come here—never brought poor Jake—never let herself be tempted by easy flying and good pay. She had been stupid to fly a cargo into the Levant, innocently believing that the Famiglia Rosa ran their business the way the powers in other countries did. Nothing in the Duchy was the same as in other countries.

Especially not the dispensation of justice.

"Alice, we must move," Maggie said urgently, rolling to her knees. "They may have seen us fall."

Well, since there was nothing else to do now, she might as well humor the girl. She rolled over and, on hands and knees, crawled after Maggie toward the distant goal of the dorsal vane in the stern. But it didn't matter. "We're not going to get away, you know," she called to her. "They have to know we abandoned ship."

"Perhaps," Maggie said over the bag still on her shoulder. "But they mayn't know precisely where. We can hide until dark."

"And then what?" she asked curiously, though really, there was only one answer: They would have to surrender.

"I don't know," Maggie said. "Honestly, Alice, buck up. We're alive, and that's more than we can say for some we've seen on this voyage."

"Lot of good that will do us," Alice told her, stung. "We're alone on an island in the middle of the sea with a team of marksmen who saw us go down. You tell me how long it will take them to find us."

"About half as long as it will if you don't stop moaning and put that famous brain to work!" Maggie snapped. "Here is the dorsal hatch. Get yourself down there and be quiet if you have nothing useful to say."

Alice's temper, buried in the ash of grief and loss and hopelessness, stirred with a spark of annoyance. "You sound just like Claire."

"I am delighted you think so. Move."

Grumbling, Alice scrambled down the ladder to the coaxial catwalk inside the fuselage, and before she could even release the last rung, one of the bags landed on her head. "Ow! Watch it!"

"Carry your own," came the voice from above as Maggie closed the hatch and descended swiftly.

The nerve of the little minx. Alice pressed her lips together and jogged forward away from her, her burst of temper—and maybe the smack of the bag landing on it—clearing her head a little.

"This is a military vessel," she said, noting the numbers stenciled every so often on the supporting ironworks. She took a good look at one as they passed. "Hey."

It couldn't be. What a horrible thought if it were. But clearly it was.

"What?" Maggie passed her and reached for the forward hatch, and they stepped directly into the deserted crew's quarters. It was cold in here, and dusty, with cabin after cabin neat as a pin despite their state of neglect.

"Look." In the small canteen, Alice pointed to a framed portrait over the door. "The Kaiser. This is a *Prussian* military vessel. And you know what else?"

Maggie shook her head, and Alice felt a moment of triumph that she knew something Miss Bossy Britches didn't. "The numbers we've been seeing? Those tell me it was made by the Zeppelin Airship Works five years ago, and in fact this is a B2 long-distance airship. The first transoceanic model the count ever made."

"We saw one of these in Santa Fe," Maggie said immediately. "The Texas Rangers were testing it, weren't they, because it was so fast. And then it shot at us."

"The question is, have they stripped it and disabled it?" Alice thought fast. "Maggie, run back astern, to the bombing bay. See if there's anything left in there, and release both lines while you're at it. I'm going to try to fire her up."

Instead of jumping to it, Maggie planted her feet and stared at her in challenge. "Alice Chalmers, we've been shot out of the sky once already this morning. Are you really going to quit whining and try again?"

"Gloating is a very unattractive quality in a young lady," Alice retorted, nettled. "The Ministry men are probably on their way over here to investigate while we stand here blabbing. If they're not in that tower with a clear shot, and if this old girl has anything left in her, then, yes, we have a smidge of a chance to get away. Now, go!"

So much dust. So little maintenance. But if Alice knew her onions, the B2 ship came with two beautiful Daimler 954C engines. She'd read all about them, back at home in Resolution, when they'd first come out, never dreaming that she'd actually get the chance to see one, never mind fly a ship powered by one.

The thought of those engines blew away the last of the ash, and she bade farewell in her mind to the faithful *Lass*. Maybe the old girl had had a trick or two left in her as she died—and dumping them on the B2's fuselage had been her way of giving her captain a parting gift. Having never been the recipient of a dying legacy before, Alice was not about to waste this one.

She took in the B2's flight console in one sweep. It was a lot more complicated than that of the *Lass*—and more organized, too, since it hadn't been pieced together with parts from wrecked ships. Vanes—thrust—ignition—all here, coming easily to hand under a curved front viewing port so that one man could fly the entire vessel while the others were engaged in attack and defense.

Outside, Maggie swarmed up the mooring mast and released the rope. Then she vanished below the gondola.

"Bless you, Count von Zeppelin," Alice murmured, her hands busy on levers and switches. There was no time to do a pre-flight check, so she had no idea if there was even oil or water in the chambers. If there wasn't, they might float for a little before they were shot down. But that was better than sitting here like a stone and simply waiting to be discovered.

The ready lamps came on. That was good. The needles tilted to the right. So there was fuel, and water pressure. *A miracle. Please—please—*

Her hand hesitated over the ignition lever, and then she set her teeth and drew it down.

Under her feet, the great Daimler engines coughed, still waiting for the water in their boilers to heat. Part of the reason for the B2's speed was its sleek fuselage, but the other part was the superheated coils inside the boilers that brought the water to steam pitch faster than any engine had done before. The floor vibrated, shaking Alice to the knees. *You need a tune-up, don't you, darling? Well, if you get us out of here, that will be the first thing I do to say thank you.*

The needle in the last gauge slammed over to the right, and Alice rammed the vanes full vertical. Through the viewing port she saw half a dozen figures in the distance, rapidly closing in on the *Lass*'s position.

# A LADY OF INTEGRITY

"Maggie," she said into the speaking horn above the console. "Where are you? Are we cast off?"

The speaking horn clacked, as though someone had dropped something into it. "All clear!"

"Do we have bombs?"

"No! Just the ones we brought with us."

"Good enough, then. Up ship!"

The engines coughed again, and then caught, and the ship rose gracefully into the sky.

The figures below took aim, but Alice set the vanes full horizontal and pushed the engine controls into forward position. They began to make way, like a bird that has been injured and isn't sure if the air currents will hold it up.

"Come on girl," Alice urged. "You can do it."

But something was wrong. The B2 should have been halfway to Venice by now, but she was inching through the sky as though still tied down, her decks shaking in earnest under the strain.

*Should have taken ten seconds for a pre-flight check.* Alice snatched up a length of rope and tied the manual helm easterly, then dropped like a monkey down into the engine compartment.

"What's the matter, ladies?" she crooned to the hulking Daimlers, both shuddering with the effort of moving again. "Something holding you back?"

She levered herself into the gearbox between the two engines and saw the problem immediately. Like a stove whose flue has been closed, oxygen was not getting in and already the heat levels were too high for comfort. She tore off her shirt to cover her hands, and grabbed the long lever that opened up the air intake to full.

Immediately the vibrating stopped and the sound of the engines changed to an altogether different hum—the hum of a dedicated, well-designed machine getting down to business. Something pinged and ricocheted off the metal below her feet, and Alice scrambled back up into the navigation gondola, tugging her shirt on as she went.

"Maggie?"

"I got one!" came a shriek. "Two!"

But there was no longer any need for their gaseous capsaicin bombs, for in the time it had taken Alice to climb out of the engine room, the lovely sleek ship had left the Lido behind and was already out over open water.

"You beautiful thing," Alice told it, her heart swelling with love and gratitude. "You've saved us."

"And not a moment too soon," Maggie said, coming in with her bag, her face alight with the hungry, predatory expression of a woman whose aim has been true. "Is she truly able to fly?"

"Like a bird." Alice patted the wheel. "She had a little trouble getting off the ground—someone had closed the oxygen vents to keep the rats out who knows how many years ago, and she couldn't breathe. But listen to her now."

"Swans are like that," Maggie said.

"What, as silent as our beautiful engines?"

"Well, that—but they have a hard time getting off the ground. Once they're in the air, though, it's like watching a poem to see them fly."

"And this has what to do with anything?" Poor girl, the shock of evading death by a hair was finally catching up with her.

# A LADY OF INTEGRITY

"A ship has to have a name—even a stolen one," Maggie informed her. "We should call her *Swan*."

"*Swan*," Alice repeated thoughtfully. "Her fuselage is blue, and not white, and she's spent more time surrounded by water than any ship should, but you're right about that takeoff." She looked up into the cabling. "What do you say, girl? Would you like to be called *Swan* instead of ZAW-eighty-nine-dash-three?"

The ship purred through the air, as sleek and comfortable in the sky as though she had never left it.

"I'll take that as a yes," Alice said, and smiled at Maggie. "*Swan* it is." She leaned toward the starboard viewing port. "Now, chances are they've already sent a pigeon to the commercial field, so if we try to land, we'll have a welcoming committee armed with rifles and an arrest warrant. But I need to check her water pressure, and we need to find out what's happening with the others. Any suggestions?"

Maggie peered down as well. "There are a lot of little islands in this lagoon," she said. "We could land on one just long enough to be sure we aren't going to fall out of the sky. I already checked the communications cage—there isn't a single pigeon there. That was probably the first thing they confiscated so that no one could send for help."

Alice nodded. "Inconvenient, but first things first. Let's set down on that little island there, with the tree. At least the *acqua alta* hasn't swallowed it up yet. And I think the two of us could do with some of that lunch, don't you?"

## 25

Claire and Andrew hung from the harness inside the diving bell, as limp as a pair of wet sheets on a line.

She must not give up hope. Intellectually, she knew that. But when she idly catalogued her body's reactions, she wondered if it had not already happened, and her mind was simply not yet ready to admit it. Her shoulders slumped, her face felt slack, and her very bones were beginning to chill under her wet clothes. She felt, in fact, very much the way Captain Hollys looked.

Her eyes narrowed, and the salt drying in her eyelashes stung.

"Captain Hollys," she said, "what is your opinion, upon hearing our various options? Which course of action seems to offer the greatest chance of our survival?"

It took a moment for his gaze to connect with hers. "None of them," he finally replied. "I still cannot fathom why or how you are here. Of all the foolish things I believed you capable of, Claire, this tops them all."

"They are trying to save our lives, ye great numpty," Jake snapped, with no regard whatever for Ian's rank or position. "Though I don't know why she should bother, since you're not the least bit interested in the effort."

"Shut up, you young scamp," Ian said, but he didn't sound very convincing.

Claire widened her eyes at Jake as if to say, *What on earth is wrong with him?*

But he only shrugged. "It takes some of them this way," he said, as if she had asked the question aloud. "I suppose they can't believe that one human being can treat another the way the Ministry treats the people it captures. It sets a man adrift, like."

Captain Hollys was certainly adrift. "If we are to survive, then we all must be fully in our senses," she said. "And that includes me. I apologize, Jake, for burdening you with my brief loss of hope."

She had never thought to see that rapscallion's half-smile again, and to see it now brought another flood of salt to her eyes. She blinked it away.

"That's all right, Lady. The captain's been in command of others for so long that I suspect having no say in his destiny is a new state of affairs for him."

Andrew stirred from a contemplation even deeper than Claire's had been. "Now, now. No need for personal remarks."

But something in Jake's deliberate tone told Claire there was more going on here than personal remarks. This was a cue for her—and one she had better pick up, for Jake had already made it clear it was only a matter of minutes before the Ministry men came down to find out what had gone amiss with their errant bell.

"Yes," she said now. "I am certainly familiar enough with the captain's air of command. Some women find it attractive, I suppose."

"You didn't," Ian murmured.

"I enjoy and appreciate a man in control of his emotions and his environment, as might any woman. It is when he attempts to control mine that I object."

Ian glanced at Andrew, who had left off thinking and was now staring at her in some consternation. Claire stifled a niggle of guilt and promised herself she would explain it all to him later, when they got out of this.

"You've got your hands full," Ian observed to Andrew, and then lapsed back into apathy.

Andrew's gaze came fully into the present. "I am lucky that I do," he retorted. "For if I were all you had to depend on, you might be in trouble. You place far too little value on the abilities of women, sir."

"On the contrary," Ian said with a sigh of annoyance at being made to converse. "I value them a great deal. They just don't seem to value me."

"I find that hard to believe, given the swath you cut through the debutantes of London. Oh, yes," Claire told him archly, "we all read the society columns."

Ian gave a snort. "Silly girls and desperate bluestockings. Not one of them was as fine as you."

"I say," Andrew began, but Claire cut him off.

## A LADY OF INTEGRITY

"I suppose it was much easier to carry a torch for me than to risk actually becoming acquainted with a young lady—to see into her heart and realize her good qualities?"

"No time," Ian muttered. "Estate needs looking after and none of them seemed capable."

"Ian Hollys, I am ashamed of you," Claire exclaimed. "If you want someone to look after your estate, hire a housekeeper. But if you want a worthy partner to share the sky with you, to be your helpmeet when you need care, and to care for and protect in your turn, anyone with an ounce of sense knows that you must raise your eyes to someone who is worthy. Someone to whom *you* matter."

He shifted under the lash of her tone, making the harness twist and turn, and sloshing his pale bare feet in the water. "A lot you know about it. Where am I going to find a woman like that?"

"I can think of two right off the bat," Andrew said, clearly realizing what they were up to. "Though from the look of you now, they might not be quite so convinced about your abilities as a protector."

"Who?" he demanded.

"For goodness sake, Ian, are you blind?" Claire said with an air of throwing up her hands. "Have you not seen how—" She stopped herself just in time, belatedly realizing that perhaps Alice might not wish her to reveal the deepest secrets of her heart—secrets that she might not even have admitted to herself but that had been clearly visible to the loving eye of a friend.

"Seen how what?" A spark had come back into Ian's eyes, and his spine had regained a little of its iron—

enough, at least, to make his harness increasingly uncomfortable.

Good. Her ruse was working.

"Seen how Gloria looks at you and hangs all over you, of course," Andrew said. "My stars, man, while it started as a blind to distract her father, I think the girl quite believes it."

"Gloria?" Ian said, quite as though he had been thinking of someone else.

Well, let him. If he had awakened to the fact that there might be *two* women in the world who could stand beside him without shame, then all the better.

"Enough of this hanging about feeling sorry for yourself," Jake said impatiently. "We are running out of—" A brilliant flash of light made him flinch so badly that he bumped into Claire's harness, setting them both swinging.

"What was that?" she whispered, blinking away the dazzled spots in front of her eyes. "Are they coming for us with lights?"

A line of bubbles zipped past outside the bell, like the tail of a falling star, and another flash seared their eyes from the depths below.

"Did you see that?" Andrew cried.

"I can't see anything." Jake rubbed his salt-encrusted lids. "It's not the Ministry men, I'll tell you that much."

*Flash!*

"We are under attack," Ian said with conviction. "We must get out of here at once before we are struck."

"No, that's just it!" Feverishly, Andrew began to pull at Claire's buckles, then his own. "Those are my Short-Range Dazzling Incendiaries!"

# A LADY OF INTEGRITY

"Yours, sir?" Jake said blankly. "What if one of them hits us?"

"There is no charge—they are simply for distraction." He had Claire out of her harness now, and treading water. With one tug of Ian's last buckle, he dumped him unceremoniously into the water as well. "And for getting one's attention. It means that Lizzie and Tigg are directly above us in *Athena*. It means we are saved!"

Before he even finished speaking, Claire's mind had calculated the angle of the incendiaries' descent and triangulated *Athena*'s approximate position. But then, when another incendiary zipped through the water and detonated, she realized something else.

"They are moving away!" she cried. "They are clearly searching for us—quickly, we must get their attention!"

"Take the rucksack and surface," Andrew told her. "Now!"

"I am not leaving you!"

Jake grabbed her hand and yanked on it to get her attention. "The air hose. Go outside and disconnect it, and aim it at the surface. We'll have one minute of air after you do."

Andrew clapped the breathing globe upon her head, hooked up its hose, and thrust her under the lip of the diving bell. It only took a couple of kicks before she landed on the top of it, and a few seconds more to disconnect the air hose.

The thing came alive in her hands like a very angry python, writhing and blowing huge bubbles of oxygen every which way. She flung her body upon it and wrestled it into submission, finally using her own weight to point it up toward the surface.

How many seconds of her companions' air had she lost? How long would it take before someone on the ship observed the boiling of the water? Would they understand its significance?

Someone banged on the glass and she let go of the hose. It whipped away from her and wrapped itself around the cable on which the bell ascended and descended. By the time she had swum to the base of the bell, all three men had come out from under it, and she saw at once what they intended.

They had only one choice, after all.

And only one chance.

Andrew clasped her to himself, and Ian wrapped his arms around both of them. Jake grabbed Andrew's waist and pressed himself to his back, and then Claire released the cord on the rucksack.

They rose toward the surface like an unwieldy comet, trailing bubbles behind them.

Torn between watching where she was going and terror lest they attract a kraken, Claire glanced frantically in every direction. The green of the water grew lighter ... its quality changed as sunlight penetrated ... wavering light surrounded them like a nimbus ...

And they exploded from the water into the warmth of the Venetian day.

*

"Tigg—Claude—what is that?" Lizzie had opened the viewing port and hung halfway out of it, scanning the waterways with every ounce of concentration she possessed. Every time she launched one of the walnut-sized bombs Mr. Andrew had left with them, she waited at least a minute, in case by some miracle somebody under the water could respond. "Look, there, to the west of that great fancy church."

Tigg spun the wheel to come about, and *Athena* tilted into the turn.

"It's a bloody great kraken again, is what it is," Claude told them grimly, from his position on the other side of the gondola. "Remember? All that boiling about and the poor devil shooting up out of it?"

Hardly had the words left his lips than something exploded out of the depths like a waterspout. Something with eight legs, but oddly disciplined. There was no kicking here, no frantic near-death movements that would draw the kraken, simply a smooth, last-ditch flight into the air.

And, since the laws of physics again dictated that what went up must come down, they began to fall back toward the water. Four heads—one in a glass breathing globe—turned desperately toward *Athena*.

Lizzie shrieked so loudly she was sure even the fish could hear her. "Tigg! It's the Lady! And Mr. Andrew and the captain and Jake!"

"Get back to the basket!" Tigg shouted. "We've got to get them out of there before a kraken comes!"

Claude pounded behind her as she practically flew down the corridor to the hatch in the stern where the rescue basket lay ready and waiting. "What can I do?" he shouted.

"Winch me down—I'll throw Incendiaries to distract the kraken." For it was not a matter of *if* they came—it was *when*.

He grasped the handle and Lizzie scrambled into the basket, her pockets full of the little bombs Mr. Andrew had made—bless Mr. Andrew's inventive mind, to make something so useful! The wind caught the basket and swung it out like a pendulum as Tigg completed the turn that brought the ship about and positioned it above the roiling water, where it was clear the four figures were doing their level best not to splash while they struggled to stay afloat.

Down—down—oh, please let her be in time—

In the clear water two hundred feet away, a shadow swam up from the depths and began to move toward the little group at a speed at which no ordinary creature should be able to travel.

"No!" Lizzie screamed, yanked the pin from a bomb, and threw it as hard as she could. Even from up here she could see the flash under the water, and the kraken halted, temporarily disoriented, its tentacles waving as it backed away. "Claude, faster!"

The line sang out as the winch got away from him and Lizzie dropped like a stone. She screamed his name to no avail ... the basket hit the surface as though it were flagged pavement ... and she was flung out and into the water, directly into the kraken's path.

# A LADY OF INTEGRITY

26

Claire tore the now useless breathing globe from her head and struggled out of the spent rucksack. "Lizzie!" she shrieked. Had she been knocked unconscious? Had she broken something in the fall?

There was no time to lose.

Claire had not grown up on the Cornish coast without learning how to swim, thanks to lessons from the second footman about which her mother had never been told. She blessed that footman now as she stroked evenly through the choppy water to where she could just see Lizzie's sleek wet head.

"Lizzie!"

She could feel the danger rising up through the water—*feel* it, like electricity in her legs and arms, the way a lightning storm made the hair rise on the back of her neck. She had no clear idea how she was going to protect her girl from the kraken, only that she must try, even if she died herself in the attempt.

The basket was rising drunkenly, seawater pouring out of it as it swung in the air, as *Athena* came about again. With no one in it to provide a weight, getting it close enough to save one of them would be a matter of sheer luck. "Andrew!" she shouted over her shoulder. "The basket!" But he and Ian and Jake were already ahead of her, surfacing and reaching for the webbing of rope on the bottom.

She plunged face-first through a wave and came up next to Lizzie.

Who was floating on her back in a boiling calm—the kind that meant something very large was coming up from beneath.

"Lizzie—dear Lord help us—you must swim!"

Lizzie turned her head at an odd angle, her arm drawn in protectively across her chest. "It's all right, Lady."

"I will not let you die!"

"It's too late for that. I did something to my arm—I can't swim. You need to get in the basket while I distract it."

"*Distract* it!" Fear and love swamped her. "You will not!" Tears fell, warming and then chilling her cheeks, as the waves' agitation increased. "Come, I will pass my arm around your chest and—"

The first of the tentacles rose, curling and testing the air, as big around as Claire's leg. She couldn't help herself—she screamed.

"Lady, please—leave me—save yourself—"

## A LADY OF INTEGRITY

"Stay away from my girl!" Claire shrieked at the monster as it rose and rose, and now she felt something wrap around her leg, and her arm, and a tentacle slid lovingly between their bodies to encircle Lizzie's waist. "No! You can't have her! You can't!"

And now the creature's head breached the surface, exposing a black, fathomless eye.

It examined its prey.

A shudder seemed to pass through its gelid flesh—a subtle movement that Claire could feel even in the extremity wrapped around her calf.

Lizzie drew in a breath. "Why, hullo," she said.

"Lizzie—dear girl, please—try—" But Lizzie did not seem to hear Claire's frantic, tearful whisper.

"I didn't expect to see *you* again," she said to the creature, as though delighted to have met an old acquaintance on the street. "If you plan to eat me, I hope you will make it quick, and let the Lady here go."

"Why are you talking to this creature?" Claire hissed.

"It knows me," she said simply. "It's the one Tigg and I rescued the night of the Minister's ball. My, how big you've grown in such a short time," she told it.

Though she was nearly in shock with fear and cold, Claire could see an opportunity when it rose up in front of her. Slowly, she reached down and detached the unresisting tentacle from her calf. It clung briefly to her hand before sliding away. The second one unwrapped itself from around her arm, and then the one around Lizzie's waist loosened.

"So we are even, then," Lizzie said with approval. "Thank you." She leaned on Claire, who was treading water as best she could with one arm while she cradled

Lizzie's head against her shoulder. "You might think about leaving," she advised it. "This is not a very healthy place for your kind. I recommend the West Indies."

A sound that vibrated in Claire's very bones seemed to issue from the beast, resonating through the water, and then it sank slowly beneath the waves. The foam closed over the last of the tentacles—Claire had the impression of something moving very fast and very powerfully beneath her—

—and they were alone.

*

The creature's spell faded abruptly and pain rushed in like an explosion in Lizzie's brain. She cried out, spots dancing around the edges of her vision.

"I'm sorry, darling," the Lady said, half sobbing, as Jake and Captain Hollys reached down to take her. "It is going to hurt."

It did.

Dreadfully.

Like nothing ever had before in her life.

Lizzie fell into the bottom of the basket, retching and weeping, hardly even aware of Mr. Malvern heaving the Lady in and then climbing in himself. The Lady flung herself next to her with Mr. Malvern's shirt and wadded it up under her head. Far above, Lizzie's dazed eyes could see the underside of *Athena* and the long filament of the rope as they were winched with agonizing slowness into the air.

Claude had let the basket go, and she had fallen into the water and broken her arm ... or her shoulder ... or something. He would likely be as sore as she by this time tomorrow from the effort of winching up five people in a wet basket.

A crack like a tree branch breaking sounded in the distance.

The Lady gasped. "Andrew—what was that?"

"Claire, keep your head down."

"I see them," came Jake's grim voice. "Four degrees off *Athena*'s stern."

"Are we under attack?" the Lady squeaked. "Can nothing go right in this godforsaken place?"

"It appears the Ministry has discovered the abandoned bell and seen *Athena* where she should not be," Andrew said.

*Crack!* Two holes appeared magically in either side of the basket's corner above Lizzie's head.

The Lady flung herself over Lizzie's body, which made her see stars of pain. "Can he go no faster?" she moaned into Lizzie's hair.

*Crack! Ping!*

"That went off the gondola," Jake said grimly. "They're getting closer."

Twenty feet to go. Now Lizzie could see Claude and Mr. Stringfellow at the winch, cranking like fiends, even as *Athena*'s engines changed pitch and she began to make way. Dear Tigg was taking an awful risk, sailing when the basket was not secure, but given the choice, she would have done the same. Better to dock the basket in flight than be shot down.

*Crack! Crack!*

*Crrrraaaackle—boom!*

"What on earth—" Captain Hollys stared, gripping the woven rim of the basket so hard it creaked.

"Now there are *two* of them," Mr. Andrew moaned. "Ten feet. Why did no one tell those boys the automatons will run the winch!"

"Malvern, that is a B2 military transport," Captain Hollys said suddenly.

"I don't care if it's a flying squid! We are outnumbered. Why isn't Tigg pouring on the steam and getting us out of here?"

"Because he cannot until we are docked," the Lady moaned. "We are so heavy that it is a wonder the ropes have not broken already."

"But—"

*Crrraaaaaackle!*

"That is not a rifle!" The Lady leaped to her feet, leaving Lizzie staring upward at poor Claude, whose body had probably never been called to such a degree of physical labor in all his life. And now she realized, belatedly, that it was she who had not told either of them it was not a manual winch.

Oh, dear. She hoped he would not hurt himself.

Neither could she lie here like a broken doll. If she were going to die for the second time today, it would be on her feet, beside the Lady, staring death in the face.

Lizzie rolled to her knees, holding in the groan of pain even as tears spurted from her eyes. She grasped the woven edge of the basket with her good hand, and pulled herself upright. And then she saw what had silenced the others.

The sleek military ship with the blue fuselage designed to make it nearly invisible against the sky was firing—not upon *Athena*, but upon the Ministry ship sailing to intercept them.

Firing with … lightning!

# A LADY OF INTEGRITY

"They've got a lightning rifle," she said, nearly delirious with pain and wonder, to the Lady.

"Not a rifle," the Lady said. "The bolt is finer—more delicate—the range shorter. Like a—"

"It's Maggie!" Lizzie shrieked, and clutched the edge of the basket as it rocked into the dock. Mr. Stringfellow looped its ropes around the stanchion, and Claude slammed the winch handle into the closed position. "It's Maggie's lightning pistol!"

"Jake, get Lizzie and yourself into a cabin at once." The Lady leaped from the basket and ran, dripping water all over the decks and down the corridor. But Lizzie did not want to go, and made a terrible production of pain that was three-quarters truth—just enough to delay him until they got to the navigation gondola, where the Lady was stationed at the viewing port with the lightning rifle.

"I'll show them not to fire on unarmed women and children," she said grimly. "Tigg, bring her around and flank them. I want a clear shot at their engines."

The Duchy ship was a quarter mile off their stern, the B2 flanking it with tendrils of lightning crossing the gap and leaving smoking holes in her fuselage wherever they touched. *Athena* made the turn in short order, giving them all enough time to lower the viewing glass.

Lizzie got a clear view of the pandemonium on the bridge of the Duchy ship as they realized they were under attack on two fronts—they got off a few shots that went wide—until the Lady brought the lightning rifle up and sighted down its deadly barrel.

The bolt arced across the air space between them, catching the Duchy ship's starboard engine dead in the center. Tendrils of blue light flickered joyously all over it before the boiler detonated, blowing a hole in the side of the gondola. Two aeronauts fell out, screaming, to land with a splash in the canal below.

The Lady took aim again, this time at the fuselage.

The bolt passed through canvas and iron substructure, burning as it went, and thence into the gas bag. With a sound like a feather pillow striking one's head, the gas ignited, and within seconds the entire fuselage was engulfed in flame. The ship fell out of the sky in a burning fireball and landed with a crash in the canal, bits of its structure falling on it in a rain of destruction.

Shadows moved deep below the surface, as the kraken came in to finish what the lightning rifle had begun.

Lizzie said something—she was not sure what—as the swarm of black spots moved into her vision, buzzing like bees.

Tigg leaped from the helm and caught her just in time.

# A LADY OF INTEGRITY

27

While her own small airfield in Vauxhall Gardens still remained Claire's favorite, there was something to be said for the broad, sunny field in Geneva built by the Swiss, whose attention to the finer things in life extended to the installation of a lovely fountain in the central water holding tank. Flowers lined the broad avenues between the ships, and poplar and lime trees made splotches of brilliant gold upon the green of the field and the gray of the gravel.

Lizzie, whose fall from the basket had resulted in a dislocated shoulder, had her arm in a sling thanks to the field doctor who had attended her. Claude had not yet made up to her for his mistake with the winch, and catered to her every whim to the point where Maggie had determined to take him aside and inform him that being served so assiduously was every bit as bad for one's character as neglect.

The gentlemen had brought some of the chairs out into the sunny area between the moorages of *Athena* and *Swan*, and they were presently relaxing after an excellent lunch. Tigg lay at Lizzie's feet, entertaining Holly, who was not convinced that everything that could be eaten had been eaten. Ivy sunned herself in Maggie's lap in the chair next to Claire's, while Jake lay on the blanket on the grass with his eyes closed. In this position, of course, he could not tell either Claire or Maggie not to look at him as though he were about to die then and there, which he had already done at least twice.

Both of them had made sure that he had not only seconds of lunch, but thirds, too. It was no wonder he was half asleep. He had borrowed one of Andrew's shirts and had found a pair of breeches that fit in the crew's quarters aboard *Swan*. Claire had wasted no time in cutting up his prison rags for polishing cloths—a much more profitable use of cotton.

Voices proceeded from within *Swan*'s engine compartment, where Captain Hollys believed himself to be assisting Alice in repairs.

"Dadburn it, Ian, be careful with that wrench! These Daimlers are calibrated as fine as a Swiss clock, and I won't have you banging around in there as though they were clunky old Crocketts!"

Claire did not hear Ian's reply, but she had no doubt that Alice was enjoying bossing him around. Turnabout, after all, was fair play. She could not say that he was a changed man after his experience in the prison, but how could anyone be unchanged after such fear and hopelessness? They had only been here a day. Perhaps banging about in an engine compartment was more therapeutic for him than Alice, and that was why she had consented to it at all.

A whirring sound in the air made them look up, and Maggie said, "There's the pigeon. But I can't get up."

"I'll get it." Claude unfolded himself from his chair and loped up *Athena*'s gangway, reappearing a few minutes later with a letter in his hand. Claire took it, broke the count's seal, and read it aloud.

> *My dear Claire,*
>
> *Words cannot express the relief of the baroness and myself to hear of your safe departure from the Duchy and subsequent return to civilized parts. It would almost balance my dismay at learning you had gone, if not for the realization that the journey was only to be expected of a woman of your character.*
>
> *Have no fear—your position awaits you when you choose to take it up. While the baroness smiles at the thought of my swallowing my pride, I look upon it as good business. I do not let go of my investments so easily.*
>
> *And now to the subject of your inquiry. The B2 airship you describe was built in 1889, as Captain Chalmers surmised from the serial number, and completed three transoceanic voyages before inexplicably disappearing on its return from Cape Town in 1890. I cannot believe that any members of its crew still survive—in fact, services for those lost at storm were held, and all the families compensated ... as much as such a loss ever can be.*

*You may assure Captain Chalmers that I do not wish the ship returned to my fleet. If she and Maggie were brave and resourceful enough to liberate her, then they deserve to fly her with my blessing.*

*We look forward to your safe return.*

*With affection and regard,*
*Ferdinand von Zeppelin*

Claire folded up the letter and handed it back to Claude. "Run this over to Alice. She will be glad of the news."

"Does this mean I own half a ship?" Maggie asked from under the brim of her straw hat.

"You would need to take that up with Alice, darling," Claire suggested, "but it rather sounds as though the count thinks so, and I cannot imagine Alice would disagree."

"Then I give Jake my half," Maggie said, her hand slow and gentle on Ivy's feathers.

"What's that?" Jake's eyes opened, and he sat up. "What ship?"

"*Swan*, of course. What am I going to do with half a ship? You're the one flying her—though she's awfully big. You're going to need Mr. Stringfellow's help for certain."

That individual had already nearly come to blows with Jake the evening before over the privilege of who ought to wear an aeronaut's colors. Since Jake was the larger and more experienced—and had not a stitch to call his own—he had appropriated a lieutenant's britches more out of expediency than expectations of rank. This had offended Mr. Stringfellow deeply, and he was not over it yet.

"Silly blighter," Jake said affectionately. "Ship hasn't even been commissioned into the Royal Aeronautic Corps and already he's putting on airs."

"And may never be," Mr. Malvern said on Claire's other side. "The *Stalwart Lass* was registered in Charlottetown. But Alice is a Texican citizen. *Swan* may fly the Lone Star and Snake yet."

"Not on my watch," Jake muttered under his breath. Then, more loudly, "Anyhow, Mags, you ought not to give away your half so easily. You and the captain might want to go into business together."

"I doubt it," Maggie said. "The Seacombe shipping empire will be enough for Lizzie and Claude and me. No, I've made up my mind, so I'll thank you to take me seriously."

"Better talk it over with Alice before you go giving ships away hither and yon," Claire advised. Then she shaded her eyes. "There's another pigeon. It can't be Snouts, not so soon. Perhaps the Dunsmuirs have finally received Ian's ransom demand."

Once again Claude fetched a letter and handed it to her. Claire turned it over, unable to place the masculine hand. Finally she slit the seal.

*Lady Claire,*

*While our acquaintance has been brief, I hope you will forgive my trespassing upon it and importuning you in this peremptory manner.*

*I will come straight to the point. My daughter is missing, and despite the assistance of the Duchy's finest officers in the last twenty-four hours, all attempts to locate her have been unsuccessful. It is my understanding from the concierge at your hotel that you were the last person in whose company she was seen, the day before yesterday.*

*I am informed by that same individual that you have quitted Venice. I hope that this letter finds you and that you are willing to vouchsafe any information you possess on the matter. Though we have been estranged from one another of late, she is still my only child and heir.*

*I remain,*
*Your servant,*
*Gerald Meriwether-Astor*

## THE END

# A NOTE FROM SHELLEY

Dear reader,

I hope you enjoy reading the adventures of Lady Claire and the gang in the Magnificent Devices world as much as I enjoy writing them. It is your support and enthusiasm that is like the steam in an airship's boiler, keeping the entire enterprise afloat and ready for the next adventure.

You might leave a review on your favorite retailer's site to tell others about the books. And you can find the electronic editions of the entire series online, as well as audiobooks. I'll see you over at www.shelleyadina.com, where you can sign up for my newsletter and be the first to know of new releases and special promotions.

# ABOUT THE AUTHOR

### The official version

RITA Award® winning author and Christy finalist Shelley Adina wrote her first novel when she was 13. It was rejected by the literary publisher to whom she sent it, but he did say she knew how to tell a story. That was enough to keep her going through the rest of her adolescence, a career, a move to another country, a B.A. in Literature, an M.F.A. in Writing Popular Fiction, and countless manuscript pages.

Shelley is a world traveler who loves to imagine what might have been. Between books, she loves playing the piano and Celtic harp, making period costumes, and spoiling her flock of rescued chickens.

### The unofficial version

I like Edwardian cutwork blouses and velvet and old quilts. I like bustle drapery and waltzes and new sheet music and the OED. I like steam billowing out from the wheels of a locomotive and autumn colors and chickens. I like flower crowns and little beaded purses and jeweled hatpins. Small birds delight me and Roman ruins awe me. I like old books and comic books and new technology ... and new books and shelves and old technology.

## A LADY OF INTEGRITY

I'm feminine and literary and practical, but if there's a beach, I'm going to comb it. I listen to shells and talk to hens and ignore the phone. I believe in thank-you notes and kindness, in commas and friendship, and in dreaming big dreams. You write your own life. Go on. Pick up a pen.

# AVAILABLE NOW

The Magnificent Devices series:
*Lady of Devices*
*Her Own Devices*
*Magnificent Devices*
*Brilliant Devices*
*A Lady of Resources*
*A Lady of Spirit*
*A Lady of Integrity*

*Caught You Looking* (contemporary romance, Moonshell Bay #1)
*Immortal Faith* (paranormal YA)

To learn about my Amish women's fiction written as Adina Senft, visit www.adinasenft.com.
*The Wounded Heart*
*The Hidden Life*
*The Tempted Soul*
*Herb of Grace*
*Keys of Heaven*
*Balm of Gilead*

A LADY OF INTEGRITY

# COMING SOON

*A Gentleman of Means*, Magnificent Devices #8
*Caught You Listening*, Moonshell Bay #2
*Caught You Hiding*, Moonshell Bay #3
*Everlasting Chains*, Immortal Faith #2
*Twice Dead*, Immortal Faith #3

CPSIA information can be obtained at www.ICGtesting.com
Printed in the USA
LVOW08s1629060516

487046LV00007B/509/P

9 781939 08